Protecting You

Hayden Falls

Book Eight

By:

Debbie Hyde

Cover Design by: Debbie Hyde
Couple Image by: myronstandret @ depositphotos
Background Photo: Carrie Pichler Photography (Facebook).
Photographer Website: https://carriepicherphotography.weebly.com
ISBN: 9798321262887

To the men and women in law enforcement. Thank you for protecting us. You are a Hero. May Angels guard every step you take.

Chapter One

Leo

Sunday dinners with my family are my favorite time of the week. The only time I miss it is when I'm on duty. Even then, Mom and Grandma will send my brother and me a plate to the Sheriff's Office. Naturally, Dad gets a plate if he's there. It's rare for the Sheriff to be at the office on Sundays. Dad only shows up on Sunday if there's an emergency.

My dad became Sheriff when I was in middle school. He was a deputy before my brother and I were born. My twin brother, Lucas, will follow in Dad's footsteps and be Sheriff someday. Me? I'm happy keeping my hometown safe.

"You ready to hit the town this week?" Granddad rubs the hood of my truck. I think he's talking to me *and* the truck.

Maybe I should call this our truck. Granddad gave me his old '72 Ford F250 when I turned twenty-one. I keep the truck in the barn here at my parents' house during the winter. I also work on it here so Granddad can help. Helping consists of him sitting behind the wheel or walking around supervising everything I do.

"Yeah. I have the evening of the Fourth off. A bunch of us are going to Cowboys." I set the oil and filter on the work table. We're just doing an oil change today.

"I'm ready." Granddad rubs his hands together and grins.

Of course, he's ready. I promised him at Christmas we'd take Darlin out during the summer and paint the town. We've painted more towns 'than just Hayden Falls. Granddad thinks he's helping me find a girl. I've already told him if there's a girl out there for me, she's not in Hayden Falls.

I'm not looking for a girl, so I don't put much effort into the task when we're out and about. Finding someone is pointless. I wouldn't ask an outsider to move here. Small-town living isn't for everyone. Women nowadays want the fast life big cities offer. I've heard too many stories of failed marriages in our town because this life wasn't enough for one of them. It's usually the woman who leaves.

Most men wouldn't enjoy going to bars with their grandfather. I love spending time with mine. It doesn't matter to me if we're hanging around here, hunting, or going to town. Taking him outside of Hayden Falls is interesting. A few times, he meddled and picked out a girl for me. He even went as far as introducing me to them. It was a bit embarrassing.

Taking him to one of our little bars is easier on me. Grandma calls up his friends and secretly gets them to join us. She doesn't have to, but she says she's giving me a break. Granddad can be a little overbearing when his mind's set on something. That something right now is helping me find a girl.

"Wednesday night it is." Granddad rubs his hand across the hood again. "Darlin is going to help you find your girl."

Granddad named his truck Darlin after meeting my grandmother. She loved a country singer named Conway Twitty. Darlin was in the opening line of one of his songs or something. I heard that song so many times growing up. I tune the song out now when he plays it. And yes, he plays it often. Still, it's cute to watch my grandparents sit in the old truck and play their favorite song. Granddad swears his truck caught Grandma's eye first. She denies it, but I think he's right.

I can't help but laugh. "You think so?"

"Yes." He gives me a firm nod. "We got a feeling." He leans close to the truck and whispers, "Don't we, ole girl?"

Our town is small, but we're big on festivals. This year's Fourth of July Celebration lasts for nine days. When the Fourth falls in the middle of the week, we celebrate the weekend before and the one after. My shift ends at four on Wednesday. With the extra tourists in town, Dad wants a few deputies at Cowboys and O'Brien's Tavern in the evenings. Off-duty deputies don't mind the assignment. Hopefully, Willows Bend won't need any help at their bars this week. I hate having to go to Pete's Saloon. With Slone Security monitoring Pete's now, the calls for assistance have dropped.

I'll pick Granddad up on Wednesday around six. The moment we walk into Cowboys, he'll head to the bar to join his friends. I'll sit with my friends at a table on the upper level. From up there, it gives me the best view of the entire bar. The upper level is where most of the guys sit. The women usually stay on the dance floor level. I won't have to talk to a woman. Well, except for our server to order drinks. Granddad will enjoy seeing his friends. I'll have a few drinks and make sure nobody gets out of line. The night will be perfect.

"You boys ready for dinner?" Grandma walks into the barn.

"We're working on Darlin." Granddad puts an arm around her and beams proudly at our truck. "We're taking her out Wednesday night."

Grandma gives me a sympathetic look. "You have to eat until then."

"Come on, Granddad. We can do the oil change after dinner."

"She has to be ready," he says.

"She'll be ready," I assure him. "But I'm starving."

"But." He looks at Darlin. He hates walking away from her.

"I hear there's roast beef," I tempt him. We both love roast beef with cooked carrots and potatoes.

"There is," Grandma confirms. "And Mitchell's looking for you."

"Okay." Granddad pats the side of the truck. "After dinner."

He hurries to the house to find Dad. My dad probably isn't looking for him. Grandma has used this line so many times. Dad will think of something to talk to Granddad about when he finds him.

"Well, beautiful lady, allow me to escort you to dinner." I hold my arm out.

"All your country boy charm is going to waste on me." Grandma slides her hand around my elbow.

"It's never a waste. You're special." I lean down and kiss the top of her head.

"You make an old woman happy." She smiles up at me.

"I never want to disappoint you."

"Oh, please." Grandma tosses her other hand in the air. "All four of you boys make us all proud."

"Luke! Stop it!" Riley, my brother's girlfriend, comes running around the side of the house. "Don't you dare!" she shouts over her shoulder.

Luke chases after her with a huge water gun in his hands. My little brother will never grow up.

"Not a chance, Rocky!" Luke yells as he pulls the trigger.

"Aaahhh!"

Target hit. Grandma and I try to stifle our laughter.

Poor Riley didn't make it around the other side of the house in time. She spins around and runs straight for Luke. She crashes into him, knocking them both to the ground and lands on top of him. Riley breaks out into a fit of squeals when Luke tickles her. She's as weird as he is. They're perfect together.

"I want that for you," Grandma whispers.

"Grandma, I have a water gun."

She laughs and nudges me with her shoulder. "I'll call your Granddad's friends tomorrow. They'll be waiting for him at Cowboys Wednesday night."

"Thanks, Grandma."

I help her up the back steps and into the house. For a moment, I watch Luke and Riley in the backyard. It's Luke's fault my grandfather is trying to find me a girl. Luke was the first of us to fall in love. My parents and grandparents think the rest of us need to settle down, too.

My twin brother fell a few months ago. It shocked us all. Lucas was so focused on his career that he didn't notice Hadley for a long time. Luke had a hand in opening our older brother's eyes. Yep. It's all Luke's fault. I want what my brothers have. I'm not a fool, though. My woman, if I have one, isn't in Hayden Falls. Sadly, I'm not leaving this town to find her.

Chapter Two

Kyleigh

Mondays are crazy. I don't know anyone who looks forward to Mondays. Well, except for my mother. When I started college, Mom chose Monday nights for our mother-daughter dinners. At first, I thought she was crazy. Well, she is crazy. Don't believe me? Just ask my dad. My mom is a fun kind of crazy and not the type who needs medication or a mental hospital. The mental hospital might not be true. She did leave my dad. He's a great man. I don't understand why she left him.

I don't understand a lot of the things my mom does, but she was right about Monday night dinners. Spending the evening with her has a way of bringing me happiness and peace after a stressful day at work. Those nights gave me back my sanity during college. Mom insisted we continue our dinners after I graduated.

During my final year of college, I interned at Hillsworth Financial. I was officially hired the week before graduation. I've had an amazing year with the company. Well, next week will be fourteen months, but who's counting? I love this company and plan to spend my entire career with them.

"Are you sure you don't want to change your mind?" Mom pouts. "I can still get us a reservation at *Six Seven Restaurant*."

What she means to say is she already has a reservation. I knew she'd do this. I told her two months ago we'd have to have our mother-daughter dinner on another night this week. Wouldn't you know she'd choose my favorite restaurant tonight?

I love everything about the *Six Seven Restaurant*. The food is amazing. Their clam chowder and salmon are simply divine. Oh, and they have the best Lobster Mac-N-Cheese in the world, not that I've been around the world to test others. I love seafood. Mom doesn't. She'd prefer to be downtown where all her high-society friends can see her. The *Six Seven Restaurant* is fancy, but I've never seen her friends at the pier.

"Mom, you know it's mine and Scott's anniversary."

She doesn't need reminding. I don't know why she's trying to sabotage this night. She likes Scott. At least, I think she does. She's always been kind to him. Not once in the two years we've dated has she said a bad word about him. I've seen Scott roll his eyes a few times when we visit Mom, but I never asked what it was about.

"Who knows, maybe after tonight, I'll officially be on my way to being Mrs. Jensen."

"Oh, please," Mom mumbles.

That's strange. I pause. It's the first bad response she's given me when I mention my boyfriend. Maybe I misunderstood her.

"What was that?"

"Nothing, dear." Mom's back to her cheery self. "If you change your mind, let me know."

"Okay." I laugh, letting the odd moment go. She knows I won't change my mind. "You should ask Mrs. Fitzgerald to go to dinner with you tonight."

Her nosy neighbor is probably on standby as we speak. The woman is pleasant when you're in a crowd with her. If she ever gets you alone, she'll spill the dirt on everybody she knows.

"Maybe." Mom dramatically sighs.

I'm not letting her guilt trip me tonight. "Mom, I really need to go. I want to have dinner on the table before Scott gets home."

"All right, dear." Mom sighs again. "But you know I'm a phone call away."

"I know. I love you, Mom."

I end the call as the timer on the oven goes off. I grab the oven mitts and carefully pull the Chocolate Souffle from the oven. I squeal and do a happy dance because it came out perfectly. This is Scott's favorite dessert. I set the filet mignon on warm and hurry to get dressed. Scott should be home any minute.

Thank goodness, I'd already showered and laid my dress on the bed. I bought the red dress two weeks ago just for this night. Red is Scott's favorite color—not mine. I slide the matching heels on before touching up my hair and makeup. The reflection staring back at me in the full-length mirror brings a smile to my face. This dress fits like a glove. It's perfect.

I quickly set the table before lighting the tapered candles. They're red, too. So is the wine. I pour two glasses. A little giggle escapes when I hear the front door of our condo unlock. Scott is going to be so surprised. With the wine glasses in hand, I stand by the table and wait. My entire body vibrates with excitement. This could be the night I've been waiting for.

"Uh, hello?" Scott calls out. That's a bit odd. He steps into the dining room. Our eyes meet. His go wide, and his mouth falls open. Wow. I know I look good. I'm glad he thinks so, too. "Kyleigh?"

That's odd, too.

"Who else were you expecting?" I nervously laugh and maintain my smile. It's hard.

"It's Monday. You always have dinner with your mother."

"Tonight's special." My smile fades a little. Does he not remember it's our anniversary?

"Yeah." He rubs the back of his head and neck.

The front door opens and closes. That shouldn't be happening.

"Scott?" a woman calls out.

"Uh." Scott spins on his heels and rushes toward the front door. "I'll meet you at the restaurant."

Who's he meeting at the restaurant? He and I didn't have plans tonight. The anniversary dinner I cooked is a surprise.

"Scott, what's going on?" I follow him into the living room.

My eyes lock with those of the woman my boyfriend is trying to push out the door. She and I freeze and look each other over. It's impossible. She's wearing the same dress and heels as I am. Our hair is almost the same shade of brown and styled exactly alike. Except hers is from a bottle.

"Who is she?" My smile is long gone now.

"I thought you said you broke up with her," the woman snaps at Scott.

"Broke up? Scott?" I blink to hold back tears.

"Kyleigh, we need to talk."

"I don't understand."

"Obviously." The woman crosses her arms and rolls her eyes.

"Things haven't been good for a while." Scott's eyes flick to the woman before landing at my feet. He won't look me in the eye.

"Since when? We were fine this morning. Last night was…" I can't even finish the sentence. I sniffle and turn my head.

"Oh, for crying out loud." The woman slaps her hand to her forehead. "If you won't grow a pair and do it, I will."

"Brenda," Scott warns.

Brenda doesn't listen. "He was supposed to have broken up with you six months ago."

"You've been dating her for six months?"

"Uh." Scott rubs his neck again.

"A year," Brenda corrects me.

"A year?" I drop the wine glasses.

"Great." Brenda tosses her hands up. "Now, I'll have to have the carpet replaced?"

"What?" I choke the word out.

"Brenda," Scott warns again. He turns to me. "Kyleigh, I want you to leave."

"Leave?" Nothing makes sense right now.

"You can go to your mom's." He gives me a little smile like it fixes everything. It fixes nothing.

"But this is my home." The first tears spill over. "It's our anniversary," I whisper.

"Good." Brenda motions to the front door. "You get to enter and leave his life on the same day."

Scott takes a deep breath and drops his head back. He's serious. They're serious. This is really happening. He's chosen her, not that I knew I had competition. I swallow hard and walk to our bedroom. I guess it's their bedroom now. I pull three suitcases from the closet and begin to shove my clothes into them. This isn't enough. I grab two more. These are his, but who cares? Brenda can buy him some more.

Scott enters the bedroom as I zip the fifth suitcase closed. "Kyleigh, I'm sorry."

"Don't talk to me," I snap.

"Let me help you." He reaches for one of the suitcases.

I jerk it away from him. "Don't touch it."

"You can't get all this to your car by yourself."

"Yes, I can." I push the luggage to the front door. Yes, it took three trips.

"Bye!" Brenda waves from the kitchen table. I hope she chokes on the dinner I made.

It took three trips to the elevator and three more to my car, but I did it by myself. Once I'm inside my car, I let the tears fall. How did two years of my life get destroyed in less than thirty minutes?

My phone lights up on the passenger seat. It's Mom. I hope Scott didn't call her. Brenda sure would if she had the number. I can't talk to Mom right now. I can't stay in this parking garage, either. I need a plan, but it can't be Mom. Oh, she loves me and would gladly take me in. I can't face her. I don't want her to know how much of a failure I am. I need someone with a level head. There's only one person I can call. No one would look for me there. I need somewhere to go to heal and get myself together. It's going to be hard, but I pick up my phone and make the call.

"Hey, sweet girl."

"Daddy?" I cry.

"Kyleigh, what's wrong?" His voice is full of panic.

"Can I stay with you for a while?"

"Always." He doesn't hesitate. "I'll come get you."

"No, Daddy. The drive will do me good. I'll see you soon. I love you."

Without giving him time to reply or ask questions, I end the call. I'll call him back when I stop for gas. I've got at least a nine-hour drive ahead of me. I won't have anything figured out by the time I get to my dad's. Sitting here isn't helping. I start the car and pull out of the parking garage. I never thought I'd be leaving Seattle, yet here I am. By sunrise, I'll be in Montana.

Chapter Three

Leo

"There's some pretty ladies here tonight." Granddad grins as he looks around the bar.

I laugh and shake my head. Most of the *pretty ladies* here tonight live in Hayden Falls. They're here nearly every week. There's no point in mentioning that to Granddad.

"Yeah, Granddad," I agree and point to the bar. "Mr. Wentworth and Mr. Gibson are waiting for you."

Granddad's friends wave to him from their usual spot at the far end of the bar. They already have a beer waiting for him.

"Okay." Granddad pats my arm. "You talk to a girl tonight."

"Granddad."

"No." Granddad points a finger in my face. "Tonight's the night. I feel it."

"Fine." It's useless to argue with him. "You join your friends, and I'll go see mine."

"And a girl!" Granddad yells over the music as he hurries toward the bar.

Several people narrow their eyes at me. A couple of them snicker. Those two know my Granddad is trying to help me find a girlfriend. They also know I'm only bar hopping with my grandfather to keep him happy. The only woman I'll talk to tonight is my server when I order another beer.

My friend, Tyler Hayes, already has a table for us. Surprisingly, he's sitting with Miles Hamilton. The rest of Miles' regular group aren't here tonight. They all must be on duty. I know Aiden Maxwell and Spencer Murphy are. They took over for Lucas and me this afternoon.

"Hey, man." Tyler pushes the chair across from him out with his foot. He can wipe the silly grin off his face.

"He's not going to stop until you find a girl." Miles pulls a beer from the bucket of ice and hands it to me.

"More like engaged." I lightly laugh.

"You'll wanna marry her quick." Tyler takes a sip of his beer.

"And have a couple of kids on the way, too," Miles adds.

My friends are jerks. As much as I hate to admit it, they're probably right. I twist the top off the beer and take a sip. I'm not big on partying and drinking, as most of the guys around here are. My younger brother, Luke, used to lead a few of those parties until he met Riley.

Riley Anderson returning to Hayden Falls was a blessing to my entire family. She settled Luke down. He's still crazy, but thank goodness the partying stopped. Mom and Grandma tried to hide it, but they were worrying themselves sick over Luke's partying ways. It's also embarrassing to get a disturbing the peace call only to discover the person leading the disturbance is your brother. Lucas and I never want to arrest a member of our family. We'll have to call Aiden, Spencer, or Chief Deputy Green if it ever comes to that.

I glance around the room and assess the crowd while my friends talk. Lucas, no doubt, has done the same. We're sitting back-to-back. Somehow, if we're not at the same table, this is how we end up. It's fine. This lets us have eyes on the entire bar. We learned long ago how to be present in a conversation and monitor the crowd around us.

"Do you think you're home for good?" Miles asks Tyler.

"I'm not sure yet." Tyler runs his hand through his hair and looks away.

Tyler's a professional photographer. He's traveled the world and has done a few photoshoots for *National Geographic*. It surprised everyone, including his family, when he came home at Christmas. Usually, he only stays in town for two or three days when he visits. He's been home a little over six months now. Maybe he's getting restless. I, for one, hope he never leaves. His parents and sister are the happiest I've seen them in years.

Miles doesn't push the issue. He glances down to the lower level and smiles. His pregnant wife is sitting with her friends across the dance floor. Lucas' girlfriend is down there too. Katie and Hadley's friend group is growing rapidly. It started with five best friends. There are at least a dozen women in the group now.

Their group is large, but they don't cause any trouble. Beth Murphy raises a shot glass and shouts. The rest of the ladies do the same. Well, a few of them are drinking nonalcoholic drinks. Wait. I take it back. When Beth has too much to drink, she can get out of hand. She hasn't broken any laws yet, so we let Spencer handle his little sister. If Beth doesn't settle her partying down soon, Spencer will one day be arresting one of his family members.

The crowd tonight seems to be under control. It's only Wednesday, but it's double what a Friday night crowd usually is here. The Fourth of July Celebration always brings in a huge number of tourists no matter what day it falls on.

A shout comes from the pool tables. I groan and drop my head. None of us have to look to know it's Four and Pit. Four's been drinking a lot lately, too. He gets thrown out or arrested on a regular basis. We've been trying to give him a little slack since he's been shot and beaten up this year. Mick Calhoun is taking advantage of our kindness. Lucas has told Dad several times that we need to stop letting the little things slide. In Four's case, I believe my brother's right.

Miles, Tyler, and I spent the next couple of hours laughing and talking. We jump in a few of the conversations at the tables around us. The men don't pull their tables together like the women do, but we're still a big group.

"Leo!" Luke rushes into the bar. He grabs my arm and tries to pull me from my chair. "Come on, man."

Great. The night was going fine until now. It's nice when I don't have to go into cop mode and settle someone down. I thought this was going to be a quiet night. However, when Luke's hyped up, anything can happen. It's usually Four and Pit causing a scene at our little country bar. Luke's his own hyped-up ball of drama. He's nowhere near as bad as Four. Tonight, he's a bit agitated. This is bound to be bad or stupid. Knowing Luke, it's something stupid.

"Go find Riley." I shove him away and grab my beer.

Luke's been in and out of the bar all night. I'm not sure why. I'm not asking why, either. Well, since he's pulling on my arm, maybe I should ask. No. He's being stupid. Riley can handle this. She's sitting with Katie and Hadley's group. I quickly find her across the dance floor. My eyes plead with her to come get this fool.

"No, bro." Luke grabs my arm again. This time, he pulls me out of the chair. "You gotta come now."

"Why?" I shake off the beer that spilled from the bottle onto my hands.

"Luke, go dance with Riley," Lucas orders.

Luke ignores our brother and grabs my arm again. Unbelievable. This idiot is dragging me toward the front doors. Luke never listens.

"Luke, stop!" I jerk my arm free and glare at him. Half the guys on the upper level are staring at us. The next words out of my brother's mouth slam into me like hitting a brick wall.

"It's Darlin."

"Darlin?" No. I run for the door, losing Luke somewhere along the way.

The sound of chairs scraping on wood doesn't register. Every man I know jumps up to follow me. What's wrong with my truck? I'd swear Luke is pranking me, but he knows better than using my truck, or rather our grandfather's truck. If this is a prank, Lucas will have to arrest me for beating up our little brother. Riley won't even be able to save him tonight.

Chapter Four

Kyleigh

"Shh." Zoe gives Jenna a playful shove. "They'll hear us."

Jenna shoves her back. "No, they won't. They're all drunk by now."

The people inside Cowboys aren't the only ones who are drunk. Both of my friends are plastered. I have a little buzz, too, if I'm being honest. It's the only reason I let them talk me into this.

The night air is warm. Excitement electrifies the air around us. I'm not sure what kind of excitement it is just yet. Hopefully, in about twenty minutes, the three of us will be sitting on the couch at my dad's house, laughing about this. A feeling of uncertainty settles over me. Maybe we should leave and forget this crazy idea. Sadly for everyone, we're fully invested in this mission and a little drunk. My friends giggle and stumble into each other. Okay. We're more than a little drunk.

The sound of country music gets louder when somebody opens the front doors. I grab both their arms and pull my friends down. Slowly, I lift my head to peek over the hood of a white Prius. Hopefully, whoever owns this car doesn't live in Montana. It wouldn't survive a winter here. Someone must have gone inside. I don't see anyone in the parking lot.

I crouch back down to find my friends giggling on the ground. These two idiots are going to get us caught. Right now, we're just three drunk girls in the parking lot of a bar. We might survive that. If we go through with our plan, we could get into some serious trouble.

"If you two can't straighten up, maybe we should go home."

"No." Zoe sits up and tries to act sober. "We have to do this."

Jenna nods. The movement causes her to wobble. "Monica is depending on us."

Our friend, Monica, doesn't know we're here. She has no knowledge of our plans tonight. We came up with this idea twenty minutes ago, so we're winging it. Monica is curled up on her couch, wrapped in a blanket, with a container of ice cream on her lap. Seeing her red, tear-filled eyes and hearing her sobs broke the three of us. It's what sprang us into action tonight.

Monica had a date with her boyfriend tonight. He was supposed to drop her off at our little pajama party after their date. Skip was late, but Monica waited patiently for him. After two glasses of wine, Zoe blurted out that Skip wasn't going to show. Still, Monica held on. They've been dating for a little over a year, and she's devoted to him.

I'm not the best person to ask for relationship advice right now. I was an excellent source until two days ago. I would have happily shared some of my wisdom with Monica. Tonight, after two glasses of wine, my gut instincts agree with Zoe. The proof we needed came less than an hour ago. Monica received a text from one of her co-workers. Skip was stumbling around the parking lot at Cowboys with a redhead all over him. The second picture was of them sucking faces. Skip is not the smartest man on the planet. If you're going to cheat, you shouldn't do it in a town twenty minutes from your girlfriend. Skip is a stupid nickname, anyway. Needless to say, Monica is an emotional mess right now.

"What kind of truck does he drive?" I scan the parking lot. Seventy-five percent of the vehicles here are trucks. Another twenty percent are SUVs. Four percent are cars. The final one percent is a white Prius. I still can't wrap my head around that.

"Uh." Jenna scrolls back through Monica's text messages. "An old blue truck," she happily shouts.

"Shh." Zoe clamps her hand over Jenna's mouth. They fall over laughing.

I roll my eyes. If we're going to do this, we need to hurry up. If these two don't settle down, we're going to get arrested before we can deliver payback to the two-timing douchebag.

Old blue truck? Okay. That narrows it down drastically. There are about five blue trucks in the parking lot. Three look fairly new, so I scratch those off the list. One older truck is a little too close to the front doors. We definitely don't want to take a chance on that one.

"Does she know the make and model?" We need more information.

Jenna scrolls through the messages again. She sends a quick text. A reply comes within seconds.

"No." Jenna scooches close to me. "But here. Look at the truck they're leaning on."

We zoom in on the picture Monica sent us earlier. It's a Ford. Crouching low, I move past the black truck parked next to the Pruis. A slow grin crosses my face. The exact truck in the photo is parked three spots down. How nice of Skip to park off to the side, away from the other cars. His truck is in the corner space. Only one car can park next to him, and that space is empty. He's so stupid.

"Got it. Come on." I hurry toward the truck.

Zoe and Jenna crouch low and follow me. They've switched to serious mode, thank goodness. Their giggling was going to give us away.

"Should we really do this?" Zoe walks around the truck.

"Of course, we should," Jenna snaps. "It's for Monica."

"But it's a pretty truck." Zoe motions to the truck like we can't see it.

It is a pretty truck. Maybe we should rethink this. I'm surprised an idiot like Skip owns something this nice. I expected his truck to have faded paint with rust spots and dents. This truck has been well taken care of.

"Here." Jenna angrily holds up a picture of our friend. Why she took a screenshot of our video call with Monica is beyond me. "This is our friend." She shoves the phone toward Zoe and me. "She's upset and crying." She slaps her hand on the side of the truck. "This jerk hurt her."

"He broke her heart. The truck didn't," Zoe mumbles.

"Ha!" Jenna tosses a hand up. "He's a man. They don't have hearts."

After what Scott did to me, I agree with her. Men are cold and heartless. I also agree with Zoe. Even though this truck isn't one of the super old ones you see in car shows, it is pretty.

"Men only love their cars and trucks," Jenna continues her rant. She slaps her palm against the truck again. "Since this is where his heart is, we're going to punch him in the throat."

Okay. Her analogy isn't working. The heart and throat are two separate things. Well, they are connected. If you can't breathe, your heart will stop. Never mind. It's too much for my wine-tipsy brain to figure out.

"He doesn't get to get away with this." Jenna hits the truck on each word.

"But." Zoe scrunches up her face and stares at the truck.

"Oh, for goodness sake." Jenna snatches the bat from Zoe's hand. "Why don't you get the car and pull it to the side of the road? You can be the getaway driver."

"Good idea." Zoe's more than happy with this plan. She pulls Jenna's car to the side of the road in front of us. She's less than ten feet away.

"Now." Jenna grins at me. "Time for some payback."

"Jenna, wait!" My words are lost to the wind.

Jenna swings, and the passenger side headlight shatters to pieces. She bounces to the driver's side and swings again. Oh, this is bad, so so bad. She continues to swing and hit the truck as she makes her way to where I'm standing at the rear.

"Here." She shoves the bat into my hands. "Your turn."

"But."

"Hit it, Kyleigh!" Jenna screams. "Hit it! Hit it for what Scott did to you. Hit it for Monica. You remember our broken friend. Don't you?"

Of course, I remember our friend. I remember Scott and Brenda dropping the worst news of my life on me two days ago. But this doesn't feel right anymore.

"Hit it!" Jenna screams again.

I scream, too. I should have dropped the bat and run to the car. Drunk, angry me swings instead. Red pieces of plastic fly from what used to be the taillight.

"Hit it again!" Jenna claps her hands and squeals.

Did I drop the bat? Nope. I scream again and take out the other taillight.

"Hey!" a man shouts.

"Hey yourself!" Jenna shouts. "Tell your buddy this is what he gets for cheating!"

"Jenna," I snap.

"Let's go!" Zoe yells.

"You'll regret that!" The man rushes into the bar.

"Uh oh." I freeze when the realization of what we just did hits me.

"Come on!" Zoe shouts.

A group of men rushes out of the bar. Tires squeal behind me. I look over my shoulder to see Jenna's car racing down the road. Really? This was Jenna's idea. How can they leave me?

"What are you doing?" The deep, almost inhuman growl makes my entire body tremble. I might just die tonight.

Chapter Five

Leo

The sight before me has my blood running hot. What in the world? Somebody has destroyed my truck. Broken pieces of headlights and taillights lay scattered on the ground. Dents pepper the driver's side.

The smell of burning rubber fills the air as a car peels away, but I don't look. My eyes zero in on the culprit standing at the back of Darlin with a baseball bat in her hands. A woman. A woman I've never seen before has destroyed my truck.

"Oh no," she cries.

Her eyes are as wide as saucers. She drops the bat, spins on her heels, and starts running after the car that just left her behind. Her friends are the least of my worries right now. I want *her*. Running is pointless for her little legs. Within four long strides, I have her wrapped in my arms from behind. She's not going anywhere.

"Darlin." My grandfather's cry buries into my soul. It's a sound I'll never forget.

"Let me go!" She wiggles in my arms and kicks me in the leg.

"Not a chance, Sweetheart," I growl in her ear.

"Leo," Lucas says my name, calm and slow.

Usually, my twin can calm me down. There's nothing he can say tonight that will help. I've never been this mad. I take deep breaths through and out my nose. If I open my mouth, I'll pop off something hateful. Why should I care? She just destroyed my truck. Sirens pierce the night. The woman gasps and jerks in my arms.

"That's right, Slugger," I say next to her ear. "You're under arrest."

Her head drops in defeat. Her body shakes as she silently cries. It rips me apart when my mom and grandmother cry. I'm numb to this woman's tears.

"Leo, you've arrested her." Lucas holds a hand out towards us. "Let me have her."

"Nope." I hold my hand out and wiggle my fingers. "Give me your cuffs."

The woman gasps again. Granddad falls to his knees and starts picking up the broken pieces of the headlights. Luke pulls him to his feet and away from the truck before he cuts himself on the jagged pieces.

"Leo," Lucas pleads.

Aiden pulls into the parking lot. He kills the siren but leaves the blue lights flashing. He and Spencer get out. Their eyes widen when they see my truck.

"Aiden." I hold my hand out to him and keep one arm wrapped tightly around the woman. Since my brother won't help me, I have to ask another deputy. "I need your cuffs."

"She did this?" Aiden's as shocked as the rest of us. Unlike my brother, he hands me a set of handcuffs.

"You can't arrest me."

She tries to pull away when I loosen my hold on her. My hand slides down to her wrist. With a little more force than necessary, I pull her back and spin her to face me.

"You're already under arrest. Or did you miss that part?" I loom over her and clamp the cuff around her wrist. Before she has time to comprehend what's happening, I spin her around and grab her other wrist. "Maybe this will help you understand." The metal closes around her tiny wrist, securing her hands behind her back.

Aiden reaches for the woman's upper right arm. "I'll take her now." Our eyes meet. Every other man here shies away from me, but not Aiden. "Trust me. She won't get away. I'll drive her to the station, and we'll call your dad."

"Sheriff's on the way," Spencer calls out as he ends a call and pockets his phone.

"Leo, I don't want to use force. We'll hurt her if we do. I need you to let her go." Aiden stands a little taller. He'll use force if he has to. I've seen him do it.

"Why should I care what happens to her?" I snap.

"You care. You're just mad." Aiden tilts his head and waits for me to make a decision.

Oh, I'm beyond mad. I'm so far beyond mad that I don't know what to call this. The look in Aiden's eyes says he's about to use force, even on me. We're about the same height and weight. I can take him.

Aiden leans forward and lowers his voice, "Please, don't."

The man has some serious detective skills. He belongs in a major city, not our little neck of the woods. I didn't realize reading minds was part of his skill set. Who am I kidding? I've seen Aiden apprehend suspects plenty of times. Most of them were at Pete's Saloon. He'd have me on the ground and in cuffs within seconds. Reluctantly, I give a single nod and release the woman to him. Aiden walks her to the SUV and puts her in the back seat.

"Leo?"

I slowly turn my gaze from the woman in the back of Aiden's cruiser to the one standing beside my brother. Ally Roberts holds up both hands. I huff out a breath, drop my head, and run a hand through my hair. I can't be mad at every woman because of what another one did.

"Sorry, Ally." I wish I could say I have myself together. I don't.

"I get it." Ally points in the direction of her dad's garage. You can't see it from here, but it's within walking distance. "I'm going to go get the rollback. If I can have your keys, I'll tow Darlin to the shop."

"You'll put her inside, right?" I toss my keys to her.

"Of course." Ally hurries to the passenger side of Aiden's wife's SUV.

Ally is the only female mechanic I know. Her mother tried to turn her into a girlie girl. Ally was too much of a tomboy. She preferred being under the hood of a car with her dad. She's an only child, but she has lots of cousins. They don't live in Hayden Falls, though.

"Come on, Leo. We'll drive you to the station," Hadley, Lucas' girlfriend, says softly.

Hadley's tucked into Lucas' side. He gives me a warning glare. I look away and run my hand through my hair again. I can't snap at my brother's girlfriend. I like Hadley. She's the best thing to happen to my brother.

Speaking of brothers' girlfriends. Riley is helping Granddad into Luke's truck. Luke gives me a firm nod, saying he's got our grandfather. Some grandson I am. I was so angry that I forgot about my granddad.

"Yeah. Thanks."

Lucas helps Hadley into his SUV. He narrows his eyes at me and points to the back passenger seat on the driver's side. Whoa. Got it. Big Brother isn't letting his mad twin anywhere near his girlfriend. It's probably for the best.

I wouldn't do or say anything disrespectful to Hadley or Riley. I would never intentionally disrespect any woman. With the way I feel right now, I should probably avoid women until I calm down. I only associate with a handful, anyway.

Chapter Six

Leo

"What's your name?" Dad asks.

The woman doesn't look at him, nor does she answer the question. We've been trying to get her to tell us her name for nearly half an hour. She sits on the metal bench inside the holding cell, trembling. She sniffles and silently cries, but she won't speak. Riley gives her some tissues. Hadley offers her water and coffee. She shakes her head on both and looks away.

Hadley and Riley stand outside the holding cell. They haven't let any of us approach the bars, not even Dad. Both of my brothers' girlfriends talk softly to the woman. She still won't open up.

Dad looks at each of us. "Anybody know who she is?" Everyone shakes their heads.

"She didn't have a phone or a form of ID on her," Lucas says.

"Her stuff must have been in the car that drove off." Spencer hands Riley a blanket to pass to the shivering woman.

"Here you go, Sweetie." Riley holds the blanket through the bars.

The woman's red-rimmed eyes glance at the blanket. More tears spill over as she reaches for it. She curls up inside the blanket with her knees pulled up to her chest and rests her head on them.

Dad tries again. "Ma'am, we need to know your name, and it would help if you'd answer a few of our questions."

"We could fingerprint her," Aiden suggests. "If she's in the system, we'll at least know her name and possibly who to contact."

She snaps her head toward us and slides to the far end of the bench. She either has a record, or she doesn't want someone to know she's here. I'm not sure how we'll fingerprint her. Hadley and Riley stand shoulder to shoulder. They're not going to let anyone inside the cell.

I'm stuck sitting at my desk. Dad and Lucas insist I stay here until I calm down. Removing me from the cell door hasn't gotten us any information from the woman. Well, I wasn't exactly in front of the cell door. My brothers' girlfriends stood in front of me. My temper might be why they appointed themselves as the woman's protectors.

"Here you go, hon." Mom sets a cup of coffee on my desk. She's been hovering around me since she got here.

"Thank you." I don't really want it, but I'll never be rude to my mom.

The woman's sad eyes meet mine. Her blue eyes would be bright and sparkling if she weren't crying. My anger's fading because looking into her eyes makes my heart feel like it's being stabbed. I quickly look away. I'm not ready to show her any compassion.

"Will you please reconsider?" Mom holds a to-go cup of coffee through the bars.

The woman slides to the edge of the bench and cautiously takes the cup. It's an improvement.

"Can I call my dad?" Her voice is so low I almost missed it.

Everyone pauses and looks around. Dad and Aiden perk up. She's finally talking. It's definitely progress.

"You don't have a phone on you," Dad says.

"I know his number by heart."

"Great," I mumble. "She's a Daddy's Girl."

Mom narrows her eyes at me. Dad shakes his head. Lucas shoves my shoulder. He needs to go stand beside his girlfriend. It makes no sense for my family to be mad at me when she's the reason we're here. At least Luke and Levi are staying out of it. Luke's wandering aimlessly around the room. Levi sits with Granddad and Grandma. Riley and Hadley have their arms crossed, glaring at me. This is not my night.

"And you're a Mama's Boy," the woman shoots back.

Everyone's head snaps toward the holding cell. Whoa. Somebody found their voice. She has no idea how wrong she is. Well, of course, I love my mom dearly, and she loves me even more than I can imagine. However, Levi is what you'd call a Mama's Boy. Is there such a thing as a Granddad's Boy? If so, that fits me better.

"Here, Dear." Mom hands a cordless phone through the bars.

The woman squeezes her eyes shut and takes a deep breath before dialing a number. Another sob shakes her body as she lifts the phone to her ear. My eyes drop to the floor. I'm not a heartless man. Watching her cry does break my heart. I'm not ready to let my caring side show yet. Yeah, it makes me a jerk, but she destroyed my truck.

"Daddy, I've been arrested." She hangs up before he can reply and hands the phone back to Mom.

Granddad stands. "Why did you do it?"

Her eyes meet mine again. "He knows why."

All eyes turn to me. I stare at her for a moment.

"I have no idea what she's talking about. I've never seen her before."

Lucas keeps his eyes on her as he walks over to stand beside Dad. "She looks familiar, but I can't figure out where I've seen her."

"Uh, guys." Luke's standing across the room, holding a picture frame.

"Not now, Luke." Lucas waves his hand like Luke's an afterthought. My twin is in cop mode.

"But." Luke points to the picture in his hand.

"Not now," Lucas says sternly.

Luke tosses his hands in the air. He sits on the corner of the desk and pouts. Levi may be the baby of the family and gets away with everything, but Luke perfected pouting years ago. Grandma and Riley hurry over and wrap their arms around him. See? Pouting works for

Luke. He and Riley whisper. She looks at the picture he's still holding and gasps. What's that about?

"What did my son do?" Dad takes advantage of Riley giving up her self-appointed post and walks up the bars.

"He cheated." She crosses her arms, leans back against the bars, and pouts. Great. Another pouter.

"What exactly did I cheat on?"

This is getting more bizarre by the minute. She knows nothing about me. I have no idea what she believes I cheated on or why she had to take revenge on my truck. We should probably call Doctor Larson and let him have her committed to a mental hospital.

"Leo?" Mom questions.

I shake my head. I'm as confused as everyone else is.

Hadley grabs the bars. "How did he cheat?"

We haven't gotten her name out of her. There's no way she's going to answer Hadley. As I suspected, she drops her head and looks away.

"What's going on?" Chief Deputy Green demands as he walks into the room.

Well, darn. Somebody must have ticked him off tonight.

"Hey, Al. You didn't have to come. Your shift doesn't start until eight," Dad says.

"I know that." He knows it, but he's in uniform anyway. "Somebody wanna tell me what's going on here?"

Granddad points to the woman in the holding cell. "She destroyed our truck."

Al's eyes widen. "Darlin?"

"Yeah." Lucas shows him a picture of my truck on his phone. "Noah's getting us the security footage."

"There has to be a mistake." Al looks to the woman. She'd buried even deeper into the blanket now.

"Nope." I lay my forearms on my desk and lean forward. "Caught her in the act with the bat in her hands."

"Why?" Al's eyes remain on the woman.

She won't answer him. We've been asking her that question and several more for nearly an hour. We still don't know her name.

I wave my hand toward the holding cell. "Because Slugger over there has lost her mind."

Al growls and snaps his head in my direction. He looks as though he's ready to kill somebody. That's strange. The man has no problem using his authority when it's needed. He'll happily arrest anyone being a jerk. He took great pleasure in arresting Aaron Bailey last month. It broke his pride when Dad told him to unlock the cell and release Aaron. Still, I've never seen him look like this.

"We've been trying to get her to answer that for nearly an hour," Lucas snaps Al out of whatever moment he was having just now. For a moment, I thought the man was about to challenge me.

"Why didn't somebody call me?" Al's eyes bounce to every cop in the room.

"You're *Chief Deputy Sheriff*, not the Sheriff. Him we called. I've been here for nearly two years. Not once has anyone told me I'm supposed to call you every time I make an arrest." Aiden crosses his arms.

Never ask Aiden Maxwell a question unless you want a blunt answer. The man will go toe-to-toe with anybody. He doesn't believe in beating around a bush and dragging things out. Aiden gets straight to the point, and he won't sugarcoat things, either. Al isn't going to butt heads with Aiden.

"I don't have to be called at every arrest, but you should have called me tonight," Al snaps.

Whoa. Looks like I was wrong. We're about to have cops fighting in the middle of the Sheriff's Office.

Aiden's eyes narrow. He takes a step toward Al. "When my Sheriff orders me to do that, I will."

"Aiden." Dad steps in front of him. "Get the fingerprinting kit and print her. Maybe she's already in the system."

Aiden gives Dad a firm nod. He glares at Al as he walks across the room. Aiden's no pushover, but he respects authority. He may disagree with Dad from time to time, but he'll follow orders. Dad's always had a soft spot for Aiden for some reason. Aiden respects my dad as much as he does his own.

Al gives up the staring contest with Aiden and turns to Dad. Good choice. "What do you mean by that?"

"She doesn't have a phone or ID on her." Dad turns to face the woman. "She won't answer our questions or tell us her name. We're hoping printing her will at least give us her name."

"No need to print her." Al walks past Hadley and up to the cell. The woman's eyes drop from Al to the floor. "Kyleigh."

Slowly, her once again tear-filled eyes lift to his. "Hi, Daddy."

Shocked gasps echo around the room, me included.

"That's what I've been trying to tell you." Luke turns the photo he's been holding around.

Oh, snap. She's Chief Deputy Green's daughter.

Chapter Seven

Kyleigh

"First." Dad closes his eyes and rubs his temples with his fingers. He sighs and looks at me again. I try to disappear into the blanket. "I can't believe we're here. Second, why are you not cooperating? You know that's important."

As a cop's daughter, I do know cooperation is important. I haven't lived under his roof since I was eight and seen a cop's life from day to day. Still, he shared his life with me whenever he visited me in Seattle. During his vacation time, he gets a room close by, and we spend the week together. I've heard so many crazy stories about this little town. I feel like I already know half of these people.

Dad would have been here within minutes of my arrest if I had told these cops my name. My arrest? This is so unreal. I never thought in a million years I'd be arrested for any reason, let alone for smashing up someone's car. Well, truck, in this case.

"I'm sorry, Daddy," I whisper.

I can't look him in the eye. I refused to cooperate because I never wanted to disappoint him, and I was trying to find a way out of here without calling him. I've cried enough in front of these people. If I look at my dad now, I'll be a crumpled heap on the floor.

As hard as I tried to figure a way out of this, I couldn't. I couldn't call Jenna and Zoe. If they show up, they'll be in trouble, too. Monica's no help. She's an emotional mess. My only other option was Mom. She'd just call Dad. When a solution couldn't be found, I gave in and called him myself. I knew he'd be disappointed. It's why I hung up before he could reply. I tried to prepare myself for seeing him. It only took him ten minutes to get here. It could have been ten years, and I still wouldn't be ready to see the hurt look on his face.

"Did you really do this?" Dad swallows hard. He wants an answer I can't give him. I nod. "Baby, why?"

Sheriff Barnes places a hand on Dad's shoulder. "She wasn't alone. The boys tell me a car raced off as they ran outside."

"Noah just sent the security footage." Lucas walks over to Dad. He points at his phone screen. "This one took the first swing and did most of the damage."

Even though I haven't been talking, I've been listening. It took a while to figure out which Barnes brother was which. Dad talks about them a lot, especially Lucas and Leo, because he works with them. The only way I can remember who's who is by the color of the shirt they're wearing. Thank goodness they all have a different colored one on tonight. Leo jumps up from the desk to watch the security video over his brother's shoulder.

"I doubt she'll give us her name." Leo narrows his eyes at me.

"It doesn't matter." I lift my head and look him in the eye.

"It doesn't matter?" Leo approaches the cell. "My truck is in pieces, and you think it doesn't matter?"

"It was my idea." I boldly lift my chin. It was Jenna's, but they don't need to know that.

"Fine." Leo's eyes harden even more as he takes a step back. "Let her take all the blame for it."

"Leo," his dad warns.

Being in this cell is probably the safest place for me right now. My dad's disappointed. Leo's mad. His grandfather is an emotional mess. Apparently, the truck used to be his and has sentimental value for some reason. Every other Barnes in the room shakes their heads when they look at me. The two girlfriends and Mrs. Barnes are being kind to me. Their grandmother looks at me with sympathetic eyes. At least the women in the Barnes family are kind-hearted.

Lucas grabs Leo's arm and pulls him back to his desk. Dad cuts his eyes at Leo. He wants to say something. For now, he's letting Lucas handle his angry brother.

"Kyleigh, why did you do this?" Dad's not just asking anymore. He's in cop mode.

"She said Leo cheated," Mrs. Barnes replies.

Dad looks between Leo and me. Once again, everyone in the room seems confused, even Leo. He can't be that big of an idiot. He's obviously playing the innocent act for his family. If I didn't know any better, his big brown eyes would have me believing him too. I know better. I've seen the proof. Well, the picture was dark and a little blurry, but there was no mistaking his truck. After the way my week started out, he gets no sympathy from me. I'm not softening my heart for a cheater.

Leo tosses his hands up. "I have no idea what she's talking about."

He's a liar and a very good one. Everyone in here believes him. Denying it doesn't change things, though. Maybe I should spill the beans and let them all know the true character of the man they're protecting.

"Kyleigh?" Dad's voice hardens even more.

"Why do you think Leo cheated on something?" Hadley's still standing outside the cell.

I chance looking at her. "Because he did. And it wasn't on something. It was on someone."

"Now I know she's crazy," Leo huffs.

Lucas gestures toward his brother. His eyes remain on me. "Leo hasn't dated anyone in a long time."

I drop my head back and laugh. This guy is a bigger jerk than I thought. He's been hiding his relationship with Monica for a year. She's going to be an even bigger mess when she finds out. She and I need to talk. How dare she not tell me Skip was a cop?

"Kyleigh, it's true. Leo doesn't have a girlfriend," Daddy says.

I finally look at my dad. Great. Even he believes the two-timing jerk. This is unbelievable.

"I saw the picture." I glance at Leo and shake my head. He's cute. I can see why Monica fell for him. Cheating makes him disgusting in my eyes.

"Kyleigh, you're going to have to be a little more specific. What picture? And who do you think he cheated on?" Dad's deeper into cop mode now.

"Monica."

"I don't know anyone named Monica." Leo won't even look at me now. Good. I don't want him looking at me anyway.

"Who's Monica?" Sheriff Barnes ignores his son.

"One of her friends from Walsburg," Dad replies.

"I only go to Walsburg when we get a call or when someone's in the hospital." Leo leans back in his chair and stares at the opposite wall.

"Kyleigh, I can't help you if you don't tell us everything. You were supposed to be having a Girls' Night at the house with Jenna and Zoe." He turns to Sheriff Barnes. "Jenna Owens is the girl in the video. I'm guessing Zoe Weber is the driver of the car. Monica is Monica Lopez. All three live in Walsburg." Great. My cop dad just gave my friends away.

"I don't know any of them." Leo continues to stare straight ahead.

"Kyleigh, we need a full explanation now." Cop Dad isn't going to let me wiggle my way out of this.

"Fine. Since he wants to play dumb." I angrily toss a hand toward Leo. I have no idea why Monica calls him Skip. It must be a pet name, and I don't need an explanation. "Monica had a date tonight. It's why she couldn't come over. She called later, crying because her boyfriend didn't show up. Somebody sent her a photo of *Skip*." I say his pet name with disgust, "He and a redhead were all over each other outside Cowboys."

"Skip?" Dad's face scrunches up. He looks at Leo. The cheater shrugs.

"Wait." Luke holds up a hand. "Are you talking about Skip Rodgers from Walsburg?"

"What?" Now, I'm confused.

"You've got to be kidding me," Leo grumbles.

"Skip Rodgers comes to Cowboys every other week. He leaves with a different woman every time. He did leave with a redhead tonight. He and I used to run the same partying groups. He's a die-hard partier and a womanizer." Luke quickly turns to his girlfriend. He holds both hands up. "It was never about the women for me, Rocky. I just like having fun."

"What does this Skip fellow have to do with my grandson's truck?" their grandfather demands. His wife cups his face in her hands and whispers to him until he calms down. It's sweet to watch them together.

"He drives an old blue truck. It's nowhere near as nice as Darlin," Luke says.

Leo's truck was given the nickname by his grandfather. No one has shared the story. Of course, I'm probably the only one here who doesn't know it.

"Kyleigh, vandalizing someone's vehicle is wrong no matter what. But why did you destroy Leo's truck?" Dad pushes for more.

"Skip had the redhead pushed up against it." My eyes drop to the floor. Oh, my gosh. We got the wrong truck.

"When did you get the photo?" Aiden asks.

"About an hour before we went to Cowboys."

Lucas pulls out his phone and heads to the hallway. "I'll get Noah to send us the security footage."

The others talk amongst themselves and ask questions. I tune them all out. Dad stands with his shoulder against the bars. Not only did I commit a crime and disappoint my dad, but Skip gets away with hurting my friend. This is so embarrassing.

Lucas comes back into the room. "Got it."

Leo, Luke, and their father rush over to watch the video with Lucas. My father quietly watches me. Dad will probably ask me to leave when this fiasco is over. Maybe I should have gone to Mom's.

"Great," Leo huffs and returns to his desk. "I'll have to disinfect the whole truck after that."

Luke points to the phone screen. "That's Skip's truck next to Darlin."

I drop my head back and groan. The empty parking space next to Leo's truck. With all the bad luck I'm having this week, I should lock myself inside the house and never leave. Wait. I'm locked in a cell. Am I going to get to go home tonight? My eyes snap to Dad's.

He seems to have read my mind. "Can I take her home, and we sort this out tomorrow?"

"She's under arrest for vandalism. She also failed a sobriety test. We haven't decided on charging her with being drunk and disorderly yet," Lucas says. "And there's the issue that she doesn't live here. She has to see the Judge before she can go home."

Dad closes his eyes and groans. He saw the wine Jenna and Zoe brought over before he retreated to his room. It's a wonder we didn't wake him up when we slipped out of the house. Jenna isn't exactly a quiet person. The way the three of us acted tonight, you'd think we were unruly teenagers.

"She's staying with me for a while," Dad tells Sheriff Barnes.

"You're just going to let her go?" Leo's still angry. He will be for a long time.

Sheriff Barnes is unsure what to do. He has an obligation as the Sheriff to uphold the law. He's a father and wants to help his son. He's also my dad's friend.

"We could put an ankle monitor on her," Aiden suggests.

"You want to track my daughter?" Dad yells.

"Yup." Aiden shows no emotion.

"We could put her in a cell and let her stay until she sees a judge." Of course, Lucas is on his brother's side.

Sheriff Barnes looks at Leo. Leo doesn't agree, but he nods. Oh, my gosh. I want to cry. This cannot be happening.

"Spencer will finish booking Kyleigh. Aiden will get the ankle monitor ready. It's the only way she's walking out of here tonight," Sheriff Barnes' words are final.

Chapter Eight

Kyleigh

"*O*kay. Everything's working." Aiden offers Dad the monitor base. "You can hook this up when you get home."

Dad stares at the device. "Is this really necessary?"

"Sheriff ordered it, so yeah." Aiden shoves the box into Dad's hands and walks away.

"How long does she have to wear this?" Dad asks Sheriff Barnes.

"Judge Morgan's on vacation. It's up to him. He'll see her first thing Monday morning." At least Sheriff Barnes made the phone call.

Great. I have to wear this horrible-looking thing for five days. My appointment with the judge won't go well. I'm sure the man didn't appreciate being called in the middle of the night while on vacation.

"This is unbelievable," Dad mumbles. "If all of you are satisfied, can I take her home now?"

"You can," Sheriff Barnes replies.

"Come on, Baby. Let's go." Dad places a hand on my back as I stand. He steps behind me like a shield and ushers me toward the door.

My eyes meet Leo's as we walk by his desk. He glances at my ankle and grins. There's nothing happy about his little smirk. He believes I'm getting what I deserve. Who knows? Maybe I am. Darlin was a pretty truck.

Dad doesn't speak on the drive home. He lives just outside the city limits. The Wentworths own most of the land on this road. Zoe told me that Grace opened a bookstore on the square. I can't wait to visit. Reading books might be the only safe thing for me to do for a while. Dad connects the monitor base to his house phone when we get home.

Finally, he speaks to me. "Why don't you get some sleep? You can clean this up in the morning."

We glance around the room. Jenna, Zoe, and I left a huge mess. We obviously relived our wild teenage years tonight, not that I was ever wild. My friends and I had sleepovers when we were little. We had one all-night party during our Freshman year of college. Zoe went to college in Washington State. Jenna and Monica stayed at home and went to Missoula. They visited Zoe one weekend, and all three of them stayed at Mom's with me. We crammed all the silly things teenage girls do during a sleepover during that weekend. We didn't beat up anyone's car, though.

I look down at my awful new piece of jewelry. "Can I take a shower?"

"Yeah. It's waterproof."

I start toward the hallway and pause. "I really am sorry, Daddy. I can go to Mom's if you want."

"No, Baby." He walks over and wraps me in his arms. "We'll figure it out." He kisses my forehead. "You can't leave until you see Judge Morgan, and I don't want you to leave, anyway."

He has no idea how comforting it is to know he wants me here. I wrap my arms around his waist and rest my cheek against his chest. "I love you, Daddy."

"I love you too, Baby. Now, get your shower and get some sleep." He kisses my forehead again before going to his room.

After a quick hot shower, quick because I don't trust this monitor not to shock me, I go to my room. Dad has a three-bedroom, single-story brick house. The house is more modern than I expected, but you can tell a man lives here.

I sit on the side of the bed and do my best to towel-dry my hair. Blow drying is a disaster for my curls. I only do it when I'm short on time. I hate going to bed with wet hair, but I don't want to turn on the hairdryer. My dad needs some sleep. He has to be at work in a few hours. Hopefully, his co-workers won't give him a hard time tomorrow because of me. Well, later today. It's after midnight.

I'm so ashamed of myself. I came here to get myself together. After only two days, I've made matters worse. My boss is letting me work remotely for a couple of weeks. If the judge makes me stay longer, I could lose my job. Going back to the office will be hard. Scott works for the same company. It was rare for us to bump into each other during the day, but it has happened. I'm not ready to see him after what he did.

A light tapping comes on the window, bolting me from the bed. My first thought is to get Dad. Maybe I heard wrong, and it's just the wind. The sound comes again. Nope. That's a knock.

"Kyleigh," Jenna whisper yells.

I drop the wet towel on the floor and rush to the window. When I open the curtains, Jenna and Zoe wave at me. At least they didn't completely desert me.

"Hey," I whisper. Hopefully, opening the window didn't make enough noise to wake my dad.

"We're sorry we left you," Zoe apologized.

"We thought you might want this." Jenna holds up my purse. She doesn't apologize.

"Yeah." Of course, I want my purse. My phone and wallet are in there. I quickly pop the screen out.

"Did you get in a lot of trouble?" Zoe asks.

I step back and hold up my left foot so they can see the monitor. Zoe gasps and covers her mouth with her hand.

"Oh." Jenna places a hand on her chest.

"Yeah." I glance over my shoulder to the door. Dad's still asleep. "And we got the wrong truck."

"Oh, Kyleigh. I'm so sorry," Zoe apologized again.

"Do they know we were with you?" Jenna peeps behind me. She must think my dad is going to come in here and arrest her, too.

"Yeah, they know."

"We're getting arrested?" Zoe cries.

"You ratted us out?" Jenna huffs. "Unbelievable."

"No, I didn't." Her attitude is making me wish I had. "The security camera showed everything." Not that I watched the videos.

"I can't go to jail," Jenna snaps.

"We were in on it." Zoe gives her a little shove. "Besides, it was your idea."

As much as I want to let Jenna stew for a while, I can't do that to Zoe. "Nobody is coming for you. I took all the blame."

Jenna smiles. "Thank you."

"But it's not right," Zoe protests. Jenna elbows her in the side.

"It's done." I shrug. "Just leave it as it is."

"You're the best." Jenna smiles sweetly. She's just happy she's not in trouble.

Wow. I put my palm against my forehead and huff out a long breath. I've had enough drama and now criminal charges to last a lifetime. I'd call Jenna out on her pettiness, but it's not worth it. She is my friend, after all.

The three of us scream when a bright light shines on Jenna and Zoe. They freeze. It's just a light, and it's not blue. There's no siren, either.

"Girls." Dad drops the light to the ground.

"Mr. Green, we…" Jenna stumbles for words.

"They brought my purse." I hold it up.

"They could have used the front door," Dad says.

"Yes, Sir. We should have," Zoe agrees.

"It's late. You two should head home." Dad shines the flashlight toward Jenna's car at the end of the driveway.

"Yes, Sir." Zoe grabs Jenna's arms and pulls her away.

"I'm sorry, Daddy." I'll be apologizing for this night for years to come.

"Just glad it was your friends and not a burglar." He turns the flashlight off. "Get some sleep. We'll talk tomorrow."

I nod and lower the window. Dad pushes the screen back in place. I've caused him enough grief for one night. I turn off the bedside lamp and settle under the covers. I really need to rethink my life and maybe a few of my friends.

Chapter Nine

Leo

"Well, ole girl, we're going to be spending a lot of time together." I slowly rub my hand over Darlin's hood.

Things were dark and dreary last night. I thought seeing my truck in the daylight would be better. I was wrong. Seeing the damage Kyleigh Green and her friends did to Darlin almost has me crying like my granddad.

"You two need a few minutes?"

I glance over my shoulder at Ally. I'm not sure if she's being sarcastic or not. She's always been good at holding a serious expression. The only time I've seen her slip is during Girls' Night Out after a few drinks.

"I'm good." I'm not good. However, staying mad and upset won't fix my truck.

"You want me to do the work? Or do you want to fix her yourself?"

"I want to do as much of it as I can." She knows this, but I appreciate her asking. Anything I can't do, I'll gladly let her.

"Okay." She nods and hands me a parts list. "I already found the headlights and taillights for you. I'll order them if you want me to. You might be able to buff some of these dents out. If between us, we can't, my cousin knows a guy near Thorn Valley who has a couple of trucks like Darlin. We can try to buy parts from him."

Wow. It's not even noon, and she's already been working on helping me fix Darlin. Ally's uncle owns a winery in Thorn Valley. It's less than two hours away. Just looking at the driver's side of my truck is enough to know I won't be able to buff out all the dents. It's good to know a parts guy is close by.

"Thanks, Ally. I really appreciate this. Definitely order both sets of lights, and it looks as though Darlin is going to need a new door."

"The lights are already ordered. Plus, the chrome trim doors for the headlights. Those aren't salvageable, and they weren't cheap, either. The guy with the door is on vacation. He'll meet with you next Saturday at two. It's your day off, by the way." Ally hands me a billing invoice and an appointment card.

Okay. That's a little creepy. How does she know when my days off are? Maybe I should hire Ally to organize my life. She's done more in two hours than half the people in this town do in two days, possibly a week.

She's not wrong about the headlights, either. The two chrome doors are over a hundred dollars each. The lights themselves are almost the same. The taillights are the cheapest part on the list. My eyes bug out when I see the price of the door.

"He wants four hundred for the door?" Surely, that's a mistake.

"Yep. But if you had the hood for a 1970 Corvette Stingray laying around, he'd trade you for it."

Well, that sucks. I don't know anyone who owns a Corvette, let alone a 1970 Stingray. I might need to take Luke with me to meet this guy. I'm not good at bartering over prices. Luke could talk a toddler out of a sucker.

"Thanks again." I pull out my wallet and hand her my credit card to pay for the lights.

"Not a problem." She goes to the front office to run my card. "She's drivable. You should get in the passenger door, though. Or I could tow her to your family's barn."

I glance back into the bay at Darlin. "No. I won't drive her like that. Add the tow to the bill."

"Don't worry, young man." Mr. Roberts pats my arm. "You'll have Darlin looking great in no time."

He's right. Darlin will one day soon be back to her former glory. I'm a little too heartbroken to feel confident about it today, though. I nod in reply. Mr. Roberts turns to answer the shop phone when it rings. It's for the best. I'm not in the mood to talk about my truck. Maybe after I start working on her, I will be.

"Here you go, Leo." Ally hands me back my credit card. "The lights will be here this weekend. I'll make sure you have them before Monday so you can start working on Darlin. Be sure to confirm the appointment next weekend with Bryson. Take cash. That sometimes helps."

Bryson Crane will take me for every dime he can get. I have nothing to trade. He probably already knows I desperately need the door. Ally could shop around for another one at a cheaper price. My truck isn't something collectors look for. Waiting would have my granddad in pieces longer. I don't want to see him shed another tear over this. No matter what Bryson wants for the door, I'll pay it to see Granddad smile again.

"We'll be right there." Mr. Roberts hangs up the phone and hands his daughter the work order slip.

Ally takes one look at it and throws her hands in the air. "You've got to be kidding me."

"Nope. Pick the car up and move it to the front of the line." Mr. Roberts walks over to the coffee pot like nothing's wrong.

"I'm tired of working on this piece of crap, Dad."

"I know. You've told me that repeatedly." Mr. Roberts casually takes a sip of his coffee and turns to face Ally. "He's paying extra to get the work done fast."

"He needs to set it on fire and buy an American-made car." Ally tosses the work order on the desk.

"Ally Girl, we don't tell 'em what to drive. We just fix 'em when they break down." He hands the work order back to her.

"I've already told him this BMW is a lemon. He doesn't get it. He thinks I'm talking about fruit." Mr. Roberts lets his daughter continue her rant. "He's an idiot, and I'm sure the good doctor will need a ride into town too."

"He does," Mr. Roberts confirms.

"Can I set the car on fire?" The look in Ally's eyes tells me she'll do it.

"No, young lady." Mr. Roberts points at his daughter. "Pick the car up. Drop the doctor off at the office. Fix the car."

"Fine," Ally huffs. She grumbles all the way to the rollback.

Just my luck, I parked beside it. "I didn't know Matt had a BMW."

"Doctor Larson doesn't. He's got the sense to at least buy a Dodge, not my recommendation, by the way. Doctor Bennett, however, is an idiot. If he's going to move here, somebody needs to educate him."

"Doesn't he have a PhD?" Ally cuts her eyes at me. I hold both hands up in surrender. I'm laughing on the inside, though. I won't laugh openly at a woman who owns power tools. "Thanks again, Ally. I'll see you when the parts come in."

Before I'm murdered by the only female mechanic in the county, I get in my car and drive home. Monday is my day off. I didn't tell Ally that, by the way. It's more proof she's on top of things. I'll spend Monday at my parents' house working on Darlin. Kyleigh Green has an appointment with Judge Morgan on Monday. I might just stop by the courthouse first. Mom works there part-time. I'm sure she'd love a coffee from Beth's and a pastry from Sweet Treats from one of her sons. Yeah, I'll make sure Mom's week starts out great.

Chapter Ten

Kyleigh

The moment I parked in the town square and got out of my car, I knew coming to town was a mistake. Every person here, and I mean *every single one of them*, stopped to stare at me. A few huddle together in little groups, whispering. Some don't even try to hide their gossiping behind their hands.

Even the men pause and watch me walk across the street. They don't gossip, though. Instead, the men look as though they're about to burst out laughing. I've no idea why. Well, maybe I do. It must be funny to them because I mistakenly beat up one of the Barnes brother's trucks. Why they think the situation is comical makes no sense, but whatever.

I jerk the door to Beth's Morning Brew open with a huff—big mistake. Once again, everyone stops to stare at me, even the baristas. Surprisingly, Lucas Barnes' girlfriend is one of them.

"Kyleigh," Zoe calls out from the table in the front corner of the shop.

Zoe points to the to-go cup of coffee sitting in front of the empty chair across from her. Oh, thank goodness. She ordered for me. Zoe is the best. Monica waves, but she doesn't smile. It might be a while before she genuinely smiles again. She'll fake one many times, I'm sure. I've faked a few myself.

"Thanks." I quickly drop down in the chair. At least from here, my back is to all these nosy people.

"You okay?" Monica asks.

"I should be asking you that question."

She's the one who just found out her boyfriend is cheating on her. I know the heartache she feels right now. My boyfriend cheated, too. I've had a couple more days than her to process things. It's not enough time to offer her any advice on healing. I'm not healing. I'm deflecting.

"I'll be okay." Monica shrugs one shoulder. "I suspected Skip was seeing someone else. I just didn't want to believe it."

I totally get where she's coming from. A part of me wants to deny Scott cheated on me, too. It hurts, and it strips you of your confidence. No matter how much it hurts, knowing the truth is better. If I hadn't stayed home Monday night, I'd still be in Seattle living a lie.

"You two need to forget both of those good-for-nothing jerks and move on." Zoe waves a finger between Monica and me.

"I'm not ready." Monica drops her head.

I nudge her with my shoulder. Monica leans toward me until our heads touch. Scott and Skip are good-for-nothing jerks. However, sometimes, moving on is easier said than done.

"Forgetting will never happen. The moving on will take a little time," I tell Zoe. Monica nods.

"I get that." Zoe nods, too. "I hope it doesn't take too long, though. You both deserve better."

Mine and Monica's eyes meet. We sigh and nod. We do deserve better. I don't know about her, but I won't be looking for better for a while. All men, right now, are in the jerk category with me. Well, not my dad. He'll always be my hero.

I grab my coffee and take a sip. A loud moan escapes me after the first swallow of minty chocolate goodness. Several people look my way, but I ignore them. My eyes bug out as I gawk at Zoe. She got me a Peppermint Mocha in July.

"I know. Right?" Zoe laughs and points toward the baristas behind me. "Beth keeps it on the menu year-round for her friend Katie."

I lift my cup in a celebratory salute. "Thank you, Beth and Katie." I'll definitely be visiting the coffee shop more often.

Monica leans close and whispers, "Do you really have on an ankle monitor?"

"Yeah." I'm embarrassed to admit it. "I'd show it to you, but enough people are staring at me already."

"I'm sorry."

I quickly take Monica's hand in mine. "It's not your fault. You didn't know what we were doing. This was our bright idea. Well, it was Jenna's." I look past Zoe out the front window at the square. "Where's Jenna?"

"She has a date tonight." Zoe gives her head a little shake. I guess she doesn't like the guy.

"She's meeting a guy in Missoula," Monica adds.

"Well." I don't know what to say. Jenna hasn't mentioned she has a boyfriend. "I hope she has better luck with her guy than we did."

"Oh, she's not dating this guy." Zoe lifts her eyebrows.

I'm confused. She has a date, but she's not dating the guy? That makes no sense.

"She's just looking for a good time," Monica explains.

Jenna? No. I would never imagine in a hundred years that Jenna would be wild.

"Does she even know this guy?" Alarm shoots through me when my friends shake their heads. "And she went alone?"

"I offered to go and hide in the shadows, but she turned me down," Zoe replies.

"I let her brother know. He's going to follow her tonight," Monica says.

"Good." That makes me feel better. I've heard some horror stories in college of dates that went bad. A woman can't be too careful.

"What are your plans tonight since you can't go with us to O'Brien's?" Zoe props her elbow on the table and rests her chin in her hand.

She called a little while ago to see if I wanted to go to the other bar in Hayden Falls. O'Brien's is technically a Tavern. It's the only other bar in this town. O'Brien's and Cowboys have a better reputation for bars than any of the others in the area. None of us think it's a good idea for me to show up at Cowboys anytime soon.

"I'm not sure. Dad called before you did. Someone invited us to dinner. I texted him after you called and told him I'd meet him here."

I can't go out with my friends tonight, but I wanted to see them. The coffee shop was the only place I could think of. I've been wanting to stop in here from the moment I drove through the square on my way to Dad's house.

It's already five. Dad had to stay late at the Sheriff's Office to file some paperwork. The coffee shop and every other store in town will close by six. Only the restaurants stay open late in this little town. It's so weird and will take some getting used to if I stay with Dad longer. I'm used to stores staying open until nine or eleven. Some were even open all night.

My friends and I laugh and talk for twenty minutes. Monica's laughs are light, but at least she's smiling. Zoe points out people she knows as they walk past the window. There's still a lot of activity going on in town even though the official Fourth of July Celebration is over. It's easy to figure out who the townsfolk are. The tourists smile and go about their business. The wonderful citizens of Hayden Falls stop and stare. Two old women stop on the sidewalk behind Zoe and point at me through the window.

"Really?" I toss both hands up. I hope they get their eyes full. I'm so tired of this nonsense. Once again, I've drawn the attention of everyone in the coffee shop.

Hadley walks over and pulls the blind down. It's thin, more like a screen. We can still see the two old biddies outside.

"Sorry about that." Hadley smiles sweetly. "Ms. Taylor is the worst gossiper in this town."

"Thank you." I return her polite smile. I like Hadley. She was really nice to me at the Sheriff's Office. I motion toward the window. "Do they always stare openly like this?"

"I'm afraid so." She lightly laughs. "You'll eventually learn to ignore them. If you don't, you'll be arguing with ninety percent of the town."

"They all know about the truck." It's not a question. Of course, they all know. I sigh and shake my head.

"It's not just the truck." Hadley grits her teeth in a weird smile.

"Oh, no," Monica gasps.

"What?" I look around quickly.

Zoe laughs and looks at Hadley. "She's in Hayden Happenings. Isn't she?"

Hadley nods. I look at the front counter. All of the baristas and customers are nodding, too. It's proof you can't have a private conversation in this town.

"The gossip blog?" Dad mentioned it to me, but I never looked. I thought it was a joke.

Zoe is already pulling up the website. Okay. It's not a joke. Me being in it is. Zoe's eyes widen, and her mouth falls open as she reads.

"What?" I don't know why I'm asking. I could look it up on my phone.

"Here." Monica hands me her phone.

A Fourth of July Hit

There were some bigger hits at Cowboys Wednesday night than there were at the town's baseball game. Apparently, bats are used to introduce yourself to the community. Our newest resident thinks so, anyway. Who knows? And by a cop's daughter. Mistaking someone's identity is one thing. Mistaking a man's truck in something totally different.

The quietest deputy on the force can actually get pretty loud when he has to. That temper might be something to watch, though. He sure had his hand, um, arms, full with his latest arrest.

Rumor has it that the quiet deputy and his Slugger were doing a lot of staring at each other at the Sheriff's Office. Oh, my. What could possibly happen once the bars are no longer between them? Stay tuned, Hayden Falls, to find out.

"Who's Megan, and where do I find her?" I demand.

Monica snatches her phone from me. Zoe grits her teeth. I look up at Hadley. Surely, she knows where to find this woman.

Hadley places her hand on my shoulder. "I wouldn't do that."

"But this isn't right." I can't let this woman get away with writing this nonsense.

"I know," she agrees. "Megan only gets worse if you confront her. It's best to let it die out."

"Hey." Zoe taps the top of the table to get my attention. "It's not worth it."

"People don't really believe this stuff." Monica doesn't sound so sure of her own words.

"Let it go for now." Hadley holds up a finger when I start to protest. "Trust me here. When Lucas can find a way to shut the blog down, he will."

This stupid blog is another reason everyone in town was staring at me. It explains why the men were laughing. The bell over the door jingles, drawing our attention.

"You ready to go?" Dad looks tired.

"Yeah." I hug my friends bye and walk to the door.

"See you later," Hadley calls out.

Hopefully, I will see her again. Maybe next time, it won't be at the Sheriff's Office or while she's working. It would be nice to make at least one friend in this town while I'm here. After beating up Leo's truck and the gossip blog, I'm afraid no one will want to be my friend, though. I nod and wave to her before walking out of the coffee shop.

Dad leads me to his truck and opens the passenger door. He parked two spaces from me. "Hop in. We'll come back for your car later."

I'm not sure if going to dinner with one of the local families is a good idea. They're bound to bring up my arrest and Leo's truck. The gossip blog will definitely be part of our dinner conversation. Hopefully, I can tune it all out and enjoy a home-cooked meal.

Chapter Eleven

Leo

The last two days have made this one long week for me. Today was a rough day at the Sheriff's Office. We spent nearly the entire morning listening to our townsfolk complain about everything under the sun. None of it was illegal, so there was nothing we could do but offer a little friendly advice. Surprisingly, they all left happy. Maybe somebody should open up an advice column or something. It was the weirdest morning I've seen. It was lunchtime before we figured out why everyone was stopping by with ridiculous complaints.

Hadley visited Lucas for lunch. My twin finally opened his eyes to see the amazing woman right in front of him. Hadley showed up with coffee for everyone and burgers and fries from Davis's Diner. She was the one to tell us about the article in Hayden Happenings. Every one of our visitors this morning was here to see me, not to file reports.

I understand why Lucas wants to shut the gossip blog down so badly. He was Megan's headline news earlier this year. I've never been headline news in the blog until today. Luke used to make regular appearances in it until he met Riley. Levi was Megan's topic a few weeks ago. He's still fuming. Maybe all four of us can find a way to shut the nonsense down once and for all.

Yesterday, I got things squared away with Ally for my truck. She towed Darlin to my parents' barn this afternoon. Guess she was tied up with the new doctor's car this morning. I feel better knowing my truck is here. Monday, I'll have enough parts to get started working on her. Not only did my granddad cry when Ally dropped Darlin off, but Mom and Grandma did, too. If I were a weaker man, I'd cry right along with them. Somehow, I've always been able to hold my emotions in.

Tonight isn't an official family dinner. Luke and Levi are on duty at the Fire Department. Lucas, Hadley, and I are here. My brothers and I don't live with our parents anymore, but we're here a lot.

Hadley's helping Mom and Grandma finish up dinner. I'm grateful for Hadley and Riley. Mom and Grandma needed more women in the family. Both of my brother's girlfriends fit in like they've always been here.

Sitting around doing nothing is making me antsy. If I had some parts, I'd be out in the barn working on my truck. Seeing her beat up hurts. I can't handle walking back out there tonight.

"You want me to set the table?" I offer.

"Sure, hon." Mom hands me the plates. "Take these to the dining room."

The old farmhouse has a huge dining room. We use it mainly for holidays and parties. Now that two of my brothers have girlfriends, we use it when everyone's here. I'm not sure why we're using it tonight. The table in the kitchen is big enough for us. There would even be an empty chair. After setting the table, I count two plates more than we need and carry them back to the kitchen.

"We don't need these." I open the cabinet door to put the plates away.

"Oh, we have guests coming," Mom says.

Nobody mentioned guests. I think nothing of it and carry the extra plates back to the dining room. As I'm heading back to the kitchen, the doorbell rings. Since Dad's greeting our guests, I help the ladies carry the food to the table.

"Come on in, Al," Dad says.

I freeze and peep around the doorframe. You have got to be kidding me. Chief Deputy Green and his daughter walk into the living room. Why didn't anyone tell me they were coming? Lucas looks as surprised as I am. I glance at Mom. She smiles sweetly. A look at Hadley tells me she knew, too. Women are so sneaky.

Mom hurries past me to greet our guests. "Al, Kyleigh, we're glad you could make it."

"Thanks for inviting us." Deputy Green offers Mom a box from Sweet Treats. "I know you said we didn't need to bring anything, but I picked up a Coconut Cake."

The women in the house practically drool. Granddad perks up a little, too. Coconut Cake is a favorite in our family. I glance past Chief Green to his daughter. She doesn't look at me or anyone else. Her eyes remain on the Sweet Treats box. Maybe it's her favorite cake, too.

"Everything's on the table." Mom kisses Dad's cheek. "I'll just put this on the counter for later."

"Okay." Dad motions to the dining room. "Right this way."

He's mostly talking to Kyleigh. Her father has had dinner with us many times. Still, we all follow Dad and take our seats around the antique oak table. My family takes their normal seats except for Lucas. He gives Deputy Green the seat next to Dad. Mom and Dad sit at the heads of the table. I'm on the corner with Mom on my right. Granddad sits on my left. Kyleigh takes Levi's seat straight across from me. This is going to be one awkward meal.

Things go well for the most part. Nobody brings up my truck. We all have little conversations with the people close to us. Hadley's next to Kyleigh. They seem to be hitting it off well. Even Mom joins in their conversation. That might be a problem later.

While Mom, Grandma, and Hadley get everyone a piece of cake and a cup of coffee, I watch the woman across from me. She's a little older than I first thought. Honestly, I didn't look at her closely Wednesday night. Was that really only two nights ago? I swear, it feels like at least a week.

I lean back in my chair and slowly rub my thumb across my bottom lip. I pegged Kyleigh Green for a bratty college kid. Now that I'm looking at her, she's about Hadley's age. From what she's told Hadley tonight, she graduated from college last year and works for some financial company in Seattle. Just because I haven't been looking at her doesn't mean I haven't been listening.

Hadley sets a dessert plate in front of Kyleigh and sits between her and Lucas. Kyleigh picks up her fork. I'm not sure if she feels me staring at her or not, but her eyes snap up to mine. Blue. I thought they'd be brown to match her hair. Usually, blondes have blue eyes. I haven't paid much attention to a woman's eyes before. I swallow hard and concentrate on my slice of cake.

"Well, Leo, when do you plan to start working on Darlin?" Deputy Green's the first to bring up my truck.

"Um." I cough into my fist. I was hoping we could avoid this subject. "Monday morning."

"Good." Deputy Green nods. "After we finish up with Judge Morgan, Kyleigh will be here to help you."

"What?" Kyleigh and I exclaim at the same time.

Deputy Green looks at his daughter. "You helped destroy that truck. You're going to help fix it."

"But, Daddy…"

"No, young lady. You're not getting out of this," he says firmly.

"Deputy Green, I appreciate it, but I don't need her help."

The woman works in a financial office. There's no way she can work on a truck. I'm not sure it's a good idea to have her around my truck anyway.

His gaze moves from his daughter to me. "Whether you need it or not, she will be here to help."

"I don't know anything about cars," Kyleigh whines.

See? I was right.

"You knew enough about them to beat one up with a baseball bat." Somehow, Deputy Green never raises his voice while he speaks to his daughter. I couldn't do it. I'd be livid. "I paid for you to go to college. You're smart, or you would've never graduated. It proves you're teachable. You can learn."

"Can't I just pay him for the damages? I have the money."

"You're going to do that too." He points at Kyleigh. "You're going to learn a lesson on character. We don't do things like this around here.

Most of the people in this town are close, like a family. We band together and help each other. You made a mistake, but you're not free of the consequences of it."

"Dad?" I look for help out of this situation somehow.

"Mitchell." Deputy Green holds his hand up to Dad. "Please."

Dad sighs. They've been friends for a long time. "If Judge Morgan agrees to it, then fine. But if it looks as though she can get hurt somehow, I'll put an end to it."

"Fair enough." Deputy Green shakes Dad's hand.

"Don't we get a say in this?" Kyleigh asks.

"You said plenty with the bat. Now, you'll fix it." Deputy Green isn't backing down.

Kyleigh's eyes meet mine again. She looks terrified. I'm not sure if it's because of me or the fact she has to work on a truck.

"Well, Slugger, looks like we're stuck together for a while."

"The judge hasn't approved it yet." She lifts her chin. She's got some spunk in her. That's cool.

"I'll see you on Monday." Something tells me her dad has already talked with Judge Morgan. It might as well be written in stone already.

Chapter Twelve

Kyleigh

Well, here we are. As hard as I tried to keep Monday at bay, the evil creature came barreling in like always. Last Monday, my boyfriend brought his mistress to our apartment and ended our relationship on our anniversary. One week later, I'm sitting on a wooden bench in the hallway of Hayden Falls City Hall. I hate Monday.

Dad walks the hallway, speaking softly to everyone he sees. They all stare as they walk by me. Their judgmental eyes have me staring at the floor. I've never seen so many nosy people in my life. The sound of a woman's heels clicks against the marble floor. Surprisingly, she stops in front of me. Her black dress shoes are nothing fancy. Definitely not designer like I saw in college. She probably bought them from one of the local shops in town. They're really pretty with a wide heel, unlike my narrow ones.

"Good morning, Kyleigh," Mrs. Barnes says.

I snap my head up and quickly get to my feet. "Mrs. Barnes, good morning. I didn't know you were coming."

"I work part-time at the front desk. Can I get you a cup of coffee?"

"No, thank you." Normally, I'd accept it, but I've already had three cups this morning.

Movement at the far end of the hall catches our attention. Dad is walking this way with Sheriff Barnes. Aiden and Spencer are with them. My heart drops when I see Leo at the back of their little group. Well, I think it's Leo. It could be Lucas. They look exactly alike, so I'm not sure. Only Lucas has no reason to be here. It's definitely Leo.

Mrs. Barnes shocks me by pulling me into a hug. "Don't worry, dear. Everything will be fine."

She releases me and meets her family members halfway down the hall. Sheriff Barnes and Leo stop to speak with her. Dad and the two deputies make their way to me.

Thankfully, Judge Morgan has agreed to see me in his chambers. It doesn't matter. I'm sure everything that happens here today will make it through the gossip circles by dinnertime.

Mrs. Barnes smiles sweetly at me over Leo's shoulder. She kisses his cheek as she steps out of his arms. Just as I thought. Leo Barnes is a Mama's Boy.

A door down the hall opens. An extremely good-looking man in a three-piece suit steps out. He's so handsome. I'd be drooling at the sight of him under different circumstances. Everything about him screams lawyer. Maybe I should have called one, too. Then again, maybe Dad called this guy for me. Way to go, Dad.

"Chief Green, Kyleigh, Judge Morgan will see you now." The handsome lawyer opens the door wider.

The others talk as we walk into the Judge's Chambers. Leo and I chance a few awkward glances at each other but don't speak. He didn't mention Friday night that he'd be here. Why wouldn't he be? It was his truck, and he was the one who arrested me.

Dad leads me to one of the chairs in front of the judge's desk. Judge Morgan motions for Leo to take the other one. It makes me extremely nervous having him so close. His presence was hard enough to deal with from across the table Friday night. Our dads stand behind us. The two deputies stand against the wall near the door. The handsome lawyer moves to Judge Morgan's side. Okay. He's the city's lawyer, not mine. Yep. I should have called a lawyer. This won't end well for me.

"First of all, even though we're in my chambers, this is still official. Unless you all would like to move this to the courtroom." Judge Morgan waits.

"This is fine, Your Honor." Dad squeezes my shoulder. The others nod in agreement.

"Okay. I've read the report and charges. I've also seen the security footage from Cowboys." Judge Morgan pauses again and watches me for a moment. "Miss Green, would you like to explain yourself?"

I shake my head. What I did is all over town. I'm embarrassed to tell the story anymore.

"I'd rather hear your version, officially," he adds the last word quickly. He's heard the rumors.

"Kyleigh." Dad nudges my shoulder. "Answer Judge Morgan."

I release a deep breath. I have no choice but to do this. "My friends and I were having a sleepover. Another friend called us crying. Someone sent her a picture of her boyfriend with another woman. Skip had the redhead pushed up against Leo's truck. I assumed the truck in the picture was Skip's. The rest you saw on the video."

Judge Morgan sits quietly. Even though his face shows no emotion, he thinks I'm an idiot. I feel like an idiot.

"Would you like to bring in your friend who did most of the damage?"

"No, Your Honor. It was my idea. I'll take full responsibility." If Jenna weren't my friend, I'd punch her.

"Very noble of you." He shifts the papers in the file on his desk around. "Your father presented a request to the court. If Leo agrees, I'm prepared to accept it." The lawyer hands Judge Morgan another paper. He nods. "Kyleigh Green, you will pay Leo Barnes for the parts to restore his truck. You'll also pay him a reasonable fee for the work. I'm sure he wants to do it himself."

Leo nods. Okay. This isn't so bad. I can handle paying for the damages and paying Leo for his time. I was worried about nothing.

"Your father proposed that you help with the restoration."

"Your Honor, that's not necessary," Leo says.

Judge Morgan glances up at Dad before looking me in the eye. "You will help with the restoration. I'm giving you three months of probation and sixty hours of community service. Leo will sign off on your hours."

"What?" I exclaim. That means I can't leave. "I can't stay here for three months and do community service. I have a job."

"It's now six months and a hundred hours." Judge Morgan's face hardens as he points at me. "Turn that down or make another outburst, and I'll send you to prison for three years."

Three years? I practically choke on air. This is not happening.

"It's fine, Your Honor. She'll accept the six months and community service," Dad speaks for me.

"Young lady?" Judge Morgan waits for my answer.

"Yes, Sir. I'll do it." I drop my head and turn toward the window. I don't want to look at any of the men in this room.

"Okay. Quinn here will write everything up and get you the community service sheet. If Darlin is finished before the hundred hours are up, Sheriff Barnes will find you something else to do." Without waiting for anyone to speak, Judge Morgan taps his gavel on the little wooden pedestal. "Court's adjourned."

I spring from my chair and push past everyone in the room. I have to get out of here.

"Kyleigh!" Dad calls out.

Nope. I have nothing to say. I love my dad. If I speak right now, I'll pop something smart off at him. I never want to do that. I run around the corner and out of his sight.

"Kyleigh?" Mrs. Barnes stands as I dash for the front doors.

I swipe a tear from my eye and shake my head. I can't speak to her either. I need to find somewhere quiet so I can get myself together. After lunch, I have to start my court-ordered community service with Leo Barnes.

Chapter Thirteen

Kyleigh

I hurry as fast as I can through a few side streets and find myself in the town square. Oh, no. I didn't want to come here. Now, the entire town will see me. People are already stopping and staring as I push past them. I'll be the talk of the town again before lunch is over.

I come to a halt on one of the street corners and finally look around to get my bearings. The diner is straight ahead. I could hide in one of the back booths. No. There will be lots of people inside the restaurant. The coffee shop is across the street. Beth's is bound to be packed with nosy people. The park is behind this row of shops. Maybe I can find a secluded spot near the river.

Before I can turn the corner, the door of the shop next to me opens. A woman grabs my hand and pulls me inside without saying a word. She leads me to a comfy leather recliner in one of the back corners. This spot is hidden from the front windows by rows of bookcases. I've been pulled into Page Turners. At least no one can see me here.

"Stay here," the woman says softly. "I'll get you a cup of coffee." She hands me a box of tissue before walking away.

When my phone rings, I dig it out of my purse. Dad's worried, but I'm not ready to talk to him just yet. I know he talked to Judge Morgan before today. Surely, he didn't set all this up.

I'm fine with paying for the damages to the truck and for Leo's time. If it weren't for my friends and me, he wouldn't have to restore his truck to begin with. I'm sort of okay with the fact that I have to help him with the restoration while I'm here. Dad knows I was only staying for a couple of weeks. Three months of probation, now six months because I raised my voice to the judge, well, it's more than I'm prepared for. If I stay here, I'll lose the job I worked so hard to secure.

"Here you go." The woman hands me a cup of coffee.

"Thank you." I take it with shaky hands.

"You probably don't remember me, but I'm Grace." She sits in the chair next to me.

"I remember your name and seeing you when I was younger."

I was eight when Mom moved us to Seattle. She never told me why she left Dad, and I didn't pry. Dad doesn't talk about it either. After fifteen years, you'd think one of them would mention it.

The Wentworths own the land next to my Dad's. I saw Grace and her brother a lot when we were little. Sadly, the main thing I remember about them is their parents died in a car accident when they were very young. Their father's parents have raised them.

My phone rings again. Dad's not going to give up. He needs to know I'm safe. I'm not ready to talk, but I can at least text him.

Me: *I love you. I'm safe.*

Daddy: *We need to talk.*

Me: *We will tonight.*

Daddy: *Where are you?*

Me: *In town. I'll go to the Barnes' house after lunch and start my community service.*

I turn the phone off and drop it back into my purse. There were texts from Zoe and Monica. I'll read them later.

"You want to talk about it?"

I shake my head. "It's a lot. I don't want to dump my mess on you."

"Sometimes, you need a safe place to release things so you can see your way through the chaos and move forward."

Wow. That's deep. Grace is a little older than me, but she's wise beyond her years. Bookworms are big thinkers. She probably read that somewhere. Then again, being raised by her grandparents probably gave her some long-forgotten wisdom, too.

Surprisingly, I open up and tell Grace everything. Not once does she interrupt me. She quietly listens to my side of everything, from Scott and Brenda to what happened in court this morning. When I finish, I close my eyes for a moment and sigh deeply. There. I did it. I released it all.

"Feel better?" Grace pulls a tissue from the box on my lap and offers it to me.

"Yeah. Thanks for listening." I dab the tissue to the corners of my eyes.

"Why don't you go to the restroom and wash your face?" She studies my face as she pulls me from the chair. "We're about the same complexion. If you don't have makeup in your purse, I'll run upstairs and get mine."

She's really sweet to offer. I'm fine going without makeup, though. Grace shows me to the employee restroom rather than the public one. This one is inside a little breakroom area behind the front counter. From here, she can see the door and cash register if anyone enters the shop.

"I'm going to order a club sandwich and fries from the diner. What can I get you?"

"Grace, you don't have to do all this for me."

She smiles sweetly again. "I don't mind. You need a friend, and yours aren't here."

"A club sandwich and fries sound great." I reach for my wallet.

Grace's hand covers mine before I can open my purse. "It's on me today. You can get the next one."

The next one? I hardly know her. Yet, here she is, offering me friendship and taking care of me. My friends in Seattle wouldn't do this. Zoe and Monica might. I'm not so sure about Jenna anymore. Grace is so kind. I feel as though I'm taking advantage of her, but she isn't taking no for an answer. I thank her again and hurry into the restroom.

After washing the tears and makeup from my face, I stare at myself in the mirror. My life has taken some serious and strange turns over the past week. The latest turn is my fault. I should have stopped Jenna from taking the first swing.

"Well, Kyleigh Elsa Green, you sure made a mess of things."

Naturally, my reflection doesn't offer me any advice. This is my mess, and I have no choice but to face the consequences of my actions. My breakup wasn't my fault. That's all on Scott. Leo's truck is my fault. I said I would take full responsibility for it. That's exactly what I need to do, and without complaining.

"Good talk." I give my reflection a firm nod and walk out of the restroom with a new outlook. Okay. Maybe I just have my head held high. It's something, at least, and I do feel better.

Grace is already setting our food on the small table. Wow. I must have been in there longer than I thought. It's fine. I needed that little pep talk I gave myself. I happily sit down next to my new friend and pick up half of my sandwich.

"So." Grace's eyes twinkle. Her grin is mischievous. That's different coming from her. "You're going to be spending a lot of time with Leo Barnes."

"I have no choice."

"Hey." She covers my hand with hers. "Leo is a great guy. Most people around here think he's grumpy, but that's not true. He's quiet and stays to himself."

"He hates me."

"Well." She looks to the ceiling for a moment. "That's not true, either. You might not be his favorite person right now, but he doesn't hate you. I've never known Leo to hold a grudge."

"Has anyone ever beaten his truck up before?"

She grits her teeth. "Good point."

"Leo doesn't want this any more than I do. It's going to be pure torture for us both."

"But." There's her mischievous grin again. "At least you'll have some eye candy through your torture."

We both laugh. Grace just became my favorite person in Hayden Falls. Leo Barnes is definitely eye candy. Too bad he hates me.

Chapter Fourteen

Leo

Court was an absolute disaster. It's nice to know I'll be paid back for the parts my truck needs and my time. But I don't need Kyleigh Green's help to fix anything. Little Miss Daddy's girl will only be in my way.

I won't lie. I can't explain it anyway. I felt a stab in my chest when Kyleigh bolted from the judge's chambers. Her father chased after her. The little woman was faster than I gave her credit for. We found Chief Deputy Green at the front doors with my mom, trying to console him. I don't think he was prepared for Judge Morgan's decision. He settled down a little when Kyleigh texted, saying she was okay and would report for community service this afternoon.

After leaving City Hall, I stopped by Ally's to pick up the last of the parts she ordered for me. The auto parts store was my next stop for a few odd and ends things I needed. Since I was heading to my parents' house, I picked up lunch for my grandparents at Davis's Diner. My grandmother is an amazing cook, but I don't want her slaving over a stove for me every time I visit. She wouldn't just make us a sandwich for lunch. She'd prepare a six-course meal.

Several shop owners were picking up their lunches while I was at the diner. Connie Green from the pharmacy huffed and turned her nose up at me. She's Kyleigh's aunt by marriage. She obviously believes everything is my fault. Sophie Lewis from the bakery looked at me with sympathetic eyes. Or was it pity? Half the people in this town give me a look of pity. Grace Wentworth smiled sweetly. Grace is quiet and sweet. Something about her today was weird, though. I'll never understand why women act the way they do.

"Do you think she'll show?" Granddad walks around Darlin with watery eyes. If he cries, I just might, too.

"Maybe not today. She was pretty upset when she left City Hall."

She told her dad she'd be here, but I'm not holding her to it today. She was struggling not to cry in front of us. Judge Morgan's decision surprised everyone in the room.

Granddad plops down on the stool at the work table and crosses his arms. "Well, if you ask me, she got what she deserved. You don't mess with a man's truck."

He has a darn good point and one I agree with. If you have a problem with someone, you should confront them. The person's vehicle should never be involved. If Kyleigh and her friends had gone after Skip, they would have never touched my truck.

"Right this way, dear." Grandma leads Kyleigh into the barn.

Well, darn. She proved me wrong. I thought she'd spend the rest of the day hiding and sulking. She follows my grandmother inside but hangs back a little. I'm not sure if she's nervous or scared. As sweet and innocent as she looks, she's probably both.

"I think I want a piece of pie." Granddad hurries out of the barn.

"I better help him, or he'll eat the whole pie." Grandma excuses herself. "I'll bring you two some sweet tea in a bit."

Once Grandma leaves, Kyleigh wrings her hands together and looks everywhere but at me and the truck. She doesn't want to be here anymore than I want her to be. Oh, well. There's nothing either of us can do about it now. We'll have to make the best of it, I guess.

"Um. Thanks for coming." I have no idea how to talk to her. Come to think of it, we haven't really talked.

"I could go if you want." The last part was a whisper.

As stern as Judge Morgan was with her today, if she doesn't do this, he'll hold her in contempt of court. Yes, I think she should pay for what she did. Prison, however, isn't the answer. As gentle as she looks, she wouldn't survive a night behind bars.

"You're already here. We can at least get started."

"Okay." She nods and releases a long breath. "What do we do first?"

"Assess the damage."

Kyleigh follows me as I walk around the truck. I've already assessed the damages. She needs to see what she and her friend did. I've watched the security footage a hundred times or more. Her friend, Jenna, did most of this. The only thing Kyleigh broke was the taillights. It's the easiest and cheapest repair on the truck. Technically, Jenna should be the one in trouble, not Kyleigh. If this hadn't been her idea, Kyleigh could have walked away with a fine and the repair cost to my taillights. Knowing this was her idea might be why Judge Morgan was so hard on her today.

"I have the parts we need for today on the work table." I point to the table along the far wall.

She looks everything over. She knows very little, if anything, about a car.

"This is just the lights. What about the dents?"

"We'll buff those out."

She walks over to the driver's door. "That's not buffing out."

Okay. She's not totally ditsy when it comes to cars, after all. Maybe I've dumped her into a cliché with most innocent looking girls. No clue. I'm not going to bother figuring it out.

"I have to see a guy on Saturday about a new door."

"Oh." She drops her head for a moment before looking up at me. "I'm sorry, Leo. I really am."

I stare into her blue eyes without moving. It's the first time I've heard her apologize. She may have apologized to her dad, but it's the first to me. The look in her eyes tells me she means it.

"Yeah." I run a hand through my hair and take a step back.

I've spent the past five days being angry with her for destroying my truck. What do I do now? Granddad says if someone asks for forgiveness, we're supposed to grant it no matter how we feel. How do I feel? The situation still ticks me off. Looking into Kyleigh's eyes has me second-guessing how I feel about her. I just won't look into her eyes anymore. Problem solved.

The best thing I can do is dive into working on the truck. I won't have to think about my feelings if I'm working. Will I ever forgive her? Openly? Yeah, that's easy enough, even if I don't mean it. In my heart? I'm not so sure I can. This truck is a part of my grandfather's spirit. Seeing Darlin beaten up broke something in my grandfather. Seeing him broken broke a part of me. How does a man move past something like that?

I spend nearly an hour telling Kyleigh my plans for the restoration and pointing out the parts as we walk around the truck. When I turn around, I'm surprised to see her with a pad and pen in her hands.

"What are you doing?"

"Taking notes." She shrugs. "I don't know how to work on cars."

Oh, I knew that. I run a hand through my hair again. She'll have me pulling it out before this is over. People will be able to tell Lucas and me apart for sure then. I'll have to wear a hat all the time.

"Why don't we call it a day?" Maybe if she leaves, I can get some actual work done.

"Okay." She pulls her keys from her pocket. "I don't have the community service form for you to sign."

"Quinn gave it to me this morning. It's over there." I motion to the work table over my shoulder with my thumb.

"You'll sign it for today, right?"

"Yes, ma'am. I'll sign it for two hours."

"Thank you." She turns to go.

"I'll walk you out."

"No." She holds her hand up. "I can find the front yard by myself."

With that, she spins on her heels and rushes out the door. I have no idea what makes her run from situations like she does. Kyleigh Green is a mystery to me. Oh, well. She's gone for the day, and not my problem. Tomorrow is another story because she'll be back and in my way. This restoration is going to take three times as long as it should. Maybe I should find Skip and punch him in the face. After all, it was his cheating that caused this mess.

Chapter Fifteen

Kyleigh

My head throbs the moment I open my eyes. I don't want to think about yesterday. Nothing went my way. Mondays should be officially outlawed worldwide. We should skip it completely. Tuesday is a better day to start the week.

As much as I hate to, I climb out of bed and make my way to the kitchen. I'm still half asleep, but I don't care. The smell of freshly brewed coffee pulls me along. My body protests with every step. The call from the magical goodness is too strong to stop me.

Dad's refilling his cup. He's already dressed in his uniform. Thank goodness he took the ankle monitor off when he got home last night. Hearing me walking into the room, he smiles over his shoulder and reaches for another mug. He sets the cup in front of me before sitting down. His kitchen table is small. It's an even wooden square with only one chair on each side. Even though he's at the head, he's still sitting next to me. He waits to speak until I add the cream and sugar and take a couple of sips.

"How did it go yesterday?" He means with Leo. He knows how court went.

"I can't do this, Daddy."

"You have no choice."

"Can't I pay a fine or something?"

Dad rubs his eyes with his thumb and index finger. "I asked the judge that yesterday." He sighs and shakes his head.

"Did you know the judge's decision beforehand?" It would break my heart if he did.

He leans back in his chair. "Not all of it. I called him Friday morning. I offered for you to pay for the damages and labor fees. I also suggested that you help with the labor." He looks me in the eye. "I didn't know about the probation part. Did you have any problems at the Barnes' yesterday?"

"Not really." I shake my head. "Leo's grandmother was really nice to me. His grandfather can't stand the sight of me. He left the barn the moment I arrived. Leo?" How do I put this into words? "I guess the best way to say it is he tolerates me."

"They're a good family. It'll take the men a little time to get past what you did, but none of them will be mean to you. Leo's grandfather will probably be the last to come around. He believes the truck is why his wife fell in love with him." Dad lightly chuckles and shakes his head.

It's highly unlikely the truck is why she fell in with him. But now I understand why the man is so attached to the old truck. It broke my heart to see him cry at the Sheriff's Office. I did my best not to look at anybody that night.

"I'm sorry, Daddy. I should have stopped it."

"It wasn't your idea, was it?"

If I answer that, I'll be telling on my friends and breaking a promise. I said I'd take full responsibility for everything we did that night, but I can't outright lie to my dad. I drop my head and stare into my almost empty coffee cup.

Dad sighs and pats my wrist. "It's okay. We'll get through it."

"We?" I fake a laugh, trying to bring some humor into our gloomy conversation. "I'm the one who has to fix a truck."

"I almost feel sorry for Leo." Dad wholeheartedly laughs.

"Hey!" I playfully shove his shoulder.

"I'm sorry, Baby." Dad laughs some more. "It'll do the quiet, grumpy Barnes some good to spend some time with a woman he's not related to."

I laugh, too. "I knew he was a Mama's Boy."

"Well, Leo's mother does spoil all of her sons, but Leo is closest to his grandfather."

Ah. That explains why Leo now owns his grandfather's truck. My friends and I really messed up when we decided Darlin belonged to Skip. I knew the lowlife cheater didn't own a truck that nice.

"What time are you supposed to meet Leo today?"

Uh oh. I forgot to ask. I'd call him, but I don't have his number. I can't miss a day of community service, or I'll be in trouble with the judge. As much as I hate working on the truck, I hate the idea of prison even more.

"Will you call him?"

"Yeah, but you two need to exchange numbers today." Dad stands. "Have you talked with your manager?"

"No. I'll call her after I finish this." I point to my cup.

"Okay." Dad kisses the top of my head. "I'll text you the time as soon as Leo calls me back."

After Dad leaves for work, I go to my room and get my phone. I'm not looking forward to this phone call. My manager is hateful to everyone. It was all I could do to talk her into giving me two weeks of remote work. She's not going to extend it for six months.

Another cup of coffee won't help. I fix it anyway and sit back down at the table. As much as I hate to, I hit the call button for Taylor Pierce's receptionist. Naturally, I'm left on hold for ten minutes. I swear, she does this to everybody.

"Kyleigh, it's good to hear from you." Taylor sounds too cheerful this early in the morning. It's not a good sign.

"Good morning, Taylor." I poke my finger in my mouth and silently pretend to gag. This woman is a pain to deal with.

"Your latest reports look great. It'll be nice having you back in the office next week." She does not mean that. She doesn't like me, or anyone for that matter.

"About that." I close my eyes and shake my head.

"Is something wrong?" Her voice loses all its sweetness. She's so fake.

"I have some things to take care of here. I need to extend my remote work."

"Let me see." I can hear her fingers tapping on her keyboard. "You have a lot of in-person appointments coming up."

"I can call them and request a video conference." It's pointless. She won't go for it.

"How long do you need?" Her perfectly manicured nails tap a steady rhythm on her desk.

"Six months?" I grit my teeth.

"No." She huffs out a little laugh. "I'll give you a month. You have until August 15th to be in the office. If you're not here, you can resign, or you're fired."

The call goes dead before I can reply. There's nothing I could have said anyway. Expressing my thoughts on things only makes matters worse. A month? I have one month to figure things out here. How do I get six months of probation within a month? I'm not sure it's possible. I'll have to contact a lawyer. If I can't work this out somehow, I just lost my job. Tuesdays are now my second least favorite day of the week.

Chapter Sixteen

Leo

This has been one long week. The process on my truck is going slow, too slow. I'd get more done if I were working alone. Unfortunately, I have to explain everything I do to Kyleigh or my granddad. One of them is always with me when I'm in the barn. Granddad leaves when Kyleigh shows up. He's having a hard time letting go of what happened. Mom and Grandma, however, make a fuss over Kyleigh. I'm not sure what to make of it.

Keleigh has shown up at my parents' house every day this week. If it's my day off, she arrives after lunchtime and stays through dinner. Naturally, Mom and Grandma insist she has dinner with us. It's awkward having her and Granddad at the table together. Strangely, I find myself hoping they can one day move past this and like each other.

I'm on dayshift right now. On the days I work, Kyleigh purposely shows up at seven to avoid having dinner with us. We work around my truck for an hour or two. We're not getting much done, but it logs community service hours for her.

Today, I get a break from it all. Well, from Kyleigh and Granddad watching over my shoulder as I work. It's Saturday and my day off. I have an appointment with Bryson Crane this afternoon to buy the door for Darlin.

It's a two-hour ride to Thorn Valley. I've decided to take my time and make a day of it. I'm not one for sleeping late, even on my days off. I got up early to make breakfast for my brother and his girlfriend. Sometimes, Hadley stays over. It's odd having a woman here overnight. Hadley's the only woman ever to do so. Having her here isn't a bad thing. Hadley brings a happier feeling to our home. One day soon, I look for them to want a place of their own. Who wants the grumpy twin brother hanging around all the time as a third wheel? I'm happy Lucas found love.

After breakfast, Lucas and Hadley clean up the kitchen while I get ready to leave. With all the laughing and squealing going on, I know they're not just cleaning. Hadley brings the fun side out in my brother. Lucas having fun? Nobody would believe it unless they saw it. It's going to be odd when they get married and he moves out. He and I have always lived in the same house since we were born.

Someone knocks on the front door as I walk out of my room. Lucas is heading to the door, but I beat him to it. Surprisingly, I find Kyleigh standing on our porch. I narrow my eyes. Why is she here? Did something happen?

"Hey, Leo." She pauses, her eyes flick over my shoulder and back to me. I look to see why she's stunned. Lucas is standing about five feet behind me. "Um. Are you Leo or Lucas?"

I glance back over my shoulder at my brother and grin. Being twins can have its advantages at times. Kyleigh didn't grow up here. She hasn't learned our little differences to tell us apart like most of our friends have. Lucas and I are identical, but we have different tastes and personalities. Lucas reads my mind and shakes his head. We pretended to be each other when we were kids. The prank worked on everyone except Mom and both of our grandmothers.

I roll my eyes at my brother and turn back to Kyleigh. "I'm Leo."

"Whew." She laughs nervously.

"Why are you here?" Yeah, I might not be the best at talking to women. Still, I don't understand it. "I told you yesterday you had today off from community service." Hopefully, the last part softens the sting of my question.

"Well, I'm going with you."

"What?" I did not hear her correctly.

"Dad and I talked. He thinks since this is a trip for the truck, riding along could count as my community service. That is if you agree." She presses her lips together and clasps her hands in a tight squeeze.

I run a hand through my hair and scratch the back of my head. I just might hurt Chief Deputy Green next time I see him for suggesting this. I was looking forward to a nice, quiet trip alone.

Lucas steps up behind me and slaps me on the back. "That's a great idea."

My wonderful twin brother will be the next person on my payback list. His weird grin is giving me the creeps.

"It's not working. It's just riding," I point out.

"Community service doesn't have to be physical work." Lucas pats my back like I'm a little kid. "As she said, it's for the truck. It'll count toward logging off the hours she needs."

I've expressed my discomfort to him every day for having to work with this woman. He tilts his head and raises an eyebrow. He's silently pleading with me to see reason. They're right. It'll log hours off for her and without actually working on my truck. Whatever. I drop my shoulders in defeat and give in. The faster the hours are logged, the faster she's out of my hair.

"Okay." I point at her. "But you best not talk the whole trip."

"Thank you, and no, I won't." She smiles and bounces on her toes.

I narrow my eyes. I already regret this. Kyleigh pretends to zip her lips and toss an invisible key over her shoulder.

"Let's go." I walk past my Camaro to Lucas' truck and open the passenger door.

"You have two trucks?"

"No. This is Lucas'." I point to my car. "We can't put a door in that."

"That's your car?" She sounds surprised.

"Yes, ma'am." After I help her up into the truck, I hurry around and get in the driver's seat.

"You like older vehicles, huh?"

I glance at her new Ford Taurus as we pull out of the driveway. I know her dad didn't buy it for her. She must be doing well at the financial company in Seattle. Unless her mom's rich and gave it to her.

"Yeah. I do." I pull onto the highway. Sadly, we have to drive through town.

"Did the Camaro belong to another family member?"

I shake my head. "I bought it at a used car lot in Walsburg when I was in high school."

The town square is buzzing with activity as we pass through. We should have taken one of the side roads and the extra twenty minutes to avoid driving straight through town. Several people stop and do a double-take when they see us. A wicked grin crosses my face. This is Lucas' truck. My happy moment quickly dies. These idiots will accuse my brother of cheating on Hadley. I want to pay Lucas back, but I won't hurt Hadley to do it. Somehow, I'll make sure everyone knows I was driving his truck today.

We stop in front of the bookstore and wait for another driver to get the spot she wants in front of the beauty salon. I snap my head to the passenger side when Kyleigh lets the window down.

"Hey!" She calls out to Grace.

Grace Wentworth is working on her sidewalk display in front of Page Turners. I didn't realize Kyleigh knew her.

"Hey, Kyleigh. Good to see you. The books you ordered arrived this morning. I still have to unpack the shipment."

"It's okay. I'll pick them up later. Leo and I are going out of town to get a door for his truck."

Kyleigh just solved the problem of how to let everyone know who was driving Lucas' truck today. The people walking by heard her loud and clear. All of them grin at me. Oh, no. One of these fools will call Megan. I roll my eyes and slowly move forward. Never mind. No one has to call Megan. She's standing next to the Gazebo, taking pictures of us with her phone.

"Hey." I tap Kyleigh's arm while keeping my eyes straight ahead.

"Huh?" Kyleigh sits back against the seat and lets the window up.

"Smile for the camera, Slugger." I motion with my head toward the Gazebo.

Kyleigh gasps. If I look over, I know her eyes are wide, and her mouth is open. Sliding down in the seat isn't going to help her. It's too late. Megan already has what she needs. I wave to the infuriating gossip blogger as we pass. I sigh with relief when we finally drive out of town. No doubt this will be on the blog before we get home with some ridiculous story attached to it. Kyleigh and I will probably be married by next weekend.

I snap my gaze to the woman slumped down in the seat beside me. Married? Me? Her? I mentally shake the thought away. I don't see it. She's pretty, though—very pretty.

Chapter Seventeen

Leo

The ride to Thorn Valley took forever. Honestly, it took less than two hours. It felt more like two weeks. Kyleigh Green is a liar. She talked almost nonstop the entire way. When she wasn't talking, she was singing along with the radio. Her singing was worse than her talking. Okay. Her singing wasn't actually bad. She has a pleasant voice. I'd almost say it's calming. I'd have to relax before that happened, though. The problem was she got most of the chorus right, but the rest of the song was wrong. How can somebody mess up so many words in a song?

We arrived in Thorn Valley an hour before my appointment with Bryson. Now, what do I do with this woman for an hour? I refuse to ask her. She'll probably want to talk—some more. She has bombarded me with questions and stories enough for one day, maybe for several days. So much for her zipping her lips shut and throwing away the key.

She reaches over and turns the radio off. "I'm hungry."

Okay. Problem solved. I'm hungry, too. Maybe if she's eating, she'll be quiet. I smile. Yeah. We should get lunch.

"Sounds great."

I take the road that will eventually lead us to Bryson Crane's place. At the edge of town, I turn onto a long driveway lined with trees, decorative shrubs, and flowers.

"Wow." Kyleigh turns in every direction as much as she can with her seatbelt on. "This is beautiful. What is this place?"

"Have you met Ally Roberts yet?"

"No." She doesn't take her eyes off the scenery around us. Her eyes widen when the main house comes into view.

"This is Amberlee Cellars. Ally's uncle owns this. Her father owns the garage in Hayden Falls."

"She's the woman you gave your keys to that night." She drops her head.

She was in the back of Aiden's car by that point. I didn't realize she noticed. All the excitement she was feeling a few minutes ago is gone. For some reason, I don't like hearing the pain in her voice.

"Yeah. She towed Darlin to her dad's shop and later to the barn." Maybe we shouldn't talk about that tonight.

I pull into a parking space and turn the truck off. For a moment, I watch her. She's no longer the bouncy singing woman I've listened to for nearly two hours. I prefer the happy version of her. Some kind of witchcraft is going on here. I've never worried about a woman being happy or sad. Well, except for my mom and grandmothers. This is a strange feeling.

I tap the console between us to get her attention. "Hey. Let's not think about that night." Her big blue eyes look hopeful. The power of how things will go between us rests on my next words. I can crush her with a harsh word, or I can offer her the hope she seems to desperately need. "It was bad, but we're working on fixing what happened. There's no sense in dwelling on it."

She gives me a small smile. Her eyes blink a couple of times. "Thank you, Leo."

That's enough of the heavy stuff. I reach for my door handle. "You ready?"

"I'd love to see the inside, but I want food, not wine." She opens her door and hops out before I can get around to the passenger side. I look between her and the closed door. "Oh, did you want to open my door?" She lightly laughs and reaches for the handle. "I can get back in."

Oh, she's funny. We're not doing this. I place my hands on her shoulders and turn her toward the main entrance.

"Next time, wait for me. For now, we're going in here. They have a small restaurant that serves lunch and dinner."

"Leo." Kyleigh gasps as we walk into the elegant lobby. "It's beyond beautiful."

I stand by the door and watch her walk around the room, admiring the pictures and decorations. She's like a kid in a candy store. Her childlike wonder makes me smile.

"Hello." A woman with long dark hair walks towards me. "I'm Mandy. Welcome to Amberlee Cellars." She holds out her hand. Naturally, I take it.

"Hi. I'm Leo." I motion across the room with my other hand. "This is Kyleigh."

Mandy clasps her hands together and smiles. "Are you here for a wine tasting or lunch?"

"Lunch. If you have a table." I didn't think about making a reservation. This place is fancy. They might require one.

"Of course, right this way." She grabs a couple of menus from the reception podium and waits by the restaurant doors.

"I'll just get her." I point to Kyleigh.

Mandy laughs. "Take your time. It happens a lot."

Kyleigh is admiring a large picture of the winery. As I get closer, I can tell it's a painting, not a photograph. There's an artist's signature in the bottom corner.

"It's beautiful," Kyleigh whispers.

I've no idea why she's whispering. The painting can't hear her. The artist's signature draws my attention. I lean closer. *S. Foster*. It can't be. Then again, maybe it can. It even makes sense. She and Ally are best friends. If Sammie Foster painted this, she's more talented than I thought. She should have her work in art galleries in major cities. She shouldn't be living above a jewelry store in a small town in the middle of Montana.

"It is." I stand up straight and place my hand on her back. That's a bit intimate. I quickly move my hand to her arm. "The hostess has a table for us."

"Oh." Kyleigh snaps out of her sense of wonderment. "Food. Yeah, I really need some food."

I chuckle and follow her through the restaurant as Mandy shows us our table. Our hostess must read more into this than necessary. This setting looks a tad bit romantic. Not that I've had a lot of experience in the romance department. I could be wrong. This could be an everyday setting. Yeah, we'll go with that. Kyleigh quickly drops down in one of the two chairs. I raise an eyebrow.

"Um." She looks up at me sheepishly. "Do I need to stand and wait for you to seat me?"

"Next time." I take the chair across from her. The hostess hands me the menus.

"Your server will be with you shortly." Mandy smiles and hurries back to the reception podium to greet the next guest.

"Lunch is on me." I hand Kyleigh a menu.

"Oh." She wiggles in her chair. "You're just all gentlemanly, aren't you?"

"Is that a problem?"

"No." She drops her eyes to the menu. "It's a lost trait most men don't have anymore."

I pause and watch her over the top of my menu. Kyleigh takes a deep breath and squeezes her eyes shut for a quick moment. Is she fighting to hold back tears? What did I say to cause her to react this way? A thought crosses my mind. Has a man hurt her? Chief Deputy Green hasn't told any of us why she's here. None of us knew she was visiting until she was arrested, not even Dad. Whatever it is, I feel like a jerk now.

Kyleigh's phone dings with a text. She looks at the notification without opening the message. She shakes her head slightly and drops the phone into her purse. I'm not sure what that's about.

"Well, it's how I was raised." Her eyes lift to mine. "Since we're going to be together for a while, you'll have to get used to it." I smile, hoping it takes the sting from my words if there were any. I don't talk to women like this, so I don't know.

"I'm sure I can," she says softly. Her cheeks pinken a little, and her eyes drop back to the menu.

What just happened? I swear the air around us shifted. I'll have to be careful of my words for the rest of the trip. Hopefully, Lucas can explain all this when I get home.

Chapter Eighteen

Kyleigh

Amberlee Cellars is one of the prettiest places I've ever seen, both inside and out. Lunch was delicious. Their Scandinavian Steak and Potatoes were tender and mouthwatering. I even talked Mr. Grumpy Barnes into getting it for lunch. His only complaint was that it needed more steak. He's probably like my dad. Throw a T-bone on the grill, bake a potato, and call dinner done.

My phone vibrates in my purse. I turned the ringer off halfway to Thorn Valley. Text messages pop in regularly. I ignore them. I open my purse just enough to read the screen. Scott. Nope. I'm not talking to him.

"Everything okay?" Leo's eyes flick to me and back to the road.

"Yeah. Everything's fine," I lie. My life is far from fine. Whatever Scott is calling about can't be good.

"If you need to take that, you can."

I should have known better than to try and hide something from a cop. My dad could always pick up on things, too. Maybe it's me. I might be more of an open book than I thought.

"It's fine." I shift in my seat to face him. Leo starts to speak, but I jump in first. "Thank you for lunch. Amberlee Cellars is beautiful. I didn't know there were wineries out here."

"Wineries are in the country," he says like I'm an idiot.

"No." I lightly laugh. "I know wineries are in the country. I just didn't know there were any in Montana."

"Oh." He nods. "Yeah. There are a few. It's mostly ranches out here, though."

"I passed a big ranch a few days ago. The H. H. Maxwell Ranch had a lot of activity going on."

"Aiden's family owns that ranch. Was something wrong? I haven't heard anything."

"No. I don't know what you'd call it. Cowboys on horses herding cows?" I know nothing about farm life.

"They were probably switching pastures." Leo points to the truck seat. "Do you mind sitting down?"

"Why?" I look around to see what's wrong.

"If there's an accident, your seatbelt can't protect you if you're sitting sideways."

"You're a regular buzzkill." I sit properly in my seat for the deputy and adjust my seatbelt.

"I'm keeping you safe." Spoken like a true cop.

Leo flips on the turn signal and starts down a long dirt road. Maybe it's a driveway. I only see one house, a shop, and lots of junk cars out here.

We pull up to a three-bay garage. A couple of cars sit inside the bays. At least this guy is trying to fix a few of them. Leo gets out and comes around to open my door. Yes, I waited for him to open it. He even offers me his hand and helps me down.

A man in his mid-thirties slides out from under one of the two cars. He wipes his greasy hands on a rag he pulled from his back pocket as he walks towards us.

"Leo Barnes?"

"Yeah. That's me. You must be Bryson Crane."

"Yep." Bryson offers Leo his hand. His eyes roam over me. "I have the door over here."

This man gives me the creeps. He looks at me like I'm his next meal or something. He's not that old or bad-looking. If he'd clean up a little, maybe he could find a girl of his own so he wouldn't bluntly stare at a stranger like he's undressing her with his eyes. Perhaps I shouldn't have come on this trip. I step closer to Leo.

"Thanks." Leo looks between Bryson and me. I'm not sure if he senses how uncomfortable I am, but thankfully, he puts himself between us.

We walk to the side of the shop. Bryson uncovers a door almost the same color as Leo's truck. This is a good find. It's a perfect fit for Darlin. Leo lifts the door off the wall and looks it over. Hopefully, the inside isn't rusting.

"How long have you two been dating?" Bryson asks.

"We're not," I reply without thinking. My eyes dart from Leo to the man standing a little too close now. Bryson licks his lips.

Leo drops the door back against the metal building with a loud bang. "You want four hundred?"

"We can talk price." The creep's eyes never leave me.

Leo steps between us again. This time, he's facing me with his back to Bryson, blocking my view of the man.

"Why don't you go wait in the truck? Maybe you can find us a good station to listen to on the way home. I'll be there shortly." He drops the keys into my hand.

"Yeah." Thankful for the escape, I hurry back to the truck. Leo doesn't turn to face Bryson until I'm inside.

I put the key in the ignition and start the engine. I'll find us a station to listen to, as Leo suggested. He can deal with the parts guy. I'm just glad to have something to do besides look at the creep.

Just as I find a country station, Leo hops in the truck. Without saying a word, he turns the truck around and starts toward Hayden Falls. Once we're out of sight of the shop, I look back. Hopefully, I never have to see this place again. I look down into the bed of the truck.

"You didn't get the door?"

"Nope." The Grumpy Barnes is back.

I guess the price negotiations didn't go well. If he didn't get the door, does this trip still count as part of my community service?

"Why?"

"He wanted too much for it."

"But you need that door. I have the money to pay for it." I didn't tell Leo, but I brought six hundred dollars with me just in case the guy went up on the price.

He holds a hand up. To silence my protesting, I guess. "He wanted a price I will *never* pay."

I watch him closely and don't protest further. Whatever happened back there has him on edge or fuming. I'm not sure which. I believe he's pissed off. A muscle in his neck twitches. Oh yes, he's mad. I'll stay quiet on the ride home. Too bad my phone doesn't stay quiet. It starts vibrating again. This is a call and not a text.

"You can answer that. They're not going to stop." Leo never takes his eyes off the road.

"I'll call them back when I get home."

The caller finally hangs up, only to call right back.

"Kyleigh, please answer the phone."

He's frustrated enough. I don't want to make matters worse. I don't want to answer this call either. However, I dig my phone out of my purse.

"Hello," I keep my voice low.

"It's about time you picked up." Scott doesn't speak softly.

"What do you want?"

"When are you getting the rest of your stuff?" he demands.

"What?" I can't believe he's asking me this.

"We need your stuff out of here. I've moved it all to the guest room, but I want it gone."

"Um. I'll talk to Mom and see what I can do." I can't do anything from here.

"I want it out of here by Monday, or I'm trashing it." Scott abruptly ends the call.

I slip my phone back into my purse and stare out the window. I can't look at Leo right now. It's all I can do not to cry in front of him. He saw me cry the night I was arrested. This is different. This is because I failed at the only serious relationship I've ever had.

Chapter Nineteen

Leo

The ride back to Hayden Falls is quiet. Well, except for the radio. Neither Kyleigh nor I speak. I don't trust my voice to do so. To say it's been a rough afternoon is putting it mildly.

When we get home, I park Lucas' truck beside the house in its usual spot. He and I have talked about building a garage. We haven't gotten around to looking at floor plans yet. Lucas wants a bonus room above the garage. I have no idea why. I want a room in the back for my tools. Not sure why I want that, either. I usually work on my vehicles in my parents' barn so Granddad can hang out with me.

I walk Kyleigh to her car and open the driver's door. "Drive safe. Let me know when you get home."

That's a strange statement coming from me. The only woman I've ever said those words to is my mom. Neither of my grandmothers drive. They know how. There's usually someone around to take them where they want to go.

"I don't have your number."

We pull out our phones and exchange numbers. I stand on the front porch and watch her drive away. A door opens and closes next door. I walk into the house without looking. My twin younger brothers live next door. My brothers and I did a great job at moving out on our own. We live next door to each other.

My head aches badly. I should take some pain medicine. Coffee first, though. I make my way to the kitchen and start a fresh pot. Doors open and close again. My mind's too messed up to care right now. I open the cabinet door and pull out a mug without looking. The events of the afternoon slam into me. I fought hard to hide my emotions on the way home. Now, I need a release.

I close my eyes and drop my head. The memories of today replay in my mind like a television show. My body vibrates. It's not a pleasant feeling.

"Ah!" I scream as I spin around and throw the mug in my hand across the room. It shatters when it hits the wall.

"Whoa, bro." Luke points at me. "That's not cool."

"Go home," I demand.

"No can do, big brother. You need us." Luke grabs the back of one of the kitchen chairs.

"What happened?" Levi gets the broom and dustpan. "We didn't see the door in the back of the truck."

"He wouldn't sell it to you?" Lucas walks into the kitchen.

"Oh, he wanted to sell it, alright." I ball my hands into fists.

Luke tosses his hands up. "Why didn't you buy it then?"

"The price was too high." I grit my teeth.

"Here. You sit." Lucas pulls a chair out from the table. "I'll make the coffee."

"How much did he go up on the price?" Levi sweeps up the ceramic pieces and dumps them in the trash.

I drop down in the chair, prop my elbows on the table, and grab my head with my hands. Bryson Crane is an evil man and one I hope I never see again.

"At one point, he doubled the price."

Luke whistles. "Eight hundred for a door. No wonder you didn't get it."

"There's more to it than that." Lucas sets a cup of coffee in front of me. He doesn't let go until I look up at him. "Be thankful that wasn't my favorite mug." I nod, and he releases the cup.

Hadley gave him a mug a few months ago. It's really nothing special. Well, to me, it's not. It can easily be replaced. It's a black mug with Deputy Lucas Barnes and the outline of Montana on it. To my brother, it's everything.

Lucas takes the chair across from me and leans back in the chair. "Now, tell us what else happened."

"Eight hundred for a door is enough to send me home empty-handed." Luke huffs. See? He can't stay quiet for long.

I release a breath and rub the back of my neck. "Naturally, I told him I wasn't paying that much. I reminded him of his asking price, which was our agreement. He said things changed?"

Levi narrows his eyes. "Since yesterday?"

"What changed?" Lucas taps his finger on the table in a steady rhythm. The cop in him is trying to piece things together.

"He said he would trade me even for the door."

My brothers look at each other. Luke and Levi shrug.

Luke leans forward and taps his hand on the table to get my attention. "Bro, you turned down a free door?"

I nod and ball my hands into fists again.

"Why?" Levi sounds genuinely concerned.

"The price was too high," I repeat.

Luke rolls his eyes. He's about to say something stupid. "Dude, I don't know who taught you math, but they did a crappy job. Free is a lot better than eight hundred dollars."

"What did he want to trade for?" Lucas' eyes meet mine. His expression has hardened. He's figured it out.

"A night with Kyleigh." I slam my fist against the table.

Levi springs from his chair to grab my cup. Lucas and Luke are on their feet, too.

"Bryson Crane. Thorn Valley. On my way." Luke turns to leave.

Lucas grabs his upper arms. "Not a good idea."

"Oh, come on, bro. You know you want to throat punch this jerk as much as I do." Luke pushes Lucas' hands away.

"I do, but I don't want to arrest one of my brothers."

"I'll be in Thorn Valley." Luke pokes Lucas in the chest. "Somebody else will be arresting me."

"Luke, you'll lose your job. You'll break Riley's heart if you go to jail." Levi knows precisely where to hit Luke to settle him down.

"I'm only not doing it for Rocky." Luke sits back down. "But if that creep shows up here, I'm turning the fire hose on him."

"Sounds like a plan." Lucas doesn't mean that. He's just appeasing our overly dramatic brother.

"Do you think he'll show up here looking for her?" Levi asks.

"I don't know." I run a hand over my mouth and beard. "He knows we're from Hayden Falls. His offer makes me believe he's a real creeper."

"I get that vibe too." Lucas nods.

"Does Kyleigh know?" Levi finally sits back down.

"No. There's no way I could tell her what he said."

"I'll call her dad and let him know." Lucas pushes his mug away. We've all lost our taste for coffee right now. "To be on the safe side, we should make sure Kyleigh's never alone for a while."

Luke leans toward Lucas. "You ready to be Chief Deputy Sheriff?"

"No." Lucas narrows his eyes. "Why would you say that?"

"Because when Al finds out this creep wanted his daughter, he's going to Thorn Valley to kill Bryson Crane."

I look at Lucas and nod. That's a good point.

"I'll get Dad to go with me to see Al." Lucas quickly changes his plans. An in-person visit for something like this is a much better idea.

"Okay." Luke slams both hands on the table. "Operation Keep Little Green Safe is a go. Who's doing it?"

I shove his shoulder. "We all are, you idiot."

Lucas points at me. "You're her main protector." My eyes narrow. "It makes sense. You're already in charge of her community service."

I don't like this idea. Protesting won't do any good. Lucas will have Dad on his side with one phone call.

"Her dad's the better option. I can't be with her all the time."

"We can get the girls to help keep an eye on her around town. They'll call us if they see this creep." Okay. Luke's not a complete idiot, after all.

Lucas nods to Luke and grins slyly at me. "No, little brother. You're perfect for this since you're practically married to her."

"What?" I choke the word out.

"Oh, man!" Luke laughs and pulls his phone out. "You're in Hayden Happenings again."

Lucas' grin widens as the three of us pull up the blog on our phones. I catch the flash of sympathy he gives Levi.

Third Barnes Down

Sorry, single ladies of Hayden Falls. The quiet Barnes is off the market. He and our newest bat-swinging resident were seen leaving town this morning for a romantic weekend getaway. They're trading those cell bars for wedding bells.
If things keep heating up with the youngest Barnes and Tabby, the Sheriff and his wife will be marrying all four of their sons off by Christmas.

"I'm killing her. I'm killing her myself." Levi storms out of the house.

"I got him." Lucas stands.

Luke pushes him back down. "Oh, no, no, no, Big Brother. He's my twin. I got him. You deal with your twin."

Luke runs out the door to stop Levi from doing something stupid. Megan Sanders is going to have our entire family after her.

"You okay?" Lucas raises an eyebrow.

I huff out a breath and run my hand through my hair. "I don't know. I just wanna keep her safe."

"We will," he assures me.

I'm not sure why my brother is grinning at me. Whatever. I've had enough for one day. I need a shower. Who knows. Maybe I'll call Tyler and Wade to see if they want to meet at Cowboys tonight.

Chapter Twenty

Kyleigh

We're back to the dreaded day of Monday. I'm on my third cup of coffee when Dad walks into the kitchen. He checks to make sure the back door is locked before going to the coffee maker. I'm not sure what's up with him doing that. The past two nights, he's been checking both doors and walking around the house once an hour until he goes to bed. Maybe he's done it all along, and I just noticed.

"Good morning, baby girl." Dad kisses the top of my head before joining me at the table. "How's your morning going?"

"Morning, Daddy." I lean back and rub my eyes. "It's going slow."

"Getting an early start, I see." He points to my laptop and files scattered across the table. I nod.

Knowing Monday was on the horizon had me tossing and turning for hours. Around five, I gave up on sleep and decided to work on a few clients' accounts.

My phone dings with a text. It's turned with the screen down in the middle of the table. Mom is going to my apartment this morning to get the rest of my things. I should say Scott and Brenda's apartment. I sent her a list last night of what I wanted, just in case Scott tries to push off the stuff he gave me. I don't want any of it. My eyes widen when I flip my phone over.

Leo: *Good morning.*

Dad snickers. I snap my head in his direction.

"What?" I tilt my head and stare at him.

His grin widens as he points to my phone. "Something I need to know about?"

"What? No," I stammer.

Since Leo and I exchanged phone numbers, he's been texting me good morning and good night. If I don't reply, he'll text every fifteen minutes until I do. I know because I tested my theory last night. Every fifteen minutes for an hour, I got a text from him. The first one said *good night*. The rest were *hey*, *you okay*, and *I'm on my way*. On that one, I replied, letting him know I was fine. I don't mind if he comes over. Trust me. I don't mind at all. I'm not sure what Dad would think about it, though. Heaven help us if this town sees Leo's car here late at night. The blog post on Saturday was bad enough to have me hiding all day yesterday. We don't need to add to that crazy drama.

Dad raises an eyebrow in questioning as he takes a sip of coffee. Did I do something to give myself away? Sure, I think Leo is cute—very cute. Sadly, nothing will ever happen between us. He's only tolerating me because the judge and Dad insisted I help restore his truck. Half of my helping him consists of me taking notes, not sure why I am, and handing him the tools he asks for. The other half I spend watching him do the work. And I silently watch every muscle he has move as he works.

Before our conversation about Leo gets deeper, my phone rings. Scott's name lights up on the screen. It's six in the morning in Seattle. Why is he calling me so early? He wanted my stuff out today, but this is ridiculous. I flip the phone back over. It's way too early for a conversation with him.

"Is that a problem?" Dad saw the screen.

"I don't think so. Mom is supposed to get my stuff today."

"Want me to talk to him?"

I shake my head. The last thing Scott wants is for my dad to answer his call. After the way he treated me, I shouldn't care what happens to him. Maybe I will let Dad deal with him. No. I'm a grown woman. I need to handle my problems. If I could leave Montana, I would get my things today rather than sending Mom.

My phone dings with three text messages within seconds of each other. I drop my head back and groan. Scott is the biggest jerk I've met in my life. He's not going to stop until my stuff is out of the apartment. Dad's phone dings with two text messages. That's odd. Scott doesn't have Dad's number.

Dad reads his messages and points at my phone. "You should answer your Mom and Leo."

Great. Now Mom and Leo are contacting Dad when I don't reply. Wait. I understand why Mom would, but not Leo. What is up with him lately? Did spending the day with him change things between us? Oh, I won't complain if it did. No, that's silly. I grab my phone. Sure enough, there's a message from Mom, Leo, and Scott. My phone rings again with another call from my ex.

"You should take his call and get it over with, too," Dad mumbles. He steps just outside the doorway to make a call.

He's right. I should handle this now. I said I was an adult and could handle my own problems. Reluctantly, I answer the call. I don't even get to say hello.

"Kyleigh!" Scott shouts so loud I have to hold the phone away from my ear. "What were you thinking?"

"Um." I have no idea what he's yelling about.

"Are you insane? You send your mother to my house at six in the morning?"

"Um." I don't know what to say. I didn't know Mom was going this early.

"You're crazy. I should have known you weren't adult enough to do this yourself. You're so childish. If I didn't need your junk out of here today, I'd throw your mother out of here!"

Dad snatches the phone from me. "Listen here, you little punk. You don't speak to my daughter that way. And you will not disrespect her mother again. You will step aside and let her and her friends get Kyleigh's things. I've already called your local police department.

They're on the way. You better find your manners. If Kendra messages me again to say you're out of line, I'll be in Seattle before the sun sets."

Dad ends the call and somehow calmly lays my phone on the counter. He turns to grab the edge of the sink for support and drops his head. His breathing is hard and fast. He's anything but calm.

"Daddy?" I slowly stand. "I'm sorry."

He takes a couple of minutes to get himself together before turning to face me. His smile contradicts the tension in his body. He's fighting to hold his anger in.

"You have nothing to be sorry for." He walks over to me and wraps his arms around me. "Just so you know. How that punk treated you isn't how a man treats a woman."

"I know, Daddy."

"What are your plans today?" He kisses the top of my head before releasing me.

"I have a few more files to finish up. After that, I'm going to Page Turners. Grace and I are going to lunch."

"You and Grace hit it off, huh?" His smile is genuine this time.

"I like her. She's really sweet, and she ordered some books for me. I need to pick them up."

"The Wentworths are a good family." He grabs his mug from the table and sets it in the sink. "I'm heading to work. You lock up behind me and stay safe when you go to town."

I laugh as I follow him to the front door. "Okay, Daddy."

Dad spins around on the porch to face me. He's in cop mode. "I'm serious, Kyleigh. Hayden Falls is a safe place, but the world is full of crazy people. You never know when one will ride through here."

That's odd. Where's this coming from? He has always been protective, but I swear he's on a new level now.

"Okay, Daddy. I promise to be careful." Agreeing is the only way to settle him down.

"You know, if you want and your job lets you work remotely, you're welcome to stay here. You don't have to go back to Seattle."

He looks so vulnerable right now. I wonder how long he's been trying to work up the courage to say that to me.

"Thanks, Daddy. I'll think about it."

He points to the door. "Lock that, and don't forget to call your mom and Leo." He waves before getting into his SUV.

I haven't told Dad yet, but my job isn't going to let me work remotely much longer. If I don't figure something out soon, I'll have to put my notice in by the end of next week. I can't leave Montana anyway until I get my community service done. But do I want this town to be my home again? It's quiet and laid back here. No one's rushing around to get somewhere like they do in Seattle.

Before I make any decisions, I need to talk with the town's lawyer and see if I can speed up my community service somehow. If I lose my job, I'm not sure I can find one in this little town. I didn't see any financial companies here. There's the bank, but I'd rather not go that route. Banks feel cold to me. I prefer working more closely with my clients. I guess time will tell. Right now, I'll finish up for the day and meet Grace for lunch. Maybe I can bounce some ideas off of her.

Chapter Twenty-One

Kyleigh

*G*race and I have become fast friends. Our friendship has come so easily. It's weird, and I can't explain it. I don't remember any of my friendships starting out this easily. It was hard for me to make friends in Seattle, even through college. Dad said Grace and I used to play together when we were younger. Maybe that's it.

Grace is also friends with a lot of other women in town. The number is shocking. She lists off at least a dozen names. The most friends I've had at one given time were three. My facial expression displays my shock. Grace bursts out laughing. Out of all of her friends, she's closest to Hannah, the dance teacher. I've been invited to Thursday night's adult class.

"Grace, I'm here," her grandmother calls out as she walks into the bookstore.

"Granny." Grace hurries around the counter to hug her. She pulls her grandmother behind the counter to where I sit on a stool. "Granny, this is Kyleigh Green. Kyleigh, meet my grandmother."

Both of their faces light up when they look at each other. Grace's grandmother doesn't look old enough to be her grandmother. If I had seen them on the street and didn't know better, I would have thought this was her mother.

"Nice to meet you, Mrs. Wentworth." I hold my hand out.

Mrs. Wentworth grabs my hand. Instead of shaking it, she pulls me off the stool and into her arms.

"Kyleigh Green, I've known you since you were born. It's Granny to you."

"Yes, ma'am."

She taps me on the top of my head with her finger. "What did I just say? Granny. Not ma'am."

I look to Grace for help. She giggles and nods. Okay. This confirms what my dad said. I knew the Wentworths when I was little. Sadly, I don't remember much about them.

"Yes, Granny." I happily call her the name she wishes. The smile on her face is priceless.

Granny turns to Grace. "Now, you two run along."

Grace hurries to her office and comes back with our purses. "Let's go."

"Go? Where are we going?"

"To lunch." Grace grabs my arm and pulls me to the door.

"I thought we were calling an order in. We can't just leave your grandmother here alone."

"It's Granny to you, Kyleigh, not *your grandmother*," Mrs. Wentworth calls out. "And this is a bookstore, not a hospital. I can handle watching it, so you two can go to lunch."

"Don't argue with her," Grace whispers. She turns to her grandmother. "Thank you, Granny. We'll be back in an hour."

"Take your time, girls." Mrs. Wentworth hops up on the stool I was sitting on.

I wave to her. "Thank you, Granny."

She beams with pride and wiggles her fingers at us as the door closes. I can tell I'm going to really love her.

Grace loops her arm around mine and practically pulls me into Davis's Diner. She waves to Miss Cora and walks us to a booth along the windows facing the bookstore. From here, we can watch through the side window and see if her grandmother needs help. A few ladies walk in, but not enough to cause problems for Mrs. Wentworth.

After Miss Cora takes our orders, Grace reaches across the table and takes my hand. "So, tell me all about it."

"Uh. All about what?"

"Your trip with Leo. You were vague in your text messages. I know there's more to it than that. At least, I hope there was," she mumbles the last part.

I can't help but laugh. "You know what was in the blog isn't true. We went out of town to get a door for his truck."

"But you didn't come back with a door." She leans back against her seat and raises her eyebrows, waiting for some juicy gossip. "It has everybody wondering what really happened."

She's not going to let me out of here without telling her everything. So I do. I tell her about lunch at Amberlee Cellars. She and I are making plans to go back soon. I also tell her about the creepy junk man. Yeah, that's gross, but it's what I'm calling him now. Even Grace cringes when I tell her about meeting Bryson Crane.

"You like him, though. Right?" She looks hopeful.

"Who?" Yeah, I'm playing dumb.

"Leo, silly."

"I don't really know him."

"Look." She leans slightly over the table and lowers her voice. "I saw you Saturday." I nod. Of course, she did. I let the window down and talked to her on the sidewalk. "When you glanced at Leo as you let the window up, I saw your face. That was longing. You may not have told anyone or admitted to yourself yet, but you like him."

"Grace, I just got out of a relationship. I'm not ready for another one." I want to call it a bad relationship, but for me, up until two weeks ago, it was perfect.

"You don't have to be ready yet to like him."

We spend the next twenty minutes leaning over our food and whispering about Leo Barnes. For somebody who isn't dating, Grace is full of advice. Some of it's crazy. I'm not about to tell Leo I like him, yet anyway.

"Hello, ladies."

Grace and I jerk back in our seats and look up at the man standing beside our booth. He's in a deputy's uniform. His badge says Barnes, but which Barnes? Leo and Lucas look so much alike. I can't tell them apart. I know this isn't the younger two brothers. They're both firefighters. Lucas has no reason to come looking for me. Actually, Leo doesn't, either. Unless this is official business, I'm guessing this is Leo.

"Hey, Leo." Grace smiles wickedly at me.

"May I join you?"

Grace nods without asking me. Leo grabs a chair from the table next to us and sits at the end of our booth. Well darn. It would have been nice if he'd let me slide over so he could sit beside me. Ugh! This is Grace and her little pep talk's fault. My body is now highly aware of Leo.

"How are the repairs on the truck going?" She knows this is the only way Leo and I are connected.

"Slow."

Miss Cora brings Leo a glass of sweet tea and offers him a menu. He doesn't take it and orders a burger with fries.

"Are you working on Darlin tonight?" Grace thinks she's being sneaky. I see right through her.

Even though yesterday was one of Leo's days off at the station, he texted to say he wasn't working on Darlin again until Wednesday. It put a damper on my plans to get my community service over in a hurry.

"I think I might for a couple of hours after dinner." He turns to me. "If you want to help, you can join me. If you already have plans, it's fine."

"She doesn't have plans," Grace says a little too excitedly.

Leo narrows his eyes at her and looks at me questionably. He's going to think my friend is insane if she keeps acting like this.

"She means, yes, I'll join you."

"Good. I'll see you around seven, then." He checks the time on his phone. His eyes lift to mine. I thought his expression was serious before. It must have been his casual expression. The look on his face now screams serious. "Where's your phone?"

"In my purse."

"It on silent?"

"It is."

"Turn that back on, please."

"Why?" I challenge.

"You're not answering your messages from your dad and me. I only knew you were here because he told me you were having lunch with Grace."

"Why are you keeping up with me all of a sudden? It's not part of my community service." Apparently, I'm snappy today.

"I just need to know you're safe." His eyes roam over my face, causing the heat in here to rise.

"Okay." I don't know what just came over me, but I take my phone out and turn the ringer back on.

"Thank you." He dips his chin. "Now, if you ladies will excuse me, I have to get back to work."

I'm not sure what the rush is. This town doesn't offer too much excitement.

"Bye, Leo," Grace calls out.

I'm too stunned to speak. *I need to know you're safe.* Can I read more into that? Or is he just being a cop? Grace, however, reads way too much into it.

"Oh, my gosh," she squeals, but in a whisper. "Somebody has caught the eye of the quiet Barnes."

Chapter Twenty-Two

Leo

I no longer have control of my body. I don't know what I'm doing, thinking, or saying anymore. Unless you count my mom, I've never had lunch with a woman, let alone two. When Chief Deputy Green told me Kyleigh was having lunch with Grace today, I headed straight to the diner.

Something in me snapped Saturday in Thorn Valley. No, that's not true. Thorn Valley and Amberlee Cellars were beautiful. I snapped at Crane's junkyard. How could a man offer to trade car parts for a night with a woman? I've been looking into the creep's records. Bryson Crane III is one sick man. When those disgusting words left his mouth, I wanted to knock him out cold. So far, Kyleigh doesn't know about it. Hopefully, she never finds out. I'm doing everything I can to keep her safe.

I haven't asked what the phone call she got on the way home was about. The man on the other end of the call was loud and demanding. From what little I could hear, I think she's going through a bad breakup. It would explain why she showed up at her dad's out of the blue. If she were coming for a visit, Al would want everyone in town to know she was coming. Asking Kyleigh about it could hurt her if she's not over this guy. I'll bring up the phone call when I can talk to Al privately. He was grateful when Lucas and I filled him in about Bryson Crane. I'm sure he'll let me know if there's another threat to Kyleigh.

Laughter comes from the barn doorway. I don't have to turn around to know it's Mom. I love the sound of her laughter. Dad told us when we were little that if Mom was happy, the whole house would be happy. Granddad confirmed this was true about all the women in our lives. From that moment forward, my brothers and I went out of our way to make Mom and both our grandmothers smile.

"Let's just settle this right now," Mom says. That has me turning around.

Kyleigh's standing next to Mom. She's wringing her hands together. Her eyes dart around the barn, but they're cast downward. Why is she nervous?

"What's going on? What are you settling?"

"I invited Deputy Green and Kyleigh to dinner this Sunday," Mom replies.

"Okay." I have no idea what needs to be settled about a dinner invitation. Deputy Green has joined us many times.

Mom glances at Kyleigh and back at me. "Kyleigh's afraid because it's a family dinner that she and her dad will be intruding, and you won't approve."

"Um." Kyleigh's eyes go wide. Guess she didn't think Mom would throw her under the bus.

"It's okay, dear." Mom pats Kyleigh's arm. She turns to me for an answer.

I set the headlight box on the work table and walk over to stand in front of Kyleigh. She faces me, but her eyes stay on my chest.

I smile at Mom. "Go ahead and plan on them being here."

"Thought so." Mom kisses my cheek. She rubs her hand up and down Kyleigh's arm. "Told you. I'll fix you two a glass of tea." She waves without looking back as she walks out of the barn.

"Kyleigh, look at me." I wait until her eyes move up to mine. "I have no problem with you and your father having dinner with my family. Why do you think I would?"

"You have to spend nearly every day with me as it is, and family dinner is for family." She drops her eyes again.

Somebody has stolen her confidence. I don't like it. Whatever alien has taken over my body reaches out and lifts her chin with my finger.

"Family dinner is for us and anyone we want to invite, no matter how many times a week we see them."

"If you're sure," she whispers.

"I'm sure, but I think there's more to it. Is there?" I can feel there is.

"I figured the blog post would make you mad." She presses her lips together and tries to look down again. I don't let her.

And there it is. She's seen Hayden Happenings. After the phone call I overheard, I started seeing just how vulnerable she really was. Someone has already hurt her heart. My next words will frame the rest of our time together. I can pop something smart off and hurt her more. Or I can give her a reason to smile.

"What?" I playfully narrow my eyes and grin. Releasing her chin, I step back with my arms held out to the side. "You didn't enjoy our romantic weekend away?"

She loudly gasps and stares at me like I've grown wings or horns. Who knows which? It proves I don't have control of my body and, apparently, my mouth, either. I would never tease a woman like this.

"It was a day." She crosses her arms and tries to hold back her laughter.

"Proves you can't believe everything you read." I wink and turn back to the work table. Oh, good gracious. I don't wink at women, either.

Kyleigh bounces up beside me and picks up one of the boxes. "You're really not mad?"

I glance at her from the corner of my eye. She's smiling. The tension in her body is gone. I won't take that from her.

"Not at you." I open the box and set the headlight on the table. "Megan makes a lot of people angry with her posts."

"I'm sorry." Her happiness is gone again. Darn it. That was not my intent.

"Not your fault, Slugger." I bump her shoulder with mine. "This town loves gossip. Ignore it if you can." I turn and lean my side against the table. She looks up at me. "If you ever hear anything that bothers you, just ask me."

"I really enjoyed lunch."

"Really?" I narrow my eyes again. "I guess you're right. Davis's Diner does have great food."

"No, silly." She playfully slaps my arm. "Well, yeah. Today was nice, too. But I meant Saturday at the winery. Thank you for that."

All playfulness leaves my body as I stare into her eyes. They remind me of the sky on a sunny day. When she genuinely smiles, her dimples show. I didn't realize dimples were attractive until now.

"It was my pleasure." And it really was. And I want to do it again. "We should go back and tour the winery one day."

"I'd like that." She turns and fiddles with the other headlight box. Her little dimples are on full display.

Oh, somebody help me. I have no idea how to navigate any type of relationship with a woman. I have to figure something out soon, though. Everything in me wants to wrap her up and protect her forever.

Chapter Twenty-Three

Kyleigh

"Grace, this is a bad idea." I try to pull away, but she squeezes my hand tighter.

"If I have to do this, so do you." Grace reaches for the door of Cowboys.

"Wait." I pull hard enough to spin her around to face me. "You don't like coming here?"

Grace huffs out a breath and looks around the parking lot. I have no clue what she's looking for. Finally, her eyes meet mine.

"I do, and I don't." She glances at the door and back to me. "I'm not fond of bars. Naturally, I'd rather be curled up at home with a good book. But when E and her friends convinced me to start joining them for their Girls' Night Out, I don't feel alone anymore."

Oh, wow. She was isolating herself. I don't pry and ask why. When she's ready, she can tell me. It appears people's assumption that bookworms prefer a night at home with a book is true. Grace loves to read. However, from the sound of her voice and the look on her face, she wasn't happy being by herself. I'm glad she found a group of friends who brought her out of her shell.

"I don't know if I'm allowed to go in here." No one has mentioned me being banned from Cowboys. Still, I'm not sure anyone in this town wants to see me here.

"If they throw you out, the rest of us will leave too." Grace smiles. "Trust me. Noah Welborn doesn't want to lose half of his regular customers to O'Brien's Tavern."

"These people aren't going to walk out because of me."

"You'd be surprised. Now, come on." Grace pushes the door open and pulls me inside.

This place is packed. It looks like half the town is here. As Grace pulls me across the upper level of the bar, I search out the band across the huge dance floor on the lower level. I don't know who they are, but these guys are good. They should be in Nashville with a record deal.

My boots slide on the steps as we move to the lower level. It's a wonder I didn't trip. I'm blaming Grace if I fall in front of all these people. She's in a hurry to get to our table. Her friends are already waiting on us. We'll have to weave through the crowd around the bar first.

I bumped into several people and apologized each time. The bar lines the right wall of the lower level. Grace is pulling me behind the bar stools. Why she thinks this is the best route is beyond me. She comes to a halt at the far end of the bar when someone speaks to her. I can't hear what they're saying over the music. I bump into the man sitting on the bar stool next to me.

"I'm so sorry, Sir," I shout over the music.

The man and his two friends turn to face me. My heart drops for a moment. I would have never thought he'd be here. Seeing him at Cowboys shouldn't surprise me. He was here the night I made a fool of myself.

"Oh, Mr. Barnes, I'm so sorry," I quickly apologize again.

"Mmmph." Mr. Barnes huffs and turns back to talk with his friends.

Leo's grandfather is never going to forgive me. Thankfully, Grace pulls me away. Her friends squeal when they see us.

"Glad you two made it." Hadley pats the empty stool next to her. Riley is sitting on her other side.

I hop up on the stool. At least I know more people here than just Grace. She takes a seat on the stool to my right and starts talking to the lady a couple of stools down. It's the woman who towed Leo's truck. My eyes drift back to the bar.

"What's wrong?" Hadley leans closer to me.

I nod toward the bar. "He hates me."

"Who?" Riley follows my gaze to Mr. Barnes. She gives me a sympathetic look.

Hadley sighs. "He's hurt and upset, but he doesn't hate you."

"Have you apologized to him?" Riley asked.

"I've apologized to Leo."

Riley points at me and nods once. Oh my. I didn't think to apologize to Leo's grandfather, too. Darlin used to belong to Mr. Barnes.

"She's right. An apology just might help." Hadley grins. "He likes donuts."

"Let me know when you need them. I'll have a box of his favorites ready for you," the woman next to Riley says. I don't know her name, but she owns the bakery in town.

"Thanks." These ladies have given me a great idea. I'll apologize to Mr. Barnes and make it special. I doubt I'll have everything ready by Sunday dinner, though, but I'll sure try.

"What can I get you, lovely ladies?" One of the bartenders walks up behind Grace and me. He's cute. The ladies at the table behind us are drooling over him. He doesn't even notice.

"A round of shots and lots of beer!" Beth shouts across the table.

Most of the women at our table nod in agreement. Well, it's really three tables pulled together to be one. A couple of the ladies order nonalcoholic drinks. I understand why one does. She's pregnant. Grace, Riley, and Hadley order a glass of wine.

"What can I get you, Slugger?" The bartender grins.

"Noah." Hadley swats his arm.

I slightly turn and look up at him. "You're the bar owner?"

"I am."

Grace turns and looks up at him, too. "Noah, this is Kyleigh Green. She's worried she's not welcome here."

Noah's expression turns serious. "Did you leave the bat at home tonight?"

Oh no. I shouldn't have come here. "Um. I don't know what happened to the bat." The bat wasn't even mine. It was Jenna's.

"Good." Noah grins again. "You're welcome here. Just don't bring any more bats." I nod. "Now, what can I get for you?"

"A glass of red wine." I'm not much of a beer drinker. I won't stick out since the three ladies next to me ordered wine.

Grace introduces me to the women at our table while we wait for our drinks to arrive. Knowing which shop these ladies own or work at helps me keep their names straight. I'll have to visit more stores than Page Turners and Beth's Morning Brew if I want to really get to know them all. Do I want to be friends with this many women? It'll make leaving Montana harder once my probation ends.

Beth makes a crazy toast to friendship and this crazy town after Noah brings us our drinks. Everyone but E and Katie down their shots. A round of cheers goes up, mainly from Beth. She seems to love to party. I should have joined E and Katie and refused the shot. Whiskey is not my thing. My throat burns. Who knows? Maybe I didn't drink it right.

"I expect to see you at dance class next week." Hannah is sitting on Grace's right.

"I'll see what I'm doing on Thursday. If Leo is working on his truck, I'll have to help him." I sigh and shake my head. "I should be helping him now."

"Leo's not working on Darlin tonight," Riley says.

"Oh," I say softly.

Leo didn't tell me what his plans were tonight. He texted earlier to say I had the night off. He's been working on the truck when I'm not around. I may not know anything about working on cars, but I know where we stop each day. I have it all written in my notebook.

"It's why his grandfather's here." Grace takes a sip of her wine.

"What does that mean?" I look to Hadley for an answer. She knows the Barnes family the best.

"Granddad Barnes has been bar hopping with Leo since early spring." Hadley covers her mouth with her hand to hide her laughter.

I gawk at her. It's cute, but it makes no sense.

"He's helping Leo find a girl." Katie laughs and covers her mouth, too.

Everyone laughs but me. I look to the bar at Mr. Barnes' back. He's helping his grandson find a girl. Wait. If Mr. Barnes is here, it means Leo is, too.

"They're here looking for Leo a girlfriend." I drop my head and lean back against my stool. The laughter around me quickly dies.

Hadley takes my hand. "Hey. It's okay. Leo's not really looking for a girlfriend. He's just making his grandfather happy by taking him along. They're very close."

"Besides," Grace nudges me with her shoulder. "Leo Barnes has already found his girl."

"What?" My head snaps up. I look from Grace to every woman sitting with us. "He's here and already found someone?"

E has the biggest grin on her face. She's so excited she's about to vibrate off her stool. "He's here, and he hasn't taken his eyes off you since you walked in."

"He's watching me?" I bite my bottom lip. She's wrong. There's no way Leo is interested in me. Sure, Grace teases me about it. Sure, I wish he was. It's not possible, though. I destroyed his truck. He's not going to ever get past that completely.

"Yeah. He is," Hadley confirms.

"Where is he?" I'm afraid to look.

"Straight across the dance floor on the upper level. All our guys sit up there and keep an eye on us," Hannah replies.

Slowly, I turn my head and look to the upper level. My stomach flips, and my heart flutters. My eyes lock with the soft brown eyes of Leo Barnes. Oh, my gosh.

Chapter Twenty-Four

Leo

"You're a goner." Wade Lunsford chuckles and grabs another beer from the bucket of ice.

"What?" I snap my gaze toward him.

"Never thought I'd see the day." Tyler laughs.

Tyler's leaning against the wood railing across the upper level. The railing is about six inches above the tables and runs the length of this level. We have a perfect view of the dance floor below.

I look between the two men I consider my best friends. We may not talk every day and spend a lot of time together, but when we do, it's like no time has passed. Right now, these two idiots are laughing at my expense. If they keep this up, I might have to rethink our friendship status. Nah. I'd never do something that drastic. Wade and Tyler have been my friends since we were practically born. Our parents are friends, so we were bound to be friends too.

"Nothing is happening," I insist. Something's happening. I just don't know how to describe it or explain it.

Tyler points at me. "You are a horrible liar."

"You like her." Wade turns serious.

I don't reply. Instead, my gaze goes back to the little brunette across the bar.

Kyleigh looks happy tonight and cute. It's the first time I've seen her wearing cowboy boots. She's done something different with her hair, too. Maybe she went to Kenny's Kuts. Instead of her bouncy waves, her hair is straight tonight. One corner of my mouth slightly lifts. She's pretty either way.

Tyler also stops laughing. "It's okay to admit you like her."

"I don't really know her."

"Lucas didn't really know my sister, but look at them now." Wade looks across the bar to his little sister. Hadley's sitting next to Kyleigh.

"And Luke hardly knew Riley when she showed up in town. Those two are inseparable now." Tyler snickers.

My brother Luke seriously dating a girl is comical, not because of Riley. She's great. Luke, on the other hand, is crazy. Our family never thought he'd settle down. And Wade isn't wrong about my twin and his sister, either. At first, I thought it would be awkward that my brother was dating my best friend's sister. Well, the first time Hadley spent the night with Lucas was awkward. I'm sure Wade knows she's doing it, but I'll never mention those nights in front of him.

"I have to protect her." Those words feel bitter in my mouth.

Wade and Tyler look at each other. They glance at Kyleigh before snapping their heads toward me. They don't know what happened yet. I haven't had a chance to sit down and talk with them until tonight. This isn't exactly the type of conversation to have over the phone.

"From what?" Tyler asks.

We lean our heads close over the table. The gossip about Kyleigh and me going on a romantic weekend is all over town. Only my family and Chief Green know what happened at the junkyard. I tell my friends about the trip with Kyleigh to Thorn Valley. Both men want to go after Bryson Crane, just like Luke did. Like I still want to.

Wade sits up straight and drops his head back. Why he's laughing now makes no sense. Nothing is funny about Saturday's trip. Tyler looks as confused as I am.

"You wanna explain?" I ask dryly when he stops laughing.

"Man, you're so crazy." Wade laughs again and shakes his head. "The woman's father is a cop. You don't *have* to protect her. Chief Deputy Green is more than capable of taking care of his daughter." He points at me. "What happened in Thorn Valley opened your eyes and probably your heart too."

"You're the crazy one." I shake my head. We're not discussing this.

"Nope." Wade clamps his hand around my wrist on the table. "That creep best never show up here." Tyler nods in agreement. "But it took a drastic event to wake you up. You've never acted this way over a woman. There's more going on than you're willing to admit. You like her."

"She destroyed my truck," I remind him. How does a man get past something like that? It's not possible. Is it?

"Wrong again." Wade holds up a finger. "Kyleigh broke your taillights. Her friend did the rest of the damage."

I run my hands over my face. This conversation is uncomfortable. He's not wrong, though. I want to bring Kyleigh's friend Jenna in and make her take responsibility for her part in beating up my truck. Dad and Lucas said no. It was Kyleigh's idea, and she's taking responsibility for everything.

Tyler taps his hand on the table in front of me. He's looking toward the lower level. "Man, if you're protecting her, you need to go protect."

What's he talking about? All the women in Kyleigh's group are line dancing with Hannah. Still, I search her out on the dance floor. A deep growl rumbles in my chest as I bolt from my chair when my eyes land on the little brunette who has my emotions messed up. I take my eyes off her for two minutes, and this idiot moves in on her. Not on my watch.

My anger builds with every step I take. Of all the things that had to happen tonight, I now have to deal with this idiot. The line dancers quickly part as I make my way across the middle of the dance floor. Is this how Aiden feels when this fool flirts with his wife?

"Come on, Bat Girl. Let's take a spin around the dance floor." Four stumbles as he reaches for Kyleigh.

"Bat Girl? Seriously?" Kyleigh takes a step back and jabs her finger at him. "It's called line dancing. Nobody's spinning anywhere."

"Oh, Bat Girl. We can spin to any song." Four's already drunk.

I step between them and place my hands on Four's chest. He stumbles backward when I shove him away. Not to worry. Pit's there to catch him before he falls.

"Keep moving, Calhoun." I point toward the front doors. Noah should have already thrown him out tonight.

"I am moving." Four does a crazy wiggle. He tries to dance around me to Kyleigh. "Bat Girl and I are gonna dance."

I step in his path, keeping Kyleigh behind me. This is the dumbest man on the planet. Maybe Hadley and her grandmother should shoot him again.

"You will stay away from her." I take a step toward him. Chairs scrape across the floor on the upper level. "If I catch you anywhere near her, the beating Aaron Bailey gave you last month will be nothing compared to what I do to you."

"Whoa." Four grins and holds both arms out. My threat doesn't faze him. It proves how drunk he is. "Guess that little romantic getaway really happened."

Great. He's read Hayden's Happenings. The whole town has read it by now.

"That's none of your business," I roar. "Stay away from her!"

Every pore in my body is on fire. I take two steps toward Mick. Finally, the fool realizes how serious the situation is.

"Gotta go." He spins on his heels and slams into Pit. They fall to the floor.

Pit's the first one on his feet. "You gotta stop doing this nonsense." He jerks Four up, and they rush for the front door.

I slap my hand to my forehead and close my eyes. After a couple of deep breaths, I realize the bar has gone quiet. No boots slide across the dance floor. No one is talking. The band has stopped playing.

Someone on the upper level starts slowly clapping. I turn my head to see Aiden on his feet. My wonderful twin stands next to him and starts clapping, too. So do both of my best friends. Soon, the entire bar joins in, including Noah. Jake Campbell nods to his band members. They start playing a slow song. Couples pair up and take the dance floor. It's back to business as usual. I now have to turn around and face the woman behind me.

Facing her sucks the air from my lungs. Kyleigh's big blue eyes stare up at me. She looks frightened or uncertain. I'm horrible at reading women. I'm not sure what to do now. My only thought was keeping Four away from her.

"Are you okay?" She's not physically hurt. I didn't let Four get close enough to touch her.

She nods. "Are you?"

"Maybe." I'm nowhere near okay. I've never felt like this. I should go to the Emergency Room and get some medication to lower my blood pressure and something for this pounding headache.

Kyleigh nervously glances at the couples dancing. She bravely steps toward me and holds out her hand.

"Do you want to dance?" She presses her lips together.

"Dance?" I feel like an idiot. I should be asking her to dance.

"You know how to dance, right?" She smiles, revealing her dimples. Wade's right. I'm a goner.

"Yeah, Slugger. I can dance." I take her hand and lead her onto the dance floor.

She steps close until our bodies touch. Her grin widens, and her dimples deepen as her other hand slides around my neck.

"Well, Deputy, spin me around this dance floor."

For the first time tonight, I wholeheartedly laugh.

"My pleasure, Slugger."

And for the first time in my life, I drown in pools of blue as I allow myself to get lost in a dance with a woman I should be running from. Something tells me Kyleigh Green is going to completely break me.

Chapter Twenty-Five

Leo

Sunday dinners with my family are usually great. Today, things are weird. Everyone is looking at me strangely. My dad and brothers grin and look away. The shake of their shoulders gives away their silent laughter. Granddad's eyes dart from me to something random in the room and back to me. He's constantly chewing on his thumbnail.

The women in my family have caused me to retreat to the barn. It's fine. Darlin's better company today, anyway. Mom, Grandma, Riley, and Hadley all smile sweetly and look at me with stars in their eyes. It creeps me out and makes my skin crawl. At times, they share a knowing look with each other. After thirty minutes of this nonsense, I had to get out of there.

I wasn't planning on working on my truck today. My nerves have been a jumbled mess since the trip to Thorn Valley. My actions Friday night intensified everything—my nerves, my feelings, and my anxiety. My body is physically paying for it. My head hurts. Pain medication isn't helping. My chest aches so badly at times I rub it to try and ease the pain. The muscles in my back, neck, and upper arms are so tight it hurts to move. I need relief. Hopefully, some physical labor will help.

Kyleigh helped me remove the front fender yesterday. Her job was mainly helping me lift the fender off the frame and carry it to the work table. We have another table set up along the back wall of the barn for the bigger parts. My original work table is in the opposite corner. It has all my tools and the smaller parts on it.

I pause for a moment and look the new work area over. Kyleigh set this up by herself while I worked on the taillights. She did a fantastic job. Everything is so organized, even my tools. I'm not a slob by any means, but I'm not this neat. I'll thank Kyleigh later for the work she's done out here. I shrug and begin buffing out one of the dents in the fender. A baseball bat can do a lot of damage.

"How's it going?"

I stop working and look over my shoulder. Granddad makes himself comfortable on the stool Kyleigh sits on. At first, I thought she'd constantly be in my way. Most of the time, she sits here and talks when she's not writing in her little notebook. Surprisingly, she's a big help. I don't have to stop working to search for the tools and parts I need. Kyleigh finds them and brings them to me. She could have organized all of this so she could find everything easily. Whatever her reason, I like it.

"It's going good." I'm not exactly lying. The restoration of Darlin is going well. I'm the bigger mess at the moment.

"You really like her." Granddad sets a glass of sweet tea in front of me.

I'm not sure if he's asking or telling. Sadly, I'm not sure how to answer him. Technically, I should stay mad at Kyleigh forever. Spending time with her almost every day and getting to know the little things about her has me seeing past what she did.

"I don't know, Granddad." I wipe my hands on a shop towel before taking a sip of tea.

"You do know," he says softly.

"But you don't." Yeah, I'm deflecting. Admitting my feelings for Kyleigh is hard. I shouldn't have feelings for her.

"I don't like what she did." He slides off the stool and walks around to the driver's side of Darlin. Tears well up in his eyes. "This hurts, Leo."

Something in me breaks every time I see him cry over this. He hasn't tried to sit behind the steering wheel since Ally towed Darlin here. He could get in on the passenger side, but he says that's Grandma's side. He has no problem sitting in the passenger seat when we ride around town together. I guess he believes it's wrong for the driver to get in on the passenger side.

"I know, Granddad. It hurts me, too." I put my arm around his shoulders.

"But you like her," he repeats softly.

"I've tried not to." My voice drops lower than his. I feel like I'm betraying him and our truck.

"A pretty girl will always get by with everything," he grumbles and walks back to the work table.

"It's not like that, Granddad."

I knew people would look at it this way. It's one of the reasons I haven't admitted my feelings for Kyleigh out loud, not even to Lucas. But my brother knows without me saying a word. Of course, my actions this past week have told everyone all they need to know. The gossip circles are running rampant right now. I made front-page news in Hayden Happenings yesterday. I refuse to read it.

"But it is." Granddad grabs his glass of sweet tea and starts toward the door. He pauses and places his hand on my shoulder. Our eyes meet, revealing the pain and torment we both feel. "A pretty girl can smile and bat her sweet little eyes at the right man, and the entire North Pole will melt."

I swallow hard and look away. It's not like that. It really isn't. But how do I explain what's happening to me? I can't. There aren't enough words to get this right. I'm even worse than Lucas when it comes to women. Well, was. My twin seems to have figured relationships out rather quickly. He's madly in love with Hadley. He could probably help me sort through my jumbled emotions if I wasn't too embarrassed to talk with him about it.

Granddad pats my shoulder twice before walking out of the barn. So much for getting any work done today. My heart isn't into working on Darlin anymore. I haphazardly put everything away and follow Granddad back to the house.

Laughter and the happy sounds of my family greet me as I walk through the back door. Surprisingly, no one is in the kitchen, so I make my way to the living room. Granddad's sitting in his favorite recliner. Dad's in the chair next to him. Chief Deputy Green is sitting on the edge of one of the couches. All of the women are huddled around Kyleigh. Each takes a turn hugging her.

"Kyleigh, sweetie, you didn't have to bring anything." Mom holds her at arm's length. "I told your dad we had the food covered."

"Oh, it's not food." Kyleigh holds the gift in her hands to her chest. "This is for Mr. Barnes."

My family looks around the room at each other. It's nobody's birthday. All eyes settle on me for an answer. I shrug and shake my head. She hasn't mentioned anything about giving anyone a gift.

"Dear." Grandma puts an arm around Kyleigh. "There are six Mr. Barnes's in the room. You'll have to be a little more specific."

Kyleigh looks at her dad. He nods. At least somebody knows what's going on. Her eyes meet mine. *Please, don't let this gift be for me.* I don't mean that in a bad way. I don't have anything to give to her. I'd be embarrassed. Besides, a man is supposed to be the one giving gifts. We might be in a modern age now. Women are free to express themselves. However, some old-fashioned traits shouldn't be messed with. She's extremely nervous. I smile, hoping it gives her the courage she needs to get through whatever this moment is.

Kyleigh takes a deep breath and nods. It appears she's silently giving herself a little pep talk. Everyone's eyes widen when she walks over to stand in front of my grandfather. Oh no. This won't end well. I didn't even realize I was moving in to save her until Mom wraps her arms around my waist.

"Give her a minute," Mom whispers.

"Do you know what's going on?"

"No." Mom shakes her head. "But I have a feeling it's important."

Oh, it's important alright. But is it a good thing or a bad one? With the way my grandfather feels about Kyleigh, he's about to break her heart. What kind of man will I be if I let him destroy her? What kind of grandson will I be if I interfere?

"Mr. Barnes, I'm very sorry my friends and I beat up your truck." Kyleigh hugs the gift tighter. "What we did was beyond wrong. I can't tell you how truly sorry I am for my part in it. I should have stopped it. My reasons and excuses are hollow.

"Being drunk and calling ourselves avenging our friend's pain isn't a good enough explanation, but it's what happened. Still, it was wrong. We shouldn't have done it for any reason. I'm so sorry. I can apologize for the rest of my life, but I'll never be able to make up for it. Darlin is a beautiful truck. She didn't deserve what we did. Leo's doing a great job at restoring her."

"Of course, he is." Granddad narrows his eyes at her. Mom tightens her arms around me. Somebody needs to say something before his temper takes over. "All three of you should pay for what you did."

"I am paying for it. I'm paying for all the parts and Leo's time. I'll be here every day to help him restore Darlin." She drops her head for a moment before setting the gift on Grandad's lap. "This doesn't make up for what we did, but I wanted to give you this."

Granddad defiantly crosses his arms and eyes the gift as though it might explode. My heart breaks for him and Kyleigh. She wrings her hands together and twists her foot. Granddad remains silent. My eyes silently plead with Mom for help.

Dad reaches over and taps Granddad's arm. "Dad, open your gift."

Granddad glances up at Kyleigh again. My need to fix things is stronger than normal right now. Mom holds firm to keep me from moving. Grandma slides under my left arm. All I can do is wait and see how this plays out. Thankfully, Lucas moves to stand behind Granddad's chair. He gives me a nod, silently saying he'll help Dad if our grandfather lashes out at Kyleigh.

Granddad finally removes the wrapping. I don't pay attention to everyone else's reaction. My eyes are glued to the gift. I suck in a breath and take a step forward. Mom and Grandma move with me. They're as shocked as I am.

Granddad holds up a die-cast replica of our truck. It's mounted on a black base with a clear cover. He lifts the blue truck to eye level and studies every detail.

"Dad, that's beautiful." Dad leans over the arm of his chair to get a better look.

Granddad turns the truck around to see the back. Tears well up in his eyes as he reads the tag. "Darlin 1."

"Check the front plate out," Chief Deputy Green suggests.

Granddad quickly turns the truck around. "Sheldon." Tears spill over this time.

"I know it doesn't make up for what we did. I hope you like it and can one day accept my apology." Kyleigh releases a nervous breath.

"Mom, she needs me," I whisper. Thankfully, she releases me.

Stepping behind Kyleigh, I wrap my arms around her waist. This is a bit intimate. She might not be ready for me to touch her like this. Since I held her in my arms Friday night, I hope she doesn't mind now. Yeah, we were dancing Friday night. She was just too vulnerable standing in the middle of the room alone, trembling. I tighten my arms when she leans back against my chest.

Granddad stands and looks her in the eye. "Leo needs one."

Shocked gasps echo around the room. Dad quickly stands. He's about to scold his father. Surprisingly, Kyleigh giggles and looks toward her father. He holds out a bag from a hobby store in Missoula. She reaches into the bag and turns to face me. She bats her big blue eyes as she places a second truck in my hands.

"I hope you like yours too."

I look the replica over with wonder. It's amazing. The back tag says Darlin 2, and the front one says Leo. She thought of both of us.

"It's perfect." The rest of the room fades away as I get lost in her eyes again.

"It's a start." Granddad huffs and heads toward the dining room. We all follow him. He waits for me at the door while everyone else takes their seats. "What did I tell you?"

"Huh?"

"She's a pretty girl," he whispers before joining Grandma at the table.

I take my usual seat and smile at Kyleigh. Yeah. Granddad was right earlier. A pretty girl changes everything. The one sitting beside me has already flipped my world upside down.

Chapter Twenty-Six

Kyleigh

August is finally here. My life is…well, I don't rightly know what is happening in my life at the moment. The life I have in Seattle is on hold. My temporary life in Hayden Falls is moving forward—at a slow pace, I might add.

Mr. Barnes hasn't fully forgiven me yet. At least he doesn't leave the barn anymore when I show up to help Leo. He sits quietly on one of the two stools and watches everything. Of course, he sits at the opposite work table from me. Hadley and Riley told me the trucks I gave him and Leo had softened Mr. Barnes toward me. I don't see it yet, but I'll take their word for it.

Leo laughs and teases more. His smiles have been rare in the past. I treasure each one he shares with me. The trip we took to Thorn Valley changed things between us. The dance we shared at Cowboys seems to have pushed us closer to the edge of something more. The question is, do I want to fall over the edge with him? Of course, I do. I don't think it's wise, though. What happens when my community service is over and I return to Seattle? Very few long-distance relationships work out. Sooner or later, someone has to make a huge compromise, or the couple parts ways. I still need to get over Scott before I consider getting into another relationship.

My manager emails me after every file I turn in. The emails are always the same. She thanks me for my work and reminds me of my return-to-work deadline. I swear she's just copying and pasting her message into a new email.

My job is what brought me to this office today. Hopefully, I can get some answers about my community service issue. I have two weeks left to figure something out. I need to set some goals. I can't keep running blind. I've always had a laid-out plan for my future.

"Miss Green, Quinn will see you now." Mrs. Banks motions to the handsome lawyer waiting down the hall at his office door.

Quinn Martin, I've learned, is the town lawyer and the Mayor's son. He genuinely smiles as I walk toward him. The lawyers I've met in Seattle all had a gloomy expression and never smiled.

"Miss Green, it's good to see you today." He motions to a chair in front of his desk.

"Call me Kyleigh, please."

"Okay, Kyleigh. What can I do for you today?" Quinn closes the door and sits behind his desk, still smiling.

"I wanted to see if there's a way to speed up my community service."

His smile fades. "I've never been asked that question." He turns to his computer and starts typing.

Oh, my gosh. Please tell me this man is a real lawyer. There are degrees inside expensive frames on the walls. Hopefully, they're not from some fake online school. If he got his degrees from good looks, he'd have hundreds of them. If he has to Google for the answer to my question, I'm in more trouble than I thought.

"Sometimes, the judge will allow a substantial fine to finish out leftover hours once the original community service project has ended. Judge Morgan stated for you to help Leo restore his truck." Quinn clicks a few more keys.

Okay. He's actually looking at a digital file of my case and not Googling law questions. Good to know. This might not be so bad. Could Leo and I finish the truck in two weeks? If so, I can go home and save my job. Home? I don't have a home in Seattle anymore. Scott and Brenda are snuggled up in my home. I'll have to live with my mom. She's great except for when she's putting on airs for all her fancy friends. I don't know why she does it. Watching her flutter around them is exhausting. She has to be tired of it.

"According to the last update Leo sent me, you have logged forty-four hours in three weeks. That's roughly fifteen hours per week." Quinn tilts his head and gives me a tight smile. Ah. There's the fake lawyer smile. "That's impressive, by the way."

"So, I need fifty-six hours." That's not happening in two weeks. Well, unless Leo takes a two-week vacation from the Sheriff's Office and spends it working on his truck.

"Yeah. If you keep the same schedule up, you'll have the community service part over in four more weeks."

I sigh in defeat and fall back against my chair. Four weeks is two weeks too long.

"Kyleigh, are you trying to meet a deadline?" Quinn's fake smile changes to a look of concern.

If I want Quinn's help, I'll have to be honest with him. "Yeah, I haven't told my dad yet, but I'll lose my job if I'm not back by the fifteenth."

Quinn whistles and leans back in his chair, too. "That's not possible."

"It could be if I can talk Leo into working on his truck more."

"The community service hours aren't the problem." Quinn leans forward and rests his forearms on his desk. "You can't get out of the probation period."

"I can still do probation from Seattle. People have moved while on probation." My eyes plead with him to help me figure out something.

"That's true. Probation can be moved to another county or state."

"So, what's the problem?" I snap.

Quinn raises an eyebrow. Okay. Getting upset with people of authority might not be a good idea. I just lost any help I had hoped for from this man.

"Your outburst in court caused Judge Morgan to lengthen your time and add stipulations to your sentence. He will not allow a fine payout to your case for any reason. Your six months of probation have to be done here in Hayden Falls. You running from the judge's chambers didn't help any objection you might have to your sentencing."

"So, I'm stuck here for six months no matter what I do?" I drop my gaze to my hands on my lap. I can't look this man in the eye anymore.

"I'm afraid so. Once you and Leo finish the truck, a probation officer will be appointed to you."

"Well, okay then." I quickly stand. "I guess we're done here."

Quinn meets me at the door and gently grabs my elbow. He waits to speak until I look up at him.

"I know this is hard for you. I want to help you. And I'm sorry I can't. I understand your outbursts. The life you know and your livelihood are on the line here."

Wow. I guess he can read me better than anyone else in this town. My perfectly laid out plan for my life is nothing but trash now. One stupid decision when I was drinking has cost me everything. I simply nod. There's nothing either of us can do.

"This town isn't so bad once you get to know us." He genuinely smiles again.

"The people in this town love to meddle in other people's lives." I don't need to remind him. He knows it's true.

"Leo doesn't."

I snap my head up. "Leo?"

Quinn smirks. "He's not the same since meeting you."

"I made a mistake and beat up the wrong truck." I shake my head. "Leo's just stuck with me until Darlin's fixed."

Quinn's expression turns serious. Is this his lawyer's face?

"Leo Barnes was content with being quiet and by himself. Yeah, you didn't get the truck you thought you were getting. Personally, I think you got the one you were supposed to get."

I drop my head back and laugh. "You say that like it was destiny, fate, or something."

"Maybe it was." Quinn opens his office door and walks with me to the front door. His secretary isn't here. "You were supposed to be here, Kyleigh."

"You're sticking to fate, huh?"

"I am." He nods once. "But it's not all I meant. Fate brought you back to Hayden Falls. If your mom hadn't left, you would have grown up here with the rest of us. Like or not, Hayden Falls is still your home."

Most of that's true. I don't know about this being my home, but the rest is true. I've often wondered why Mom left. Maybe one day, I'll be brave enough to ask her about it.

"And Leo?"

"Maybe he's been quietly waiting for you."

I shake my head again and step through the door. "That's insane."

"Maybe not." Quinn looks around the parking lot. No one is here but us. "A few months ago, Leo told his grandfather if there was a woman for him, she wasn't in Hayden Falls."

"How do you know that?"

"Someone at Cowboys overheard Mr. Barnes telling his friends about it."

"You believe Leo Barnes has been patiently waiting for me to come to Hayden Falls?" I want to laugh so badly. This is utterly ridiculous.

"Stranger things have happened." Quinn's smile widens. He really believes it.

I do laugh as I walk to my car. Quinn Martin may be smart enough to be a lawyer, but he's as crazy as the rest of this town. He lives in a fantasy world. Do I want him to be right? Yeah, a little part of me wants the fantasy.

Chapter Twenty-Seven

Kyleigh

August is now my least favorite month of the year. Nothing has gone my way this week. I've tried everything to get out of this probation period. I've talked to three lawyers in Missoula. They all say the same thing as Quinn. I requested to see Judge Morgan. My request was denied the same day. I don't know why this judge seems to have it out for me. Whatever his reason, it has me stuck in this town for six months. I'll ring the New Year in right here in Hayden Falls.

Yesterday, I finally gave up and emailed my two-week notice to my manager. It's three days short of two weeks. Thankfully, it was accepted. It's the only positive thing so far this month. Not that losing my job is positive. Dad wants me to speak with Phillip Crawford to see if the bank has a temporary position available. I don't have the heart to tell him, but banks don't hire like retail stores do for the holiday season.

My community service is going to take longer than four weeks. Leo started working second shift at the Sheriff's Office this month. We only get a couple of hours in after lunch before he has to leave. I don't think second shift agrees with Leo. Some days, he's so tired we don't get to work on the truck at all. It doesn't matter anymore. My heart's not in it right now, anyway. I have six months to finish my hundred hours. Yay me!

Really, I should hate the month of July. Before it came barreling in, my life was on course and together. Since the beginning of July, my life has become a long list of failures. Tonight is bound to add to the list. I can't believe I let Grace and Hannah talk me into this.

"Relax. It's not that bad." Grace laughs as we put on our dance shoes.

"I can't dance."

"You did at Cowboys, if I remember correctly." She giggles and nudges my shoulder with hers.

"That's different. Dance classes are formal. I'll never be a ballerina."

"We don't do ballet. The kids do, but not the adults." Grace fastens her shoe and holds up her foot. "See? Not ballet shoes."

Well, just look at Grace Wentworth. The quietest person in town has a sense of humor. A comedian bookworm? No, that's not a thing. Grace is cute, though, and she's right. Our shoes aren't ballet shoes. She loaned me a pair of hers since I only had three-inch heels. These are similar but have a low one-inch wide heel. Hannah said until her students master the dance, she doesn't let them practice in heels. I'm sure it's for insurance purposes, too.

I stand and shift from foot to foot. This might not be so bad. The shoes and outfit make me feel pretty. Grace loaned me the outfit, too. It's nothing special, so I don't know why I feel this way. Grace and I have on black leggings with a long knit top that comes to about midthigh. I laughed and told her it was a dress. She insists it's not. Several ladies are wearing similar styles. Hannah is the only one in an actual dance costume.

"This isn't tap." Hannah glances at my shifting feet. "But we can do that next." She walks out to the middle of the studio. "Tonight, we're going to have a little fun with some jazz moves a few of you requested to learn. We'll also polish up on your waltz steps. Next week, the men will be back, and we'll start the Tango."

"The men?" I whisper to Grace.

She lifts her shoulders and giggles. "Yeah. They volunteer sometimes."

That's going to be a disaster. I'm not coming next week. Nobody told me I needed a dance partner. Would I have to pay for his classes, too? Would Leo consider being my partner? He can't. He's working the evening shift this month.

Hannah claps twice. "Okay, ladies, partner up."

Naturally, Grace is my dance partner tonight. It doesn't take long for me to discover that dance classes aren't easy. Some of the moves I've seen on TV and in music videos aren't simple techniques and take weeks to get right. I don't know who asked for the moves we're learning tonight, but they shouldn't be allowed to pick what the class learns. Hannah is the only one who can do them correctly. Katie doesn't even try. She sits at Hannah's desk and laughs at the rest of us.

Hannah decides to show us one of the dances from the movie *Dirty Dancing*. She partners up with Sammie Foster. The entire class stands with their mouths open. Sammie knows these moves. When the music ends, we all cheer and quickly surround Sammie and Hannah. The applause from the doorway brings us out of our celebration.

Jasper hurries across the room and wraps his arms around Hannah's waist. "Fancy, you gotta teach me those moves." We all cheer when he crashes his lips to hers.

Jasper isn't alone. Three of the Barnes brothers are standing just inside the doorway. Luke and Levi aren't on duty tonight. They aren't identical, but I still can't tell them apart. Since this one isn't making a beeline to Riley, I'm guessing this is Levi. He can't seem to make eye contact with anyone. I swear he's embarrassed for some reason.

He points with his thumb over his shoulder and starts backing toward the door. "I'm just going to go help Luke set up the refreshments."

Leo and Lucas watch their brother rush from the room. They are on duty. I must say, Leo Barnes looks good in uniform. I just don't know which one is him. It means Lucas looks good in uniform, too. I will never say that out loud in front of Hadley. She hurries across the room and bounces into the arms of the man on the right. How does she tell them apart? Glad she knows. Now, I don't have to guess. They're wearing badges, but both say Barnes. Maybe I need to learn their badge numbers. I need to figure something out before I embarrass myself.

Class isn't over, but these women heard the word food. They quickly change their shoes and hurry to the breakroom. I can't help but laugh. Mention food in this town, and people come running.

Leo doesn't move from the doorway. He stands there, looking me over from head to toe. Heat runs through my entire body. He's checking me out. One side of his lips lift in a sly grin. I look down at my outfit and snap my head up. I haven't worn anything this skimpy in front of him, not that my outfit shows anything I shouldn't be, but I know it's cute. Well, if I look anything like Grace does in her matching outfit, I'm cute too.

Grace places my jeans and tennis shoes in my hands. I wasn't moving either. I was perfectly fine checking out the deputy staring at me across the room. I would slide my jeans on over the leggings if we didn't have an audience of men in the room. Well, only one man here makes me nervous. I dart into the dressing room instead. When I come back out, Leo is the only one here.

"I guess there's nothing exciting going on tonight."

His eyes roam over me again. "Oh, I wouldn't say that."

"I meant with crime in our big city." I nervously laugh and walk through the door.

"An emergency can happen at any minute." He turns the light off and closes the door behind us.

Grace took her dancing bag with her. It's fine. This gives my hands something to do. I hold the shoes to my chest to keep from reaching out and taking his hand. It's insane. I shouldn't want to touch him, but I can't help thinking about it. Only I'm not safe. Leo places his hand on my lower back as we walk down the stairs.

"What made you guys stop by?"

"Lucas said we were helping our brothers set up the food Mom and the Hayden Sisters sent." He chuckles. "He's really here because he hates anyone dancing with Hadley. Jasper told him the class was all ladies tonight, but Lucas didn't believe him."

"Well, it's a nice surprise." I smile up at him.

His eyes hold mine for a moment. He swallows hard and rubs the back of his neck with his hand. We walk the rest of the way to the breakroom in silence. Every man in the gym pauses their workout to watch us. Good gracious. Even the men in the town are gossipers. Leo grabs my elbow and turns me to face him before we get to the breakroom door. He takes a deep breath and looks around.

"Are you okay?" I've never seen him act like this.

"Not really," he mumbles, but I heard him.

"You obviously have something to tell me. Don't worry. I've had a lot of bad news lately. You can spit it out. I'll be fine."

He narrows his eyes. "What bad news?"

"Just everything." I wave it off. I can't change anything, so there's no point in talking about it. "Now, what's up?"

"Well, I was wondering if you'd like to go out sometime?"

The way he's fidgeting, I swear, Leo Barnes has never asked a girl on a date. Wait. He's asking me on a date? No way.

"I see you almost every day." I lightly laugh. "We were ordered to spend a hundred hours together."

"No." He shakes his head. "Well, yeah. We do have to work on my truck, but that's not what I meant."

He can't seem to get the words out, so I help him. "Leo Barnes, are you asking me on a real date?"

"Yeah, I am. That is if you want to."

Oh my. He looks like a little lost schoolboy. If he weren't serious, I'd laugh right now.

I bravely reach for his hand. "I'd like that."

"Really?" He looks shocked. Did he honestly think I'd turn him down? I nod. "We can go anywhere you want."

I think for a moment and smile. "I'd love to tour the winery if you do."

His smile widens, and his eyes light up. "I'd like that. I'll set it up next week." He motions to the breakroom and follows me inside.

Since it's their dinner break, Leo and Lucas join us. They'll need a nap after this round of refreshments. Apparently, the Hayden Sisters don't do light snacks. This looks like a buffet. Everything's fine until Leo and Lucas' radios go off.

"Willows Bend needs assistance at Pete's Saloon," Sheriff Barnes says through the radio.

"We're on our way," Lucas replies through his. Hadley gives him a quick hug and kiss.

"Pete's Saloon? Aaron." Kennedy Reed springs from her chair.

Her friend Tara hugs her to keep her from running out the door. "You can't go. You're pregnant," Tara pleads. "Aaron will be fine. Our guys are going to help."

"We got him," Leo assures Kennedy. He turns to me. "I'll call you later."

I grab his hand and quickly stand. "Be careful." I've heard how bad that saloon gets.

"I will." He winks and rushes out the door behind his brother.

Grace pulls me into a hug. "I told you. The quiet Barnes is all yours."

Yeah, I believe she's right. The question is, what am I going to do about it? What happens to us in six months if we pursue this? My heart is already breaking. If I give in to this, leaving Montana will completely destroy me. Leo isn't the type of man to date randomly. What will happen to him after I'm gone?

Chapter Twenty-Eight

Leo

"You actually did it," Lucas laughs.

"Did what?" I glance at him before calling Pete's Saloon. No answer. Ugh. I hate going to this bar. If Pete's not answering the phone, it's bound to be bad.

"You asked Kyleigh out." Lucas keeps his eyes on the road. He has the lights and siren on.

"I did."

"Good."

"I don't think Granddad's going to think so." Our grandfather's feelings toward Kyleigh are the main reason I've been hesitant. Oh, and the fact I'm not great with women.

"Once Darlin is restored, he'll come around."

Wish I was as sure as Lucas sounds. Our grandfather is a kind man. I've never known him to hold a grudge against anyone. Sure, he's been mad many times. He usually makes peace within two to three weeks with whoever and whatever has him riled. It's been a month since Kyleigh and her friends destroyed our truck. He might be softening a little, but he's not ready to let it go.

"I think you're using Granddad as an excuse." Lucas glances at me. "I think you're scared." He's insane.

"I'm not scared." I look down at my phone, hoping someone from Pete's Saloon has messaged me. Nothing.

"When you're ready to talk about it, I'm here." He totally ignores what I just said. "All I'll say for now is don't let her slip through your hands because you're scared."

"Why does everyone think Kyleigh Green is the woman for me?"

"Because you're different with her. You smile and laugh more. The whole town sees, not just our family."

"You just want me to have someone so you can move on with Hadley." I'm a jerk for saying it.

Without taking his eyes off the road, Lucas punches me in the chest. It didn't hurt. Okay, maybe it hurt a little. Lucas is strong. I rub the spot and glare at him.

"What was that for?"

"You know what it was for." He's right. I do. "Yeah, I want you to find someone. I don't like the thought of you being alone. You're quiet enough as it is. If you're alone, you'll probably go mad. I love you, little brother." He shakes his head. "But I'm not going to put my life with Hadley on hold because you could possibly become a hermit."

"You're going to marry her." I've seen it coming for months now.

"I am if she says yes."

"Don't worry. She'll say yes."

Flashing blue lights pop up in the distance. Lucas kills the siren as we pull into the parking lot of Pete's Saloon. As much as I hate going in here, it stopped the relationship talk. Maybe on our next day off, I'll sit and talk with him more. My feelings about Kyleigh have my mind and emotions messed up. For now, my mind needs to be alert. Somebody gets hurt every time we have to come to this bar.

From the looks of the parking lot, the only people here are the Willows Bend Police Department, the employees, and the people involved in the fight. It's always a fight. It's a crazy thought, but I'm beginning to wish someone would rob the place just to give us a different reason for coming here. The half-a-dozen motorcycles to the left of the front door have me concerned. It looks like the Iron Rebels are back in town. If these guys are involved, it's going to be a long night.

Stepping into the bar confirms I'm right. A couple of police officers and one of the new bouncers Pete hired form a line in front of the door so no one can leave. A row of bikers are in front of them with their hands balled into fists, ready to fight. Three more officers stand around the room with their weapons drawn. The only customers here are the bikers unless Pete has more in the back somewhere.

Aaron Bailey and Tex, one of his associates from Slone Security, have the biker, Dawg, officially known as Davey Bassett, on the floor and in handcuffs. Learning the man's real name made his biker's name laughable. I guess Dawg does sound cooler than Bassett. Each of these guys has a rap sheet a mile long.

"What? These five aren't enough to handle us? You had to call in more." Buzz, the leader, snarls at Aaron. The man literally bares his teeth. If it's meant to make him look tough, he's not fazing Aaron at all.

The five officers here are about the extent of Willows Bends Department's night shift. With as rough as the bars are here, they should have fewer officers during the day and more at night. At least on the weekends, anyway.

"I didn't call them." Aaron pulls Dawg to his feet. "But I'm glad they're here."

"I called them," the little bartender shouts. She's standing behind the bar with a knife in her hand. Her Uncle Pete, the bar owner, stands behind her with a shotgun pointed at Buzz.

"Thanks, Tink."

Tink glares at Aaron. Thankfully, she stays quiet. The situation is a ticking time bomb. There are a lot of weapons drawn in the room. One wrong word or move, and this is going to get bloody. Lucas and I put our hands on our guns but don't pull them from the holster.

"I knew you were a cop." Dawg tries to pull away from Aaron.

"He's not a cop." Lucas walks past the bikers.

"He's just someone I hired to help clean the place up," Pete says. Buzz isn't buying it.

"What happened?" Lucas asks Aaron and Tex.

Slone Security has a third man here. I don't see him anywhere. Knowing Aaron, he has the guy out back guarding the rear exit.

"This one," Tex points at Dawg, "got a little handsy with another man's wife. The two got into a fight. Bassett here stabbed the man. The ambulance left with him about ten minutes ago."

Dawg glares holes into Tex. Slone Security was the first to ID the members of the Iron Rebels. They sent us files on each of these guys. Something tells me they only gave us the highlights and what could be found in a regular security search. Slone Security is a legitimate company. They have a mysterious side, too. Unless they break the law somehow, Dad won't push for answers.

"You're not arresting him," Buzz states firmly.

"He's already under arrest," Walt Freeman, the Chief of Police in Willows Bend, says. He turns to Lucas. "They won't let us carry him out of here."

Lucas steps in front of Buzz. "Your friend stabbed a man. He's going to jail. You and the rest of your guys will step aside, or we'll arrest all of you right now. If you want to help him, this isn't how you do it. Get him a lawyer."

Buzz points at Walt. "We'll be sitting with you all night."

"No, you won't." Lucas pulls his weapon, cueing me to do the same. "Mr. Bassett won't be spending the night in Willows Bend. He's going with us."

I want to look at my brother, but I keep my eyes and weapon on the two bikers closest to me, Tiny and Snake. The officers from Willows Bend motion with their weapons for the bikers to step aside. They look relieved that they don't have to take Dawg in. Their office isn't equipped to handle these guys hanging around. I'm not sure Lucas realizes it, but he just brought this fight to Hayden Falls.

The front door opens, prompting the bouncer to turn his weapon on the newcomer. He lowers his gun as Chief Deputy Green, Aiden, and Spencer walk in. Tink must have filled Dad in on how serious the situation was for him to send more backup.

"What's it going to be?" Lucas asked Buzz. "We can take him in peacefully, and you can go through the proper legal steps to help your friend. Or we can take you all in."

Buzz looks around the room. Realizing his little gang is outnumbered, he nods once. The bikers step aside, leaving a clear path to the door.

Chief Deputy Green walks over and firmly takes Dawg by the arm. "Where's the weapon he used?"

Tex lifts his boot, revealing a bloody knife. Now I notice the blood on the floor. If all the blood is from the man Dawg stabbed, he's going to need surgery. Everyone from Hayden Falls narrows their eyes at Tex.

"What?" Tex shrugs. He nods toward the group of bikers. "They were after it. I had to secure the weapon and protect my friend at the same time."

I hate to tell the man, but Aaron Bailey can protect himself. Still, it's good to know Slone Security's team has Aaron's back. Aaron left Hayden Falls ten years ago to join the Army. He's only been back for three months. In those three months, he discovered he had a daughter and made up with his high school sweetheart. They're getting married this month and have a baby on the way. Our community can't lose Aaron.

Spencer leaves and comes back with a set of gloves. He bags the knife and passes it to Aiden. Trust me. There aren't enough bikers in here to get that knife from Aiden. Spencer, Aiden, and Walt surround Chief Green and Dawg. The bikers don't move to stop them from carrying their gang member out the door.

Lucas points to Aaron's left arm. "You're gonna need stitches."

"Yep. Taking him to Walsburg now," Tex says. Aaron wants to protest, but the look in his teammate's eyes keeps him quiet.

"Here." Tink rushes over with a clean bar towel and wraps it tightly around Aaron's arm.

"You should call Kennedy and let her know what's happening." I walk Aaron out to his truck.

"She's supposed to be at dance class. There's no point in worrying her right now. I'll tell her about it when I get home." Aaron gets into the passenger seat.

"Yeah. She was at dance class. You need to call her."

"You and Lucas were at the gym when the call came in?" Aaron's face goes pale for a moment.

"We were. Tara had to stop her from running out."

Tex hops in the driver's seat. "You call your pretty lady while I drive."

"Thanks, Leo." Aaron offers me his hand. "Tell your dad to keep extra men on duty while you have Bassett in custody. These guys are trying to get into darker businesses than just selling drugs. Don't trust them for a moment."

"We'll stay on top of it." After shaking his hand, I close the door and watch Tex drive out of the parking lot.

Chief Deputy Green has Dawg securely in the back of his cruiser. We don't leave until the rest of the bikers do. I don't know where they're heading, but it's the opposite direction of Hayden Falls. Hopefully, it's a sign they won't be camping out at our office tonight.

"They'll be back," a man says behind us. Lucas and I spin around with our hands on our guns. The man dressed in black holds up his hands. "I'm with Aaron."

"You're Smoke?" Lucas asked.

The man nods. "I'll help finish up with Pete before heading to the hospital."

"Thanks, man." Aiden shakes Smoke's hand before the man disappears into the bar.

"What are you thanking him for? He didn't show up until it was over." Lucas glares at Aiden.

"When Willows Bend's officers showed up, two bikers tried to run out the back door. Smoke tossed them back inside and bolted the door."

"How did he bolt it?" I ask.

"No clue." Aiden looks to the front door of the bar. "But nobody got past Smoke."

"I see why they call him Smoke." How the man slipped up behind Lucas and me in a parking lot full of cops is a mystery. You'd think one of these guys would have noticed him.

Lucas leaves the Willows Bend Department to finish things up with Pete and his employees. Spencer and Aiden head to the hospital in

Walsburg to check on the victim and Aaron. My brother and I follow Chief Green and our unruly prisoner to Hayden Falls.

I call Dad while Lucas drives and explain everything that happened. He'll get the full report from Walt later. He also agrees with Aaron. We need extra men at the office until Davey Bassett is no longer in our custody. Our night just turned into a double shift. Good thing Dad has a sofa in his office. Lucas and I can take turns napping through the night. As we pull into the parking lot, my phone dings with a text.

Slugger: *Dad called. Are you okay?*

Me: *I am. I'll call you once things settle down here. Are you home safe?*

Slugger: *Yes, Deputy. I'm home safe. Doors locked and everything.*

Me: *Good. Try to get some sleep.*

Slugger: *I will after you call.*

Lucas snickers and shakes his head.

"What?"

"Look at the quiet Barnes being all domesticated." My brother laughs.

I punch him in the chest as he did me on the way to Pete's. It doesn't faze Lucas. My actions only make him laugh harder. I glare at my brother's back and follow him into the station. At the door, I pause and look around the parking lot. Everything's normal right now. Let's hope it stays that way. I glance up at the cameras we have outside. They're good, but maybe I should suggest that Dad looks into one of Slone Security's systems. I huff and shake my head. That's comical. A security company monitoring a Sheriff's Office. It'll never happen.

"Lock the door," Lucas orders. I do as he requests. He points to the front desk. "You take first watch and monitor who comes in."

I'm half a mind to tackle my bossy brother. Lucas will be Sheriff one day. I got used to him taking the lead years ago, especially at work. I sit down at Miss Ruth's desk and pull out my phone. I'll make a quick call to Kyleigh so she knows her dad and I are safe. Hopefully, she'll go to sleep afterward. Her dad's shift ends in less than an hour. Thankfully, Dad isn't having the Chief pull a double shift, too. I'll feel better knowing Kyleigh isn't home alone all night. My brother's right. I have become a little more domesticated.

Chapter Twenty-Nine

Kyleigh

Hearing about the biker's arrest has caused me to be a bit jumpy this week. I told Leo I'd go to sleep after he called, but I stayed awake until Dad got home. Dad told me more about what happened in Willows Bend than Leo did. They can't tell me everything since it's an active case. I heard enough to know to steer clear of these guys if they show up in town. The women in Hayden Falls didn't venture out alone until after the guy's buddies bailed him out two days later.

Leo and his brother worked double shifts both nights Dawg was in jail. Dawg? What kind of crazy name is that? I've read enough books and seen movies to know bikers have nicknames. I'd like to think they could come up with better ones than this group did. Leo's extra shifts haven't allowed us any time to work on Darlin. It will take me forever to get these hundred hours of community service finished. It's okay. I'm not going anywhere anytime soon. The longer I work with Leo, the less time I spend with a probation officer.

"You ladies ready?" Hannah shouts as she walks into the dance studio, pulling her husband behind her. She's not really pulling him. Jasper is more than happy to follow his wife.

"I'm ready!" Jasper's daughter, Bently, bounces in behind them.

I'm surprised the little girl is here tonight. We're supposed to be learning the Tango. Bently is five. Surely, she's not learning ballroom dancing. She is a lively little girl. I'm sure she could do it. She was here last week and was Hadley's dance partner.

Grace leans against my shoulder. "Isn't she adorable?" My friend is all dreamy-eyed.

"Grace Wentworth, are you dreaming about babies?"

"No." She lightly laughs, but her eyes say something else.

I wrap an arm around her and grab her hand. "Are you ready to Tango?"

I wasn't planning on coming tonight. Grace told me a few guys randomly show up to be dance partners. The ladies will pair up if enough guys don't come. Since Leo is working, I figured Grace and I could be dance partners tonight.

"I'm afraid we can't let that happen." A tall man wearing a cowboy hat walks up to us. He doesn't really seem like a cowboy to me.

"It would be a crying shame." His friend with dark hair is a little shorter.

I don't know their names, but both were sitting with Leo at Cowboys the night we danced. Grace looks toward the door like she's expecting someone. A few men enter and go straight to their wives or girlfriends. Grace's face falls for a moment. She quickly shakes her disappointment away and smiles at Leo's friends. Who is she crushing on? Grace and I need to have a quiet girl's night at her apartment and talk about men.

"Are you two volunteering to dance with us?" Grace smiles sweetly.

"Absolutely." The taller one holds his hand out to me. "What do you say, Kyleigh?"

Of course, he'd know my name. Sadly, I don't know his. Before I can ask, Hadley bounces over and throws her arms around him. He picks her up and twirls her around.

"I can't believe you're here." Hadley swats his arm when he releases her.

"You can be Hadley's dance partner." I take a step back. Hadley seems to know him very well. I'm not about to take a dance partner from her.

"Are you insane?" Hadley looks at me like I'm crazy. "I'm not about to dance with my brother."

"Brother?" I really need to learn who people are around here. If I don't, I'll embarrass myself every time I meet somebody new.

"Yeah. This is Wade." She motions to the other guy who's standing close to Grace. "And this is Tyler Hayes. He's E's brother." She looks between them. "Since my brother never shows up here, I'm guessing Leo sent you two."

Wade rubs the back of his neck. Tyler runs his hand through his thick hair. Neither man can look Hadley in the eye. Oh, my goodness. She's not wrong. They're here because Leo couldn't be. Should I be mad? I probably should be, but I'm actually flattered. It's a sweet gesture.

Hadley looks at me and laughs. She points across the room to a couple of guys. One of them is Quinn Martin. The other man does look like a real cowboy. "Don't worry. Lucas did the same for me."

"I guess they're more alike than just looks." Next time I'm alone with Hadley, I'm asking her how she tells them apart.

"Oh, they're not the only ones." She points to another man talking with E. "Aiden sent his older brother, Colton, to dance with his wife."

"Nobody else is brave enough," Tyler mumbles.

Hannah claps her hands twice. "Ladies, grab your partners and take the dance floor."

Hadley quickly grabs my hand. "You'll be there Sunday, right?"

"Sunday? Where?"

Her eyes widen. "Oh, my gosh. Please tell me somebody invited you." I shake my head. "Well, I'll find out who messed up. You just be at the Magnolia Inn this Sunday at two."

"What's happening at the Inn?" If there's a big event, there aren't any posters around town. This town takes its special events seriously. There's no way they're not advertising it.

"We're having a surprise party for Lucas and Leo," Hadley explains.

"Why? What did they do?" Maybe the town is celebrating them arresting the biker. No. That's stupid. The arrest was a group effort.

Hadley narrows her eyes. "They were born."

"It's their birthday?" I look at Grace. She nods.

I'm as confused as Hadley looks. How did no one tell me it was Leo's birthday? Well, he and I haven't sat down and had all the get-to-know-you questions. Being a surprise party, the people here can't openly talk about it. Maybe I'm not as important as I was hoping I was to him. Surely, he would mention his birthday to me.

"I don't feel like dancing." I drop my head and walk over to the chairs we used to change our shoes.

Hadley follows me. She refuses to let me sit down. "Hey. I don't know exactly what you're thinking, but don't you dare feel bad. We all want you there."

"It's okay." I turn my head and rub the corner of my eye. *Oh, please don't let me cry in front of everyone.* "I'll cancel our date."

"Date? What date?" Grace is crowding around me now, too.

"Leo asked me out last week. We were going to tour Amberlee Cellars on Saturday."

"Oh my." Hadley covers her mouth with her hand. She has tears in her eyes.

"Don't you dare cancel that date," Grace orders. Whoa. I've never heard Grace use her voice of authority before. I don't like it. It's darn right scary.

"He didn't tell me it's his birthday." I don't know why I'm harping on this. But it does hurt a little.

"You'll be at the party. But Grace is right. You're not canceling that date. Leo is the quietest person I know. He's not a spontaneous person. That tour, the wine tasting, and the restaurant are all romantic. If this is where he's taking you on your first date, trust me, he's put a lot of thought into it. It shows how important you are to him. He wouldn't take just anybody on this date." Hadley pulls me to her. "You'll crush him if you cancel," she whispers in my ear. "Something tells me it'll crush you too."

"Okay. I won't cancel our date."

"Good." Hadley turns and hurries over to the tall cowboy. I still didn't get his name.

Tyler and Wade hold their hands out to Grace and me. Before I can take Wade's hand, my phone rings. I quickly pull it from my purse to put it on silent. Scott's name lights up the screen. I snap my eyes up to Grace's. She slightly shakes her head. I declined the call and put the phone on silent before putting it away. Grace knows everything about my breakup with Scott. She has nothing to worry about. I have no intention of talking to him.

"Is that a problem?" Wade asks as we step onto the dance floor.

"Nope. Not at all." I don't bother to ask him not to tell Leo. They're best friends. I won't put him in that position. Besides, I have nothing to hide.

"If someone is harassing you, your dad and Leo can make it stop," Wade whispers.

"It really isn't a problem," I assure him. "It's my ex. I won't pull Leo into that mess. But don't worry. I'm sure Dad will handle Scott if he becomes a problem."

"That's good. My sister's right. You are important to Leo. He'll lose his mind if something happens to you."

"Thank you, Wade, for being here tonight."

I'm thanking him for more than being my dance partner today. He has no idea how much what he just said means to me. From everything I've witnessed and learned about Leo, he's an extremely quiet and private person. He doesn't chase women. He's only painting the town with his grandfather because it means a lot to Mr. Barnes. He never intended to pick up a woman. Grace is right, though. The quiet Barnes has fallen. Hopefully, he won't regret falling for someone as messed up as I am.

Chapter Thirty

Leo

"Oh, Leo. This place is beautiful. I've never seen anything like it." Kyleigh wraps her arm tighter around mine.

"Neither have I." Of course, I'm not talking about just the winery.

This date is turning out to be something more than just a date. Who knew wineries were romantic? Beautiful? Yes, without a doubt. Romantic? Not what I expected, but I'm not complaining. The look in Kyleigh's eyes makes me want to start a vineyard in my backyard. My yard's not big enough. I'm sure I can talk Mom into letting me plant some grapevines at the farm.

At first, I was concerned about coming back to Thorn Valley. Running into Bryson Crane would have me in jail. Lucas assured me this would be the last place we'd run into the creep. The sleazy mechanic might venture to one of the local bars, but he won't show up here. He's probably never had a glass of wine.

Yes, I finally sat down and talked to my brother about dating Kyleigh. The conversation was a bit embarrassing for me. My wonderful, loving twin enjoyed every second of it. He smiled the entire time. Lucas can be a jerk sometimes. I feel like an idiot. A grown man shouldn't have to ask his brother for relationship advice. I felt better after Lucas told me he talked with Dad several times when he started dating Hadley. I'm grateful for his advice because Kyleigh is extremely happy today.

We've toured the gardens, which have more flowers than I've heard of. Kyleigh stopped to touch and smell several different ones. From the twinkle in her eyes, roses are her favorite. Good to know. I might need to stop by Petals and have Katie make a special arrangement.

Katie and Miles' first baby is due in a few weeks. They decided not to find out their baby's gender early. Katie says this is their Rainbow Baby. My brothers and I had no idea what she meant until Hadley and Riley explained it one evening. The thing about living next door to your brothers is they're always coming over to grill out or watch TV.

The vineyards here are larger than I expected. We only walked the first few rows of the one closest to the main house while our tour guide, Layken, shared the history of Amberlee Cellars. Layken makes a point of looking directly at Kyleigh and me. She even asks us questions. She doesn't ignore the other guests, though. Every question they ask gets answered.

After the vineyard and garden tour, we relaxed in the wine-tasting room. Kyleigh and I got a cheese plate and sampled three different wines. She tends to lean more toward the red wines. I've purchased two bottles of her favorite. They'll be delivered to our table at the end of dinner. When I made our reservation for today, I timed it so we'd go to dinner after the tour of the main house. It is a beautiful house. Elegant is a better word for it. I see why they cater so many weddings here. The Magnolia Inn in Hayden Falls caters for weddings but not on this scale.

Kyleigh is once again drawn to the huge painting of the winery in the main lobby. She studies every detail. She lifts her hand to touch the canvas a few times but pulls away before making contact.

"Lovely, isn't it?" Our inside tour guide, Clover, stands behind us. Yes, her name is actually Clover. Several guests asked.

"Yes, it is." Kyleigh smiles and steps back. "At first, I thought it was a photograph."

"Most guests think so. They're drawn to it just as you are." Clover smiles up at the painting with pride.

"How long did it take Sammie to paint this?" I ask.

Kyleigh's eyes almost pop out of her head. "Sammie? Sammie Foster painted this?"

I point to the signature. "She's the only *S. Foster* artist I know. And she's one of Ally's best friends. Ally's family owns the winery."

Clover giggles. "You're the first to make the connection."

"Oh, wow." Kyleigh stares at the painting with a new sense of wonder. "I think I need to trade dance classes for Paint and Sip with Sammie."

"You can do both." I'll talk with Sammie and set things up for her. I'll even pay for the painting class.

"When you finish here, your table is ready," Clover says.

"Are you ready?" I hold my elbow out.

She shyly wraps her hand around it. "I'm ready."

"Right this way." Clover leads the way to the dining room. A girl at the hostess desk hands her menus as we pass.

This time, Kyleigh waits for me to pull her chair out. Once she's comfortable, I sit across from her. Thankfully, it's a table for two. I reach over and take her hand. Lucas says handholding at dinner is sweet, and ladies love it. Kyleigh blushes but doesn't pull her hand away. I'll be thanking my brother for this little tip.

"Are you enjoying this?"

"Oh, I am. It's more than I expected. My mom has done wine-tasting tours, but I never joined her." Kyleigh stiffens and forces a smile to remain on her face when her phone buzzes in her purse.

She turned the ringer off on our drive to Thorn Valley. I hear the buzzing every time it vibrates. She's only checked three times all afternoon to see who's calling and texting her. She hasn't bothered to answer or call the person back. It's her ex-boyfriend. I'm sure of it.

Wade told me about him calling during dance class on Thursday night. I kind of feel like a jerk. She's had all the signs of someone going through a bad breakup, yet I didn't put it together until recently. Well, I was a tad bit upset about my truck, so I missed the signs. She doesn't check her phone, and I don't ask about it.

Tonight, we both enjoy a traditional steak dinner. My dad said years ago that the steak here was tender and mouthwatering. From my experience tonight, it still is. Hadley and Grace told Kyleigh the same thing. She gave up wanting the salmon dinner for steak. From her smile and the little sounds she makes, she's not disappointed.

The ride home is much like our first ride to Thorn Valley. Kyleigh talks the entire way. We lingered in the dining room after dinner. By the time we get back to Hayden Falls, it's after eleven. Yes, I drove slowly. The voice that once irritated me now calms my spirit. After the past couple of weeks I've had, I need all the calm I can get. I don't really want to take her home yet, but there's no way I'll take her to Cowboys tonight. We can't end a romantic night at a bar.

"Thank you for tonight." Kyleigh unlocks the front door. "Do you want to come in?"

"Not tonight." I'm an idiot. I do want to go inside, but I can't.

"My dad won't mind."

Chief Deputy Green is on duty tonight. He informed me yesterday that he's put cameras on the front and back porches. And yes, I got the *you better respect my daughter* speech.

"Since this is his home, I'd like to get his permission first." It's a lame excuse. Hopefully, she'll understand.

"Thank you for today. I had a wonderful time."

"So did I." I hand her one of the bottles of wine. "I shouldn't give this to you." She gasps. "Promise me, if you open it, you'll stay home and leave the bat in the closet."

"I promise." She lightly laughs. "I'm not sure my Dad owns a bat."

"Where did you get the one you used on my truck?"

"Um." She drops her eyes and takes a step back.

"It was Jenna's. Wasn't it?"

"Yeah," she admits after a long moment of silence.

The biggest problem I've had with forgiving her is the fact taking a bat to my truck was her idea. Well, to Skip's truck. Sadly, mine was the one they found. I've watched the security footage from Cowboys a hundred times. There's no sound, but it's clear that Jenna was the one set on destroying my truck. Now, I'm not so sure this was Kyleigh's idea.

147

Her phone vibrates again. It doesn't last long. It's a text, not a call. She checks it this time.

"It's my dad. He asked if you'd check the back door before you go."

"Sure." Guess I'm going inside for a moment.

I follow her inside. I check not only the back door but the rest of the house, too. Bryson Crane and the Iron Rebels have her father and me worried about her safety. The bikers don't know about her. Hopefully, they don't go digging to find out who Dawg's arresting officers loved ones are. Al obviously is watching the cameras through an app on his phone. I make sure not to linger too long. She walks me back to the front door.

"I hate to see you go," she says softly.

I face her and place my hands on her waist. She steps closer and tilts her face up. This woman is going to be my undoing.

"I really want to kiss you."

"I really wish you would," she whispers.

I shake my head. "Soon."

She drops her head against my chest. "You're sticking to some gentleman's rules about not doing things on a first date."

"I am a gentleman. I refuse to be looped into a category as most men are today."

"You'll never be in the jerk or ordinary category." She smiles up at me.

"Good to know."

"But you'll kiss me soon?"

Look who's gotten all brave.

"On our next date," I promise.

"Next date?"

"Yes, ma'am." I'm already looking forward to another date with her.

"Tomorrow?"

Whoa. We've stepped out of brave and gone for bold.

"Yeah, Slugger. I'll kiss you tomorrow." I gently press my lips to her forehead. Yes, I do linger here a few moments longer than necessary. She's become too hard for me to resist. Stepping out onto the porch, I point to the door. "You lock this up. I'll check on you when I get home."

"I'll see you tomorrow." She turns three shades of red. She's not usually this brave.

"You will."

I turn and hurry to my car. If I stay here any longer, I'll break gentleman protocol and pull her to me. I want to kiss her, but I want her to know I'm not the jerk her ex is. He has to be a jerk and a fool. Only a fool would let her go.

I glance in the rearview mirror as I pull out of the driveway. The door's closed, and I'm sure locked. Tomorrow, I have a promise to keep. Only death will keep me from it. I chuckle. I may not be able to keep Kyleigh forever, but I'll never forget our first kiss. Now, I need to plan another romantic date with her for my birthday.

Chapter Thirty-One

Kyleigh

I've had a horrible time today putting Leo off. No woman in her right mind would give him the cold shoulder. It's for a good reason today. It's actually a stupid reason, but oh well.

Not knowing today was Leo's birthday still bothers me a little. If Hadley hadn't told me, would I even know? I wanted to bring it up yesterday. Since it was our first date, I didn't want to risk having an awkward moment. I've let most of my childish hurt feelings over it go because I haven't told him my birthday either.

Today, Leo is twenty-nine. I turned twenty-three in April. I've never dated anyone six years older than me before. Scott is only a year older. I shake the thoughts of my ex away. However, it's hard to keep him in the back of my mind when he won't stop trying to call and text me. It makes no sense for him to contact me anymore. Mom already got my things from his apartment.

Today's Leo's day. I put my phone on silent and left it in my car. I won't be tempted to look at the screen if I'm nowhere near it. I send all of Scott's calls to voicemail. I delete them without listening to them. His text messages are never read, either. Honestly, I'm at the point where I want to turn my phone off. If it weren't for work, my parents, and Leo, I'd do it.

Women hurry around the Grand Room at The Magnolia Inn. They're setting up tables and chairs, decorating, or bringing in food. Seven tables, each six feet long, are lined up along one wall of the room. If people bring more food, Aiden and Miles will have to set up another table. Oh, there are three more tables with desserts. I've never seen anything like this. You don't run out of food when the Hayden Sisters get involved.

"Thanks, Kyleigh. I wouldn't have finished this without you." Katie rubs her lower back as we double-check the balloon display.

The display has blue and black balloons set up to create police officers. Oh, except for the face. Hopefully, Leo and Lucas won't think the little men are too childish. Luke paid for these guys, by the way. I'm surprised he's not here to make sure they were assembled correctly. Luke really is the fun brother. He has everyone laughing until they have tears in their eyes at their family dinners.

"Are you okay?" I grab a chair and set it behind Katie.

"Yeah." She sits and rubs her baby bump. "Three more weeks."

"Will you make it three weeks?"

I'm not so sure she will. She's exhausted from assembling the two little balloon cops. I took over fixing the huge backdrop display to keep her from reaching too high and overdoing it today.

"I have to make it. I don't want to have our little one too early." Her voice is full of panic.

E walks up and hands us a glass of punch. "When you get to thirty-eight weeks, you're considered full-term, and your little one will be just fine."

"So, another week, maybe?" I tease, hoping it'll relieve some of Katie's fears.

"Just as long as it's not the last day of the month." Katie smiles up at E.

"Oh, I don't know." E wraps an arm around Katie's shoulder. Our babies will be best friends. Caleb won't mind sharing his birthday."

These two ladies are best friends, and so are their husbands. Their babies are bound to be, too, even though Caleb will be a year older. It would be sweet if Katie had a little girl, and their babies ended up together one day.

"E, is everything ready?" Mrs. Barnes sets a plate of brownies on the dessert table. There's barely room for it.

"Yes, Ma'am. We're ready for your deputies to arrive," E replies.

"Oh, they're so cute!" Riley squeals when she sees the balloon police officers.

Hadley sighs and rolls her eyes. "Luke only got them so he could play with them." We all burst out laughing, even Riley.

"How are the guys getting here?" I ask.

"Their dad came up with a reason to go over a case at the Sheriff's Office with them. Luke and Levi are there to help get them here," Hadley explains.

I'm not so sure they've thought their plan through very well. Leo and Lucas are cops. Surely, they'll figure this out. It's surprising Luke hasn't given it away before now.

Riley's phone dings. She opens the text and shouts, "They're on the way!"

Everyone rushes into the Grand Room and takes their places. Within minutes, the five Barnes men walk through the doors. The room erupts into shouts of *'surprise'* as confetti explodes in front of the guys just inside the doorway. E refused to let Riley shoot the confetti off in the middle of the room. The last thing anyone needed was little pieces of paper in their food. Knowing Riley, that's exactly what would have happened.

Thankfully, Hadley, once again, rushes into Lucas' arms. I seriously have to figure out how to tell Leo and his brother apart. The birthday boys are quickly surrounded by their family and closest friends. I stand back and take it all in. Being an only child, I never had parties like this.

Leo eases out of the group without anyone noticing. He moves to the closest corner with his phone in his hands and sends a text. For several moments, he stares at the screen. Disappointed, he slides his phone into his back pocket.

"She's an idiot for not answering you." I lightly laugh.

His head snaps up. "Kyleigh."

"Hey, birthday boy." I offer him a glass of punch.

His hands wrap around mine and the glass. "So, this is why you haven't been answering me."

"If I did, I'd give it away and disappoint your mom."

He quickly scans the room for his mom before leaning close and lowering his voice. "We figured it out."

"How?"

"Well, Dad hardly ever goes to the station on Sunday. He just happens to be there on our birthday? Not likely. And the case we talked about could have been discussed during our family dinner. Which is what Lucas and I thought was happening tonight." He playfully narrows his eyes at me. "I've been trying all day to invite you to dinner."

"I'm sorry. My phone's in my car."

His expression turns serious. "Is everything okay?"

Darn it. I just took his happiness from him and on his birthday.

"Yeah." I wave it off like it's no big deal. "I was charging it and forgot it."

Half of a lie doesn't count, does it? I was charging my phone on the way here, but I purposely left it in the car. As much as I don't want to, I'll probably have to see what Scott wants to get him to stop calling.

"So, your dad gave the surprise away?"

"No." His happiness hasn't fully returned. He's trying to smile. "When Luke showed up, we knew something more than a family celebration was happening."

"Hey, big brother. You can't be hiding in the corner with a pretty girl at your own party." Luke pushes Leo and me into the mingling crowd. "Look at the little policemen. Aren't they cute?"

Luke rushes over to the balloons. He grabs them and has them pretending to arrest somebody. Everyone thinks he's crazy. A part of me likes his childish behavior. I wish I could be as carefree as Luke.

"See? He's a little bouncier today than normal." Leo motions to Luke.

Ah. So that was the tipoff. I'll let Mrs. Barnes know not to send Luke to get his brothers next year if she really wants to have a surprise party. Next year? Listen to me acting like I'll be here on Leo's birthday next year. Would it be so bad if I was? I glance up into his soft brown eyes. I'd love to be here every year for his birthday.

While everyone's busy fixing their plates, Leo takes my hand and pulls me to the hallway. He puts his finger to his lips, signaling me to stay quiet. A little giggle escapes. Hopefully, his family won't mind him slipping out of his own party. They still have Lucas to celebrate with.

Surprisingly, we don't go far. Leo leads me to the Inn's restaurant. Once we're inside, he locks the doors. The curtains over the glass panels in the double doors block anyone from seeing us. Even more surprising, there's a table for two set up in the corner near the front windows.

"What's this?"

"I tipped E to set us up somewhere private."

E Maxwell is a romantic at heart. Of course, she helped set this up. My guess is the candles and flowers on the table were her idea.

"But it's your birthday. Your family wants to spend it with you."

Leo steps close, never taking his eyes off mine. His hands slide around my waist, pulling me to him. "And I want to spend my birthday with you."

"Your family."

"Will understand."

His eyes slowly bounce between mine. My hands act without my brain helping them and move up his chest to slide around his neck. My heart rate increases, causing whatever protest I have to disappear.

"Happy Birthday," I whisper.

As soon as the words are out of my mouth, he lowers his head and tenderly presses his lips to mine. Who knows. Maybe I lifted on my toes and met him halfway. When a small moan escapes me, he deepens the kiss. My lips move against his, matching his pace. I swear this feels like more than just a kiss. Slowly, he ends our kiss and rests his forehead against mine.

"Best present ever," he whispers.

It's not my birthday, but I wholeheartedly agree. It was the best first kiss of my life, and I'll never forget it.

Chapter Thirty-Two

Kyleigh

*M*onday. Ugh! August fifteenth, the day after Leo's birthday. Five pm. Here, I sit at my father's kitchen table, officially unemployed with no home of my own. Of course, my parents are more than happy to have me live with them.

Absolutely nothing happening in my life right now is part of my five-year plan. A grown woman, a year out of college, is supposed to be moving up in the world. She shouldn't be jobless and moving back home. It probably makes me a failure statistic for some young adult research somewhere. All through college, I swore I'd never be a statistic. Life, however, had other plans for me. Sadly, life isn't sharing her plans with me. I don't like her kind of surprises.

With a deep sigh, I close my laptop and lean back in my chair. My last project was sent in half an hour ago. I didn't get a thank you or a farewell email from my not-so-wonderful boss. It's crazy I even thought I'd get one. Taylor Pierce is not friends with her team. Once someone leaves her department, she completely forgets them. It's like they never existed. My time at Hillsworth Financial will not be mentioned again after today.

The sound of a car pulling up and a door closing pulls me from my depressing thoughts. Dad's home. His shift ran over a little today. He called to let me know he's bringing dinner home from Gino's. I'm not about to turn down an Italian meal. Dad has raved for years about their lasagna. I can't wait to try it.

The sound of a larger truck pulling up concerns me. Dad didn't mention bringing company home. The sound is too loud to be a regular pickup, though. Maybe his SUV broke down, and Ally towed it home. He should have called me to pick him up. I spring from my chair. Before I get to the door, someone knocks. That's not Dad. I jerk the front door open and suck in a breath.

"Mom?"

What in the world is going on? We talk almost every day. She hasn't said anything about visiting. My eyes almost pop out of my head. The moving truck in the driveway greatly concerns me. Another car pulls in behind the truck. This makes no sense.

"Kyleigh." Mom smiles and throws her arms around me. "I've missed you."

"What's going on?"

"Aren't you happy to see me?"

"Of course." It looks as though my dramatic Mom showed up today. I give her another hug.

"Ms. Green." One of the movers walks up to the front steps. "If you're good for the night, the guys and I will see you in the morning."

"That's fine, Mr. Keller," Mom assures him.

"Have a good night." Mr. Keller nods once to Mom and smiles sweetly at me.

The driver of the moving truck and Mr. Keller look to be in their late twenties. They get into the car behind the truck and head toward town.

"What's going on?" I ask again.

"They have rooms at The Magnolia Inn. They'll unload the truck tomorrow." Mom leads me inside.

"But what's going on?" I ask a third time and motion to the front door. "Why is there a moving truck in the yard?"

"That's our things."

Our things? I have officially stepped into another dimension or something. Mom moves around the kitchen and pulls a kettle from the cabinet. She grabs cups, tea bags, honey, and sugar. I watch in amazement, or maybe it's disbelief. She knows where everything is.

"Mom." I grab her arm and turn her to face me. "It's not tea time. What are you doing here?"

"You're here." She looks around the kitchen, teary-eyed. "I missed you."

What has happened to my mom? My well-put-together mother isn't together.

"Why would you move our stuff here? My probation ends in January." I've explained this to her at least ten times already. "I'll be back in Seattle in five more months."

"Well." Mom takes a deep breath. I swear she's about to cry. She shakes some bad energy away and smiles. "We're here now. And it's always tea time."

She goes back to making tea like it's an ordinary day. I close my eyes and drop my head back. Mom can be hard to deal with when her mind's set.

My back stiffens at the sound of the front door opening and closing. Now, Dad's home. I've never seen my parents argue. Dad's bound to go livid over this. Maybe I should call Leo and have the Sheriff's Office on standby.

"Kyleigh." Dad kisses my temple and sets two bags from Gino's Italian House on the table. He doesn't take his eyes off Mom. "Kendra."

"Dad." How do I explain this? I don't even know what's going on.

"You home?"

"I am." Mom wrings her hands together.

"You sure about this?"

Mom straightens her back and lifts her chin. "Yes."

Dad holds his hand out. "The bags you need for the night in the trunk?"

157

Mom opens her purse on the counter. She drops her keys into Dad's palm. "They're in the backseat on the driver's side."

"I'll put them in the third bedroom." Mom gasps. Dad shakes his head. "I'm not giving you the Master bedroom."

Mom takes a breath through her nose and looks away. "Understood. I'll finish the tea and set the table."

Dad kisses my temple again. I watch as he walks out the front door. I'm not sure what I just witnessed. The kettle whistles. I turn and stare at the alien who's pretending to be my mom. I'm glad the lady from Mars understands. I understand nothing.

"Mom?" I say cautiously. Should I even try to communicate with this being?

"It's fine, Kyleigh." Mom sniffles but doesn't face me. "Why don't you wash up and help me set the table?"

Wash up? Help set the table? Okay. When I closed my laptop, I entered an alternate universe. Alien lady is *not* my mom. I leave the weird being in the kitchen and aimlessly walk down the hall.

Dad comes in with two large suitcases. I manage to find enough sense about myself and open the door of the third bedroom for him. He sets Mom's suitcases by the bed. At least they look like my mom's suitcases. Maybe I should open them and check.

"I'm getting a shower. See ya at dinner." Dad pats my arm and leaves me standing frozen in the hallway.

Maybe the aliens got my dad, too. I don't like this universe. I peek into the kitchen. The alien lady is humming and setting the table like this is some TV family sitcom. I shake my head. This isn't a family sitcom. It's a Sci-Fi movie. Dinner is going to be weird. I grab my laptop from the table and hurry to my room. I need help or at least a backup plan. I unlock my phone. I'll be committed to a mental hospital after this call.

"Hey, girl," Grace answers happily.

"What day is it?"

"Huh?"

"Grace, what day is it?" I quickly ask again.

"Monday," she replies slowly.

"Look. I don't know what's going on. Things are weird around here." I crack my door open just enough to peek out. Dad's shower is running, and the alien lady is still humming. "If I need a place to stay, can I come to your apartment?"

"Of course. What's going on?"

"My mom showed up."

Grace lightly laughs. "Awe. She missed you."

"With a moving truck and all our things," I add.

"Oh."

Yeah. Now she gets it.

"We're having dinner soon. If these two start arguing, I'm getting out of here."

"Say no more. I'll be waiting for you." Grace ends the call after I promise to call her back later.

A light tap comes on the door. Dad pops his head in. "Come on, Baby. Dinner's ready. Gino's lasagna is amazing."

Dad has a tight smile on his face. He's acting strange, too. Of course, he would. His ex-wife shows up out of the blue with a moving truck and says she's home. There are a lot of strange elements in that. At least he didn't go livid and kick her out. Maybe my Dad isn't my dad right now, either.

I grit my teeth and stand. Hopefully, I'll survive having some amazing lasagna with my alien parents. Grace can tell everyone what happened if I go missing in the night. My luck—I'll wake up on Mars in the morning.

Chapter Thirty-Three

Leo

Patrolling our little town at night can be boring. Second shift isn't as bad as third, though. I took the last patrol of our shift tonight. I should've let Lucas have it. Taking it turned me into a stalker.

My shift ended twenty minutes ago. Lucas is already home. Where am I? I'm sitting on the small street between Page Turners and the park. Kyleigh's car is parked behind Grace's. She didn't mention anything about staying with Grace. Of course, she doesn't have to tell me her plans. I called her before I went to work, and we've texted a few times tonight. The last text said it was a weird night, but there wasn't an explanation. I was going to call her when I got home. I don't want to intrude if she's having a girl's night with Grace.

Sitting here makes me antsy. Rather than driving home, I get out and let the tailgate down. I'm glad Dad assigned me a truck for a cruiser instead of a car.

It's after midnight. The lights in Grace's apartment above the bookstore are on. I'll have a hard time explaining why I'm sitting here if anyone sees me. Of course, there aren't a lot of people out this time of night on a Monday. On the weekends, Cowboys and O'Brien's

Tavern would be going strong about now. Both bars close at two on the weekends and midnight throughout the week.

A silhouette moves across one of the upper windows. With the blinds closed, I can't tell if it's Kyleigh or Grace. Movement next to the bookstore catches my eye. A surge of protectiveness shoots through me when a man walks past the building. I start to place my hand on my gun but pause. He's as harmless as a kitten. As if sensing he's being watched, he stops and faces me.

Levi glances from Kyleigh's car up at Grace's apartment and grins. His shoulders shake from silent laughter as he walks to me.

"Creeping much, bro?" Levi hops up next to me.

"Don't tell Lucas or Dad. They'll arrest me," I joke.

"Your secret is safe with me."

"Aren't you supposed to be locked in the Fire Station?"

"No, idiot." Levi narrows his eyes and nudges my shoulder with his. "This isn't high school or a church lock-in."

Sometimes, the high school clubs or sports teams have lock-in events in the gym. The church uses its huge fellowship hall for the youth group lock-ins. My brothers and I went to a few. They weren't my thing, but Luke loved them.

I know the firefighters aren't locked in. I've seen them in the park many evenings playing football or tossing a baseball around. I just like teasing my little brother. Usually, Luke is under Levi's feet if he's not with his girlfriend.

I look toward the corner of the bookstore. "Luke with you?"

"Nah. He's already in bed."

"What are you doing out here?"

"Can't sleep. Told Miles I was gonna walk around the square to clear my head." Levi drops his eyes to the pavement.

Levi hasn't been the same since Megan posted the first article about him in her blog. I've noticed him sitting on the deck late at night with his head in his hands.

"Nobody in their right mind believes the stuff in Hayden Happenings."

Levi cuts his eyes at me. "Ninety percent of the people in this town don't have a right mind."

"Sorry, little brother."

"Nothing I can do about it." He grins at me. "What are you doing out here?"

Kyleigh and Grace's silhouettes appear in the window, drawing our attention. They're about the same height and size. Their hairstyles give them away. Grace has hers in a ponytail most of the time. Kyleigh's bouncy curls fall loose past her shoulders.

"Are they dancing?" Levi chuckles.

"Yeah. I believe so." It's cute to watch.

"This one got you, huh?"

I drag my eyes from the window to my brother. "What?"

Levi stares at me for a moment. "You fell, Leo."

I look up at the window. "I don't know what I'm doing, Levi."

He laughs again. "I'm no expert, but you should probably be talking to her instead of me."

"I'm not good at talking to women."

"Neither am I," Levi mumbles.

I don't understand what he means. He talks with women all the time. He's funny and outgoing. He'll talk to everybody at a party. It's not women in general he has a problem talking to. It's one woman.

"When are you going to tell her?"

"I love you, man. But I'm not telling Kyleigh you love her." He looks at me like I'm crazy.

"I don't mean Kyleigh. I mean, the real reason you're walking around the square to clear your head."

Every muscle in Levi's face goes slack. Oh, yes. My baby brother has a huge secret.

"I…" He hops off the tailgate and runs his hand through his hair. He paces for several minutes. "Does Lucas know?"

I shake my head. "I think Mom may be the only other one who knows."

"You figured it out."

I nod again. I'm the quiet one in our family. I notice more than everyone else. I just don't talk about the things I see. Levi huffs out a breath and stares off into the distance. His mind is so tormented. He's not seeing the river across the park. It hurts to see my little brother in so much pain.

Levi is only two years younger than me. Luke was born ten minutes before him. It makes Levi the baby of the family, and that's exactly how the rest of us see him. I want to fix things for him and ease his pain. Sadly, I don't know how.

"I don't know what to do, Leo."

"I'm no expert, but you should probably be talking to her instead of me." One corner of my mouth lifts.

"I can't." He drops his head and rubs his temples with the heels of his hands. His advice to me is easier said than done.

"Why?"

Perhaps if he figures out the why, he can move past the torment and claim his girl. I'm not a big talker, but if it helps him, I don't mind talking tonight. He's quiet for a few minutes. I don't think he's going to answer me. Mom should be the one helping with this. She understands romance. It pains me to say it, but Luke would have better advice than me. Levi finally stops pacing and faces me.

"She scares me." He blinks and looks away.

I glance up at the window above the bookstore. Kyleigh and Grace are still dancing.

"I know what you mean." I drop my head in my hands. "It was one kiss, Levi. One kiss, and I'm so messed up. I don't know what I'm doing."

He hops up on the tailgate again and pats my back. "Oh, how the mighty have fallen."

"You fell too." I playfully shove him with my elbow. "You should tell her."

"If she only thinks of me as a friend, telling her will ruin that." He looks across the park. "And her dad?"

I understand where he's coming from there, too. Her dad protects her furiously. Deputy Green protects Kyleigh just as much. Still, I think I'll have an easier time with the dad than Levi will.

One of the bays at the Fire Station opens. The tones didn't ring out, so it's not a fire. My radio is in the truck. I missed hearing the call. The ambulance pulls out with flashing red lights but no siren. Luke pulls up at the end of the road behind the bookstore and lets the passenger window down.

"Let's go, little brother. Got an accident outside Willows Bend. It's not life-threatening, but they need another ambulance." Luke points at me and grins. "Big brother, you got some explaining to do."

"See ya, Leo." Levi hurries to the ambulance.

"Stay safe," I whisper as they drive away.

I glance up at the apartment window again. Grace and Kyleigh have the blinds open. Our eyes meet, and I point to the back door. Kyleigh hurries away. Grace smiles and waves before closing the blinds.

Within minutes, the backdoor flies open. The woman who torments my mind and emotions fills the doorway. I quickly close the distance between us before she steps outside.

"What happened?" Kyleigh looks toward where Luke parked to pick up Levi.

"An accident in Willows Bend. It's not serious, though."

She glances up at me with too much worry on her pretty face. "Are you okay? Why are you sitting out here?"

"I saw your car on my last round."

She grins. I want to run my thumb over the little dimple at the corner of her lips. "So, you're sitting out here like a stalker. Should I make a report?"

"You probably should." I lightly chuckle.

"Are we working on Darlin tomorrow?"

We haven't worked on Darlin in days. I don't want to talk about my truck. But since she still has community service hours to complete, we should make a schedule.

"I'm off on Wednesday and Thursday. We'll get some hours in."

"Thank you." Her smile tightens, causing the little dimple to disappear. I don't like it.

The strange feeling that pulls me to her grows stronger. My mind loses control of everything. I cup her face in my hands and rub my thumbs over the spots where her dimples are. I want to see them. She needs to really smile.

"Leo," she whispers.

"Forgive me, but I need this."

164

My lips crash against hers. When her arms circle my waist, I drop my hands and wrap my arms around her. She lightly moans. The sound goes straight to my heart, and I deepen the kiss. My arms tighten, pulling her against me even more. I've never kissed a woman like this. Nothing matters anymore but this and her.

Chapter Thirty-Four

Kyleigh

Things get weirder around here by the day. I have no idea what to make of my parents. Alien Mom has been here for three nights. My dad has always been a quiet man. Alien Dad is even quieter.

My parents didn't argue the first night Mom was here. Since they were acting weird, I thought it best to give them some space to work through whatever was going on. Grace was more than happy to let me crash at her place. Oh, I'm so glad I did. Leo showing up was a surprise. I run my fingertips over my bottom lip and sigh. The best kiss of my life still lingers. The quiet Barnes sure knows how to kiss.

Alien Mom's humming pulls me from my wonderful memory. I don't recall Mom ever humming while she made pancakes, or like ever. My parents don't talk much while I'm in the room. They watch each other, though. I glance at Dad. Sure enough, he's watching Mom cook. His eyes roam over her. I swear one corner of his mouth twitches. My eyes almost pop out of my head. What in the world? I kick Alien Dad under the table. He snaps his head toward me and raises an eyebrow. I hate it when people do that.

"Stop watching my mom," I whisper scold.

Dad smirks and reaches for his coffee. I narrow my eyes at him and pretend to be mad. I'm going to have to keep an eye on him.

"So, what's your plans today?" Mom smiles sweetly at me as she sets the platter of pancakes on the table.

"I'm stopping by Page Turners and having lunch with Grace. Afterward, I'll help Leo work on his truck."

We didn't get a chance yesterday to work on Darlin. Well, Leo may have. I spent the past two days helping Mom put away our things after the movers unloaded the truck. When she said she brought our things, she meant *everything*. I'm not sure we technically live in Washington State anymore. Mom subleased her house until the end of her lease in May. I can't figure out why she did this.

"Oh, that reminds me." Dad goes to his room and comes back with a manila envelope. We stare at each other for a moment. "I really don't want to give you this."

"Uh!" I loudly huff and fall back against my chair. Manila envelopes usually mean legal documents. Great. There's more to my Hayden Falls legal saga. I toss a hand in the air. "Go ahead. No need to put it off."

"The Sheriff gave me this yesterday. I'm waiting on a call back from the judge." He slowly hands me the envelope.

My heart sinks with each line of Judge Morgan's letter. This is unbelievable. I'm not even sure it's legal to do something like this. Since the Judge's signature and official stamp are at the bottom of the letter, it probably is legal.

"What's wrong?" Mom looks between Dad and me.

"This judge hates me." I hand her the letter without looking at her. "Do I have to, Dad?"

"Right now, it's not an issue."

He's right. For now, it's not. As long as I work at least two hours a week with Leo, there's no problem.

"Albert, can you not do anything about this?" Mom tosses the letter on the table.

"It's Al, Kendra. Just Al." Dad hates being called by his full name. Mom nods. "According to the Sheriff, Judge Morgan noticed Leo wasn't getting a lot of work done on Darlin since he started second shift. She only has to report to the Sheriff's Office for community service if they don't work on the truck that week."

"Why does this judge have it out for me?"

This is a small town. It's understandable he wants to follow up on his cases, but I feel like he's going out of his way to get me even more. This is ridiculous. In Seattle, I'd probably never hear from the judge again.

"I've known Judge Morgan a long time. I'll talk to him." Mom puts a pancake on my plate like I'm a toddler.

"No, Mom." I sit up quickly and grab her wrist. "It'll just make things worse. Please, leave it be."

My outburst in the judge's chambers, which wasn't all that bad, added extra time to my community service and probation. If Mom talks to Judge Morgan, he'll think my parents get me out of everything. He'll probably send me to jail for three years to prove a point.

"She's right. Leave it be." Dad passes me the maple syrup. His eyes stay on Mom. "It's doubtful I can change his mind. For now, if you want to do something, you two can start looking for jobs."

Mom's eyes widen. "Jobs?"

"Yes." Dad keeps eye contact with her. "Our daughter is grown. She doesn't need a stay-at-home parent."

For a moment, Mom looks as though she may challenge him. Dad raises an eyebrow. Mom nods and drops her eyes. As I said, things are weird around here.

"Kyleigh has a job. She's working remotely." Mom continues to stare at her plate.

I groan. During all the weirdness, I forgot to tell her. Dad knows everything.

"That ended a few days ago." It's my turn to drop my eyes.

"Well." Mom lovingly pats my hand. "I'm sure we both can find something."

I slowly lift my eyes and watch Alien Mom pour syrup on her pancake. Mom was an assistant at a research lab in Washington. She went to part-time a couple of years ago. I don't know everything her job entailed, but I highly doubt she'll find a lab assistant job here. Still, I'm surprised she left the lab altogether to come here.

My phone lights up with a call from Scott. I silence it and flip it over. I wish he would leave me alone.

"You need to handle that." Dad finishes his coffee and stands. His shift starts in twenty minutes.

"I have nothing to say to him."

"If that's the case, block his number." Dad grabs his Stetson hat and pauses at the door. "Leaving him access to you doesn't say you're through with him. And it's not fair to Leo if you're going to date him."

"You're right." I grab my phone. After deleting Scott's new voicemail, I block his number. I should have already done it. I look up at Dad. "And I'm not sure what Leo and I are."

"Hopefully, you two will figure it out soon. He's a cop. He needs his mind on his job, not messed up over a woman." His eyes flick to Mom before he turns and walks out.

Mom closes her eyes and takes a deep breath. I have no idea what just passed between my parents.

"Has Scott been calling you too?"

"No. I think your father scared him the morning I got your things."

"Hopefully, that's the end of him then." The way my life has been going, it's probably not.

Mom pats my hand again before carrying our plates to the sink. "He's your clone's problem now—not yours."

Ah. So, she saw Brenda when she got my things. I was right in my assessment of the bimbo. Scott cheated on me with a woman who looks like me. Oh well. Mom's right, too. Scott is Brenda's problem—not mine.

Chapter Thirty-Five

Leo

"She's coming along nicely." Granddad walks around Darlin, inspecting my work.

The truck is coming along nicely. Sadly, it's at a slow pace. If I let Ally do the work, she'd be finished by now. If it weren't for being on second shift, I'd be further along myself. I hate second shift.

"I'll have to let Ally and her dad finish the back fender." As much as I've tried, I can't buff all the dents out. Most of the damage Jenna did was on the driver's door and rear fender.

The sound of a large truck pulling up outside the barn catches our attention. Granddad and I look at each other. Neither of us knows what that's about. We rush outside.

Ally Roberts is backing the rollback up to the barn's double doors. There's a door for my truck strapped onto the back. I told her to search for another one when things didn't work out with Bryson Crane. I didn't care how far I had to go for it. Looks as though she had one shipped in. She hasn't said anything about finding one yet.

Ally hops out and begins loosening the straps. "Hey, Leo, Mr. Barnes."

"Hey." I rush to the other side to help.

"This is in great shape." Granddad's face lights up. He gives Ally a huge smile.

"Yes, Sir, it sure is. Not a scratch on her." Ally turns to me. "It came in this morning. Sorry. I couldn't get out here until now."

"It's not a problem. I really appreciate this." I agree with Granddad. This door is perfect.

It's just after lunch. Her timing is fine with me. I hadn't started working yet. I didn't even know she had ordered the door.

"Oh, wow." Kyleigh hurries out the back door of the house. I didn't know she was here. Mom and Grandma must've had her in the kitchen with them. "This is amazing."

"Yeah. It looks even better than the pictures." Ally walks up and gives Kyleigh a hug. It's nice she's making friends.

I agree with them. The door is exactly what I need. It's black, but that's okay. Darlin is going to need painting anyway. Ally helps me lift the door off the truck. Thankfully, she had it wrapped in cloth before strapping it down.

"What did this one cost?" I didn't give her a price limit. I'd pay any price not to deal with Bryson Crane again.

"With shipping from Idaho and my delivery fee," Ally gives me a sweet little grin. "everything came to five hundred."

I chuckle and shake my head. Of course, I'll pay her a delivery fee. The price is great, and the door is in even better condition than the one the sleazebag in Thorn Valley had.

"Can you take my card here? Or do I need to come to the shop?" I reach for my wallet in my back pocket.

"No need. It's paid for." Ally tosses the tie-down straps into the passenger seat.

"You have my card on file at the shop?"

"Um. No." Ally looks past me. "Kyleigh paid for it."

I turn sideways so I can look between the two women. Granddad's standing in the barn door, staring at Kyleigh.

"Thank you for getting it so quickly." Kyleigh smiles nervously.

"I'm glad the guy still had it. If you need anything else, let me know." Ally pauses before getting into the truck. She points at me. "I refunded what you paid for the other parts back to your card."

I narrow my eyes. "Why?"

Her eyes flick to Kyleigh and back to me. "Kyleigh showed me the court order saying she had to pay for the parts Darlin needed."

"Yeah." It's true, but this doesn't feel right for some reason.

"I'll see you tonight." Ally waves before getting into the rollback and driving away.

"Kyleigh." I start toward her.

The screen door on the back porch bangs shut. Kyleigh snaps her head in that direction.

"Mrs. Barnes, let me help you." She rushes to my grandmother before I can reach her.

"Thank you, dear." Grandma hands Kyleigh the tray with three glasses of sweet tea and ham sandwiches. Grandma follows Granddad inside the barn and admires the new door with him.

"Lunch or snack?" Kyleigh lifts the tray slightly and smiles sweetly.

I take a deep breath and slowly release it. I'm not an idiot. She's deflecting and doesn't want to talk about this.

"A little of both, I guess." I motion toward the barn and follow her inside.

Kyleigh sets the tray on one of the work tables. She grabs a glass of sweet tea. She's nervous but happy. I hate to take that from her, but we need to talk about this.

"Here you go, Mr. Barnes." She hands the glass of tea to my grandfather.

Granddad doesn't speak as he takes the tea. He smiles nervously at Kyleigh before turning back to admire the door. I was hoping he'd have forgiven her by now. She's apologized repeatedly and goes out of her way to be extra nice to him. Granddad's holding firm for some reason.

"Kyleigh." I gently grab her hands before she can pick up another glass of tea. She looks up at me and smiles. I love her little dimples. "Thank you for the door, but you don't have to pay for everything."

"I do," she insists. "Oh, I have this for you too." She digs an envelope from her purse on the work table and hands it to me. Gifts are great. I'm not comfortable receiving them, though. Something tells me this isn't a gift. My eyes almost pop out of my head when I see the check inside. It's made out to me. Nope. I don't want this.

"Kyleigh, I can't take this." I offer the envelope back to her.

"No." She gives her head a wild shake and takes a step back. "You have to take it."

"I'm not comfortable with this." I squeeze the envelope in my hand. "What's it for anyway?"

"Your labor." She presses her lips together and blinks rapidly a few times.

"This is too much." I close the distance between us and shove the envelope into her hands. The thought of taking this amount of money from her makes me angry. "I can't take it."

"You have to," she cries and shoves it against my chest.

"It's wrong." I can't take money from a woman.

"It's not. You wouldn't have to be doing this if my friends and I hadn't beat up your truck."

"I don't want your money, and you shouldn't be paying for parts I already paid for."

Yeah, she was court-ordered to pay for my parts and labor. At first, I approved of the judge's decision. After letting her into my heart, this feels like a knife cutting through my soul. I freeze. Levi's right. I fell. I let this cute, annoying little woman into my heart.

"Please, take it, Leo." Tears spill from her eyes as she pushes against my chest. "I have to pay it all. This judge hates me. He just keeps adding to it. If he finds out I haven't paid your labor, he'll send me to prison."

Oh, my gosh. She's frantic. She's going to fall apart right here on the barn floor. She cried the night I arrested her, but she didn't fall apart like this. The check is no longer my concern.

I cup her face in my hands. My eyes bounce back and forth between hers. I practically feel the pain radiating in her eyes. My chest tightens.

"What do you mean, he keeps adding to it?"

"It's nothing. Please, take the money. I'm so sorry for what we did. I should pay for it, and I don't mind. But I've lost enough lately. I don't want to go to jail. Please, Leo. Please take it." She falls apart a little more with each word.

I wipe her tears away with my thumbs. "Your friends should be helping you pay for this."

She shakes her head. "It was my idea."

I hold her face firmly in my hands, refusing to let her step back or look away. "No, Kyleigh. It wasn't your idea. It was Jenna's." Her lips part with a little gasp. "It's noble of you to take the blame, but this was Jenna's idea. I'm a cop. I see the signs. You can't deny it. You're covering for your friends."

"It doesn't matter." She sniffles.

"Legally, it doesn't because you've already claimed responsibility. But knowing the truth matters to me. I'm only taking the check because the judge ordered it." I wrap my arms around her and pull her tightly against my chest. "You're not going to jail. You're not losing anything. I won't allow it."

"Thank you," she cries into my chest.

"Don't worry, Slugger. I got you."

I kiss the top of her head and let her cry. I'm not sure what she meant by the judge doing more. I'll talk to Dad and Lucas to see if they know. I glance over Kyleigh's head and see my grandparents slipping out of the barn. Granddad's eyes meet mine for a moment. His sad expression guts me, too. He drops his head and leaves. As much as I want to comfort him, I'm needed here more. I rest my chin on top of Kyleigh's head and let her find a little peace and comfort in my arms.

Chapter Thirty-Six

Kyleigh

After my meltdown today, I shouldn't be here. Thankfully, the only people who saw me fall apart were Leo and his grandparents. I hope it never happens again. I've cried in front of people before. Doing so bothers me, but I can live with it. Usually, I fall apart when I'm alone. Not that I've had a lot of moments in my life that caused me to fall apart. Up until this past July, I lived a pretty sheltered life.

Scott breaking up with me the way he did really threw me for a loop. I pulled over several times during the drive to Montana because I couldn't see beyond my tears. I called Dad each time. He was the only person I could pour my heart out to that night.

"Cheer up, girl." Grace slips on her dance shoes and nudges me with her shoulder. "You look like you lost your best friends." She wiggles in her chair. "I'm right here."

I lightly laugh and nudge her back. "You sure are."

It's sweet she's appointed herself as my best friend. She just might be from the way things look. The three women I thought were my best friends seemed to have deserted me. Well, Zoe still calls and texts every couple of days. It's what she and I have always done, so I still have her. She works at the hospital in Walsburg and has some crazy schedules. I can't fault her for working.

Monica may text once a week. Zoe's last text said Monica is, once again, taking Skip back. The two-timing jerk swears it wasn't him in the photo Monica got that night. Since he was leaning on Leo's truck and not his own, he's getting away with the lie. I haven't told Monica that Luke and his brothers confirmed it was Skip from the security footage. It's her life. She has to live it. I'll be here when she needs me.

Jenna is totally MIA. No calls. No texts. No messages sent between friends. It worries me she's dating men she meets online. No matter how bad of a friend she's being to me right now, I do care about her. Her brother knows what's going on. He'll keep a close eye on her.

Grace feels like more than a friend. The way she and her grandmother have taken me in makes them feel like family. I'm so glad she pulled me off the sidewalk the day I ran from City Hall.

"So, do you know how to Tango?" I stand and shuffle my feet a few times. You'd swear I'm the five-year-old instead of Hannah's daughter.

"No. But it should be fun." Grace shuffles her feet, too, causing us to giggle.

"May I be your partner?" a voice I don't recognize asks behind me.

Grace grabs one of my hands and squeezes tightly. She bats her eyes. The smile on her face is fake. I turn and look up at one of the handsome bartenders from Cowboys. Throw a Stetson on him, and he'd belong on a Cowboy calendar. I might need to find one of those. Calendars, that is—not cowboys.

Ally's friend Beth was all over this guy at Cowboys. From his sly grin and dreamy eyes, I'm sure a few more women are too. A couple of the ladies in the room are eyeing him now. Beth glances at him. I can't tell if she's upset he's talking with me. I'm not about to step on another woman's toes, especially with a man. Even if I didn't like

Leo, I wouldn't dance with this guy. Before I can turn him down, a hand clamps down on his shoulder.

"Keep moving, Carter." Leo shoves him away. He puts an arm around me and pulls me into his side. "Slugger already has a partner."

"Oh, I see." Carter snickers. "Laying claim, huh, Barnes?"

"Yep."

I snap my head up. Leo's eyes stay focused on Carter. Surely, he didn't mean that. Do I want that? Oh, yes, I do.

Carter holds his hand out toward Grace. "How bout it, Grace? You need a partner?"

"Wrong again." Wade Lunsford puts his arm around Grace's shoulders. He points at Carter. "First of all, that's not how you ask a lady to dance. Second, Grace already has a partner, too. So, move along, Theo."

Theo? Carter must be his last name. I really need to learn people's names around here. Theo laughs and holds his hands up before turning around. He makes a beeline to Beth. What a jerk. He saves her for last. I hope Beth wakes up and sees through him. He's no better than Skip and Scott.

"Spencer is going to kill him one day," Wade says.

"Not tonight. Spencer's pulling a double shift." Leo huffs and rolls his eyes when Theo twirls Beth around, making her laugh.

"You camping for Labor Day and the Fall Festival?" Wade looks at each of us.

Grace laughs. "I don't camp."

"I think Dad took me when I was a kid." I vaguely remember sleeping in a tent.

"Lucas and I will be back on day shift. We'll be on duty both weekends, but we'll be at the lake at night." Leo smiles at me. "You should join us."

I look at Grace. "I'll go if you will."

"I'll think about it." She grits her teeth. "I don't know about spending the night, but I wouldn't mind going out there for a few hours after we close the shop."

I nod. That might be the best plan until I see what's involved with camping. Would I share a tent with Leo? If so, I might enjoy camping.

"Wait. Are you working with Grace?" Wade asked.

"I'm going to help those two weekends, so she doesn't have to hire another part-time person." Grace couldn't afford to hire anyone full-time. She felt bad when she found out I lost my job. She immediately offered me the holiday position. It won't pay any bills, but it makes me feel like I'm doing something.

"I think that's great." Leo steps away and holds his hand out. "Now, Slugger. May I have the honor of being your dance partner?"

I tilt my head. "You know how to Tango?"

He grins. "Not at all. That's what the class is for."

I slip my hand into his. "I'd be delighted."

Like I'd dance with anyone else when he's around. That's comical. I've only danced with Wade because Leo sent him to be my partner.

"Oh, that's gotta work for me too." Wade steps away and turns to face Grace. He holds his hand out and slightly bows. "Miss Wentworth, may I have the honor of being your dance partner tonight?"

Grace slides her hand into his and gives him a little curtsey. "Of course, you may, Mr. Lunsford."

Grace laughs as Wade twirls her into the middle of the dance floor. Several people around the room watch them. A few look at each other and grin.

"They make a cute couple." I sigh and lean into Leo's side.

"Yeah, but Wade's not who she dreams of," Leo whispers.

"Wait. What?" I grab the front of his shirt and pull him to me. "You know who Grace is crushing on?"

He lightly laughs. "I have an idea."

"Tell me."

"Oh, no, Slugger." Leo wraps his arms around my waist. "Grace can tell you when she's ready."

"But."

"Nope." He shakes his head and leans in close. "Just know. He's not here tonight."

I quickly scan the room to see who is here, not that I know all their names. I look over my shoulder at my new best friend. We need to have another Girl's Night at her apartment soon. I need details and a name.

Chapter Thirty-Seven

Leo

It's Thursday. Tomorrow is the last day of the month, and Monday is Labor Day. It's hard to believe the month is almost over. With it being a holiday weekend, we're switching shifts tomorrow morning. A day early is fine with me. I'm ready to get back to day shift.

Today is technically my day off. Dad has us all at the Station going over our schedules and the areas we'll patrol for the weekend. Even though the Fall Festival is next weekend, we still get a lot of tourists for Labor Day.

Dad's office door bursts open and hits the wall with a loud bang, causing us all to freeze. Dad rushes into the room. He looks happy, not upset.

"Murphy! Maxwell!" Dad shouts.

Every deputy in the room jumps to their feet. We all move toward Dad behind Spencer and Aiden.

"Sir?" Aiden and Spencer say.

"Hamilton needs an escort to Walsburg. Wife's in labor." He looks at Aiden. "Your wife is driving her to hospital. Chief said Miles just ran out the door. Catch up with him and keep him from getting a ticket."

Aiden and Spencer grab each other's shoulders and grin. You'd think they were the expectant father, not their best friend.

Only in a small town would a deputy be ordered to give police escort to the Assistant Fire Chief on the way to his baby's birth. No one knew until recently that Miles and Katie had miscarried a baby years ago. Baby Hamilton is a true blessing. After today, we'll finally know the baby's name and can stop calling the little one Baby Hamilton. It's safe to say Miles won't be camping with us this year.

Ms. Ruth steps into the room, wringing her hands together. "Um, guys. We just got a call. There's a fight at Cowboys."

Every deputy in the room groans. Fights are usually at Pete's Saloon. Cowboys usually have drunk and disorderly calls. None of us want to go. We all know what this call is about.

"Dad, can we just go ahead and arrest Four and hold him all weekend?" Lucas asked.

"It would save a lot of trouble," I add.

"It's not Four." Ms. Ruth looks between Lucas and me. "It's Roman Crawford." She takes a deep breath and adds, "And your brother."

"Luke." I bolt for the door.

"Not again." Lucas is on my heels.

More deputies follow us, but I don't pay attention to who. I jump into the passenger seat of Lucas's SUV. We hurry across town. It takes less than ten minutes to get to Cowboys.

Lucas beats me inside the bar. We come to a halt at the edge of the upper level. Three steps down, and we'll be on the main level with the bar, stage, and dance floor.

Jake and Wyatt Campbell have Roman Crawford sitting at a table at the edge of the dance floor. Wyatt must have been here to help his brother set up for the weekend. The Jake Campbell Band is the main entertainment at Cowboys. Wyatt is Luke's friend. It explains why our brother is here so early in the day. Roman's left eye is bruised. It'll be black in a few hours.

Luke's sitting on a stool at the bar with Levi and Riley next to him. Noah hands Riley two ice packs. She wraps one around Luke's hand.

Luke and Roman have been going at each other for years. They usually save their fighting for the football game during the Fall Festival, where it's considered tackling and not fighting. It's really not surprising we're here now. It was only a matter of time until their little feud came to blows.

What surprises us all is Phillip Crawford standing between Luke and Roman. Well, his being here isn't the surprising part. What I didn't expect to see is Phillip protecting Luke. Phillip's a changed man now. He's nothing like his little brother. He no longer has anything to do with his family because of the horrible things they did to him.

"You're a disgrace!" Roman yells at Phillip.

"Sadly, you're mistaking me for you." Phillip crosses his arms and holds his ground.

"What happened?" Lucas demands.

I step in front of Luke. "Did you really have to hit him?"

"Yeah, I did." Luke doesn't bat an eye.

"Never mind." Lucas glares at both men. "Who threw the first punch?"

"Your brother." Roman snatches the ice pack from Noah. He wobbles, almost falling off his stool.

"I hit him once." Luke tosses his hand toward Phillip. "His brother got him the other three times."

"He's lucky I didn't break some bones." Phillip gets in Roman's face. Lucas pulls him back.

"Why did you hit him?" After examining Luke's hand, I wrap the ice pack around it again.

Levi moves to Riley's other side. He's quiet but glaring holes into Roman. Levi isn't as hot-headed as his twin.

That was one hard punch for Luke's hand to be swollen after one hit. I want to scold him. He knows better than to get into fights like this. A criminal record could cost him his job.

Luke's expression hardens. "He grabbed Rocky."

I snap my head to Riley. She's holding the second ice pack Noah gave her under her wrist. Levi's examining her injury. Red finger marks are visible on her skin. Riley's family. Nobody has a right to hurt her. Now, I want to punch Roman.

182

"I don't think it's broken, but I'm pretty sure it's sprained. We should get her to Doctor Larson's office." Levi wraps the ice pack around Riley's wrist.

"Let's go, Rocky." Luke slides off the barstool and puts his arm around Riley.

"You can't go, Luke." Lucas stops him from leaving.

Luke pokes Lucas in the chest. "My girl needs medical attention. I'm taking her to the doctor."

"You're part of a fight. We have to take you to the Station and let Dad sort this out." Lucas is only making our little brother madder.

"My girl needs medical attention!" Luke yells.

Riley slides between my brothers. "Luke, no. Please listen to him."

Luke glares holes into Lucas. Great. Now, my brothers are about to fight.

Levi moves next to Riley in front of Luke. "I'll take her to see Doctor Larson."

"We've got her." Hadley walks in. She walks up to Lucas and gives him a hug and a quick kiss. My twin's temper settles a little.

Kyleigh and Grace come in behind her. They rush over to Riley but don't pull her away from Luke. Luke's still mad.

"What are you doing here?" I take Kyleigh's hand. I don't like her being in a room with so many men ready to fight.

"Grace and I were at the coffee shop when Hadley got the call."

"Who called you?" Lucas puts a protective arm around Hadley. He's not happy someone put his girlfriend in a room full of angry men.

"I thought Riley would need a friend," Levi replies before Hadley can.

That settles Lucas down. I understand how he feels. I don't like Kyleigh being here, and Grace is too soft-hearted to be around angry men. But Levi's right. Riley needs a few friends with her.

"Thanks, bro." Luke gives Levi a fist bump.

"We'll take Riley to the Emergency Room. You guys go settle this." Hadley kisses Lucas on the cheek. "Your mom is on her way to the Sheriff's Office now."

"Somebody called Mom?" I can't believe the people in this town. My brothers groan.

"You know they did." Grace moves closer to Riley. She casually looks around the bar. The guy she's looking for isn't here.

"I don't need to go to the Emergency Room. Doctor Larson's office is fine." Riley cradles her bruised wrist in her hand. She gives Luke a quick kiss. "Don't give your brothers a hard time. You'll only make things worse."

"I'll try, Rocky." Luke gives her a tight smile. He turns to Grace. "You'll take care of her?"

"Of course," Grace assures him.

"We're going to have to go to the Emergency Room. Matt is already at the hospital with Katie. After a doctor sees you, we'll check on her and the baby." Hadley moves to Riley's other side and ushers her toward the door.

"Call me after you see the doctor!" Luke calls out. Hadley and Grace already have Riley out the door. His eyes fall on Kyleigh.

"I promise to make sure she calls you." Kyleigh looks up at me. "I'll see you later?"

"Absolutely, Slugger." I walk her to the door and watch as she gets into Hadley's SUV. She and Grace plan to have dinner with us at the campsite tonight. We're setting up camp a day early.

"Now, let's get these three to the Sheriff's Office," Lucas says.

"Three?" Luke looks at Phillip. "Sorry, man. Guess you're going too."

Lucas looks at me. "You get Luke. I'll walk Roman out."

"Am I arresting him?" I'm not arresting my brother. One of the other guys will have to do it.

"We'll leave that decision up to Dad. Just walk him to the car. I'll put Roman in Deputy Walker's cruiser. Phillip can drive himself." Lucas and Deputy Darwin Walker escort Roman out. Naturally, Roman threatens to have their jobs for it.

"I'll email you the security footage." Noah walks to the door with me. "Since Luke was involved, I called Ms. Ruth's cell phone and not the Sheriff's Office."

"Thanks, man." I shake his hand and escort Luke out. At least nothing is official yet. Hopefully, Luke doesn't end up with any charges today.

Dad won't be happy having these two back at the Station for fighting. Both times, Luke was protecting Riley from Roman. Last time, Luke and Riley weren't officially dating. Riley's family now. Dad will be livid.

It makes no sense for Roman to even speak to Riley. He has a wife at home. If Brittany shows up, we'll have our hands full. Lucas should probably go ahead and call his friend Quinn just in case Luke needs a lawyer. This could get ugly fast.

Chapter Thirty-Eight

Kyleigh

Riley's wrist was sprained, as Levi predicted. Thank goodness it's not broken. She told us what happened on the way to the hospital. Some men are such jerks. I don't like Roman Crawford at all. He deserved to be beaten up. His older brother I do like.

Luke, Levi, Wyatt, and Phillip were helping Jake Campbell set up his band's equipment for the weekend shows. The rest of the band had to work at their day jobs today. I like hearing stories about how the people here band together to help out when someone needs help.

Roman was already drunk when he showed up at Cowboys. He sat at the bar a few stools away from Riley. After three beers, Noah cut him off and offered him a burger with fries. Roman knocked over the cup of coffee Noah set in front of him and demanded another beer. He turned his attention to Riley when he didn't get his drink. Roman grabbed her wrist and jerked her off the barstool, causing Riley to fall to the floor. Luke rushed across the bar, but not in time to stop Roman from hurting Riley. Luke punched the jerk in the face. Before he could swing again, Phillip pushed Luke out of the way and nearly knocked his little brother out cold.

Riley calls Luke as we head upstairs to the waiting room outside the Maternity Ward. No one has been arrested so far. Lawyers are on the way to the Sheriff's Office, though. Sheriff Barnes is beyond mad.

I can't describe the scene in the waiting room. It's packed. People are even sitting in camping chairs in the hallway. Beth has a table set up with coffee. Sammie has one next to her with donuts, cupcakes, and cookies. Some are from Sweet Treats. More than half of the sweets were sent by the Hayden Sisters. Someone just walked in with a platter of brownies. I've never seen anything like this.

"Here you go, ladies." One of the teens and his friends stand, offering us their chairs.

"Thanks, Elliott." Hadley takes his hand and gives him an encouraging smile. "Any word on how they're doing?"

Elliott runs a hand through his hair. "Yeah, but I don't understand the medical terms. She's about halfway. Whatever that means. I just hope she's okay."

Poor kid. This must be the first birth he's been to. Katie has dilated five centimeters. She's got a way to go. This being her first baby, it could take hours.

"Hey." Grace puts an arm around him. "Your sister is in good hands back there."

"I know." Elliot nods. "But I'm still scared."

"That's understandable." Hadley looks over his shoulder to the guy behind him. "Chase, why don't you take Elliott for a walk?"

Elliott's head snaps up. "I'm not leaving this hospital."

"You don't have to leave. Just walk the halls or go to the cafeteria." Grace points across the room. "Aiden's right there. We'll get him to call Chase if Katie needs you."

"Come on, man." Chase clamps his hand on Elliott's shoulder. "They're right. Let's step outside for some fresh air. Then we'll go to the cafeteria for a burger. I'm tired of donuts and cookies."

"You're never tired of donuts and cookies," Elliott says.

"I am today." Chase nudges Elliott toward the door. He nods to us. "I got him."

Once again, I need to learn who everyone in this town is. I didn't know Katie had a little brother. The only person I know anything about their family is Grace. I really should get to know Hadley and Riley better. They protected me from the onslaught of questioning men the night I was arrested. We are dating brothers, after all.

Wait. Am I truly dating Leo? I think I am. The whole town says we are. But what about Leo? His actions make me believe we're dating. Actions are often taken the wrong way. Maybe I should ask him. Leo doesn't talk about his feelings, and it's hard to read him at times. He really is the quiet Barnes.

"Why don't you two sit? We'll get coffee and donuts." Grace grabs my arm and pulls me toward the refreshment tables.

"My wrist is sprained, not broken," Riley says.

"Yeah, but you're worried about Luke. Let's see if there's an update." Hadley convinces her to sit.

"So, do you think you'll actually camp this weekend?" I get the donuts while Grace gets the coffee.

"I don't know." She carries two cups of coffee to Hadley and comes back. "Will you?"

"I'm thinking about it." I grin.

Grace lightly laughs. Oh my. She's blushing. Why is Grace blushing over going camping? I watch her from the corner of my eye. She glances across the room. Her blush deepens. That's not from camping. I take Hadley and Riley their plates with donuts and a cookie. Grace glances across the room again when she thinks no one is watching.

Aiden Maxwell is talking with a group of six men across the room. I know Grace isn't crushing on Aiden. He's a happily married man. Leo said the guy she likes wasn't at dance class last week. I don't know all their names, but the other six men weren't at dance class. Well. Well. Well. I've narrowed Grace's crush down to six men. That's a weird thing to say. But still, this helps a lot. Now, I need to find out who these men are.

"Which one?" I whisper when I get back to the table.

"What?"

"Come on, Grace. Which man over there has you blushing?"

"I'm not blushing." Grace laughs it off. She's lying.

"Oh. I'll figure it out." I love a good mystery.

"Kyleigh, no." Grace grabs my arm and leans close. "Please don't. Not here."

"Okay, but we're having a Girl's Night soon, and you're telling me everything." I keep my voice low so no one can hear us.

Grace glances nervously across the room again. She nods, but she doesn't want to tell anyone who she likes. None of those men look our way. My heart breaks for Grace. I don't think the man knows she's interested in him. She's going to have to make the first move.

Hannah Ramsey walks in with three more boxes from Sweet Treats. The way people are coming and going, none of the treats will go to waste. She announces dance class is canceled tonight since most of the class is here for Katie and Miles. She joins us in our little corner by the windows.

Hadley taps my arm. "Riley and I are going outside so she can call Luke. Texts aren't enough, and the reception in here is crappy. We'll leave in about an hour."

"Sounds good." Texts aren't doing it for me, either. I'm not about to call Leo in front of these people. The fight at Cowboys will be enough for them to gossip about for a few days.

Every thirty minutes, Katie's friends switch out who's with her. Of course, Miles and both of their mothers rarely leave her side. So far, everything is going as expected. With any luck, Baby Hamilton will arrive by midnight. E Maxwell is hoping after midnight. She wants Katie's baby to share her son's birthday.

"Okay." Hannah motions between Grace and me. "We need a Girl's Night. And I don't mean a night at Cowboys with everybody. We need a sleepover."

Grace and I laugh. We're already planning another sleepover. Will Grace still tell me who she likes if Hannah's there too? It shouldn't matter. Hannah is her best friend. She's been trying to get the three of us together for weeks. A sleepover sounds perfect.

"I'm in." I really like Hannah. It would be great if the three of us were friends.

"I thought you liked married life," Grace teases.

"I do. It's amazing. You should try it." Hannah wiggles her eyebrows at Grace, causing her to blush again.

"You're insane." Grace nudges her with her shoulder.

Hannah winks at me. Oh, my gosh! Does she know? I glance at the group of men and look at Hannah questionably. She shrugs. Well, darn. I'm not sure she knows, either. We definitely need a Girl's Night. Hannah and I might need to bring some wine to get Grace to spill the beans. I noticed she does talk a little more after a couple of glasses.

"Seriously, though. Jasper and I agreed we should spend time with our friends. It'll be good for us. We're together all the time."

"Jasper's going to have sleepovers with his friends?" Grace giggles.

"Not like us. He'll camp at the lake with them. He's planning hunting trips in the fall and winter with Lucas and Leo." Hannah places her hand on my arm. "I hope you don't mind losing your guy for a few days."

"Oh." I cover my mouth with a napkin to keep from spewing coffee on her. "Leo's not mine."

"It's sweet you think that, but he really is." Hannah turns to Grace. "We should plan something in a couple of weeks."

"But you like camping," Grace says.

"I do, but one night is all Bently can handle. We'll do that with everyone as a family. Jasper will have the rest of the weekend with his friends."

"Okay. Let's plan a night the weekend after the Fall Festival," Grace suggests.

Hannah and I agree. We give each other a knowing look. We're definitely buying some wine.

"After we leave here, we can meet up at the lake and help set the campsite up." Hannah's phone rings. She steps into the hallway to answer it.

Grace and I say our goodbyes to everyone. We meet Hadley and Riley in the parking lot. Things are still a little uncertain at the Sheriff's Office, but Luke hasn't been arrested. Riley's antsy and ready to see him. I love watching their relationship. As silly as Luke and Riley are, they have the sweetest relationship I've ever seen. Pain hits my chest. I want that, too.

Chapter Thirty-Nine

Leo

I'm so glad this day is over. Luke and Roman's fight was all over town within an hour. Chief Deputy Green was stationed in the lobby with Ms. Ruth to send gossipers on their way.

More than a dozen ladies showed up with platters of pastries and sweets as gifts to our deputies for all their hard work. A few men made reports of missing tools. Kyleigh's dad refused to let anyone in the back. He filled out all their reports from Ms. Ruth's desk.

As much as we tried to keep rumors from spreading, a few people left with some juicy information. It's hard to keep things quiet when Edward Crawford is shouting and threatening the entire department.

Megan Sanders made matters worse. Naturally, the gossipers reported what they heard to her. Hayden Happenings ran an Emergency News Story. Once the article was posted online, Deputy Green stood outside the front doors with his arms crossed. He threatened to arrest everyone who didn't have an actual crime to report. Needless to say, our wonderful citizens left immediately and were highly disappointed.

"Here you go." Kyleigh hands me a plate with a burger and chips. She sits next to me when she comes back with her own plate.

"You ladies did a great job."

The ladies are grilling out burgers and hotdogs tonight. They set up most of our campsite this afternoon. The only thing they didn't set up were the tents. The guys worked together and assembled those when we got here.

"Hadley and Hannah did most of it. The rest of us followed their instructions." Kyleigh slides her chair closer to mine so Grace can sit on her other side.

We have several tables around the camp. Most of us sit outside our tent doors in camping chairs. It's the first time I've had a woman sitting in front of mine.

"Are you ladies spending the night?" I'll give them my tent if they do. I can bunk with one of the other guys.

Grace nervously laughs. She glances around the campsite. Her guy isn't here yet. I don't tell her the tent next to mine, just to her right, is his.

"Do you want to stay?" Kyleigh asks.

Grace drops her eyes and shakes her head. "Not tonight. I don't want to get up early and rush to the shop."

"So, Saturday night then?" Kyleigh teases.

"Maybe?" Grace grins.

If they're out here Saturday night, I'll do my best to convince them to stay. Even if Grace doesn't, maybe Kyleigh will. Hadley and Riley will be here this weekend. I like that she's becoming good friends with my brother's girlfriends.

Levi is my only brother who won't be camping with us this weekend. He's on duty at the Fire Station. Luke is supposed to be there too. He wasn't charged today. However, he is suspended until he sees Judge Morgan on Tuesday.

Roman was charged with being drunk and disorderly. He should be charged with a lot more. Riley called Dad from the hospital. She was frantic and scared Luke would lose his job. She begged Dad not to charge Roman for hurting her if it saved my brother's career. Dad's letting Judge Morgan sort things out next week. Luke's only suspended to shut Edward Crawford up. Dad's about to lose his patience with the entire Crawford family.

Kyleigh's phone dings with a text. She quickly pulls it from her pocket. She no longer avoids looking at her phone when she gets a call or text. Hopefully, it means her ex is leaving her alone.

She lightly laughs and tilts her head toward Grace. "Alien Mom wants to know if I'm spending the night here."

"Alien Mom?"

I don't get it, but Grace does. She covers her mouth with her hand to hide her laugh. Kyleigh said things at her dad's house have been weird. She hasn't gone into details about what she means.

"My mom is acting really strange since she got here. Dad is, too. Is he acting weird at work?"

If her expression weren't serious, I'd laugh, too. It's cute. She thinks her parents have been abducted. She bats her eyes a few times. Nope. I can't make a joke here.

"Well, he's been happier since you and your mom got here." I think for a moment. "You could say he's got a little spring in his step."

"See? That right there." She jabs her finger at me on each word. "My dad does not springy step."

Lucas drops his head back and wholeheartedly laughs. Hadley has to catch his plate before he drops it. Grace can't hide her laughter this time. Everyone who knows Chief Deputy Green is well aware he does *not* springy step.

"Seriously, y'all." Kyleigh tosses her hand up. "And Dad's watching Mom. They're weirding me out."

This time, I laugh. "Oh, Slugger. I think your Dad might still have feelings for your mom." It explains Deputy Green's attitude lately.

"Noooooo," Kyleigh dramatically whines and falls against my shoulder. Everyone in hearing distance bursts out laughing.

"I thought all kids wanted their parents together." Hadley takes our empty plates and throws them in the trash can.

"Yeah, but I'm not nine anymore and asking Mom to move back."

"You wanted to come back to Hayden Falls when you were nine?" Grace is no longer laughing. According to my mom, Kyleigh and Grace were friends when they were little.

"Yeah," Kyleigh replies softly. "At first, I hated the city and begged Mom to come back. She said pigs would fly first."

"Oh!" Luke raises his hand like he's answering a question in school. He jumps to his feet, startling a few people. "We can make that happen."

"Luke." I stand and hold my hand out. "Don't do it."

The stupid wheels in my brother's mind are spinning out of control. This is going to be so bad.

"Oh! This is going to be epic!" He claps his hands and points at Grace. "Does your Grandpa have pigs?"

"Luke! No!" Lucas is on his feet, too.

"No." Grace shakes her head.

Luke doesn't listen to Lucas or me. He rubs his hand over his beard. This fool is seriously planning this.

"Okay." Luke nods. "We'll have to get one from the Calhouns or the Maxwells."

"Luke!" I raise my voice. Finally, he looks at me. "You're not stealing a pig and throwing it off a building."

"Of course not." He laughs and waves his hand in my direction. "That would be animal cruelty. That's illegal."

"Yeah, and I'd happily arrest you for it." I wouldn't happily arrest him. I never want to arrest a family member. If he goes through with this stunt, I'll change my mind and happily do it.

Luke tosses his hands out to the side and looks at me like I'm the crazy one. "Well, I can't get a ham at the market and put costume wings on it." He snaps his fingers. "Actually, we could. Floyd can advertise them as Heavenly Hams for Thanksgiving and Christmas."

Lucas and I slap our palms to our foreheads and run our hands through our hair. Luke is an idiot. He'll definitely put wings on all the hams at the market come Thanksgiving.

"Um." Hadley lifts her finger. "I think that's an actual company name. Floyd would get sued if he did that."

Luke tosses his hands up. "So, a live pig it is."

Kyleigh stands and slides her hand into mine. She leans close and whispers, "He won't really do it, will he?"

"Oh, he would." I have no doubts. "You're not making a pig fly," I say sternly.

"We have to. Her mom will move back here if a pig flies." Luke crosses his arms. He seriously believes it.

"Luke." I rub my temple with my fingertips. I don't know what to do with my brother when he's like this. He will never grow up. "It was a figure of speech. Ms. Green isn't going to move back to Hayden Falls because she sees a pig fly. They're just visiting."

Those last words are hard to say. I almost choke on them. No matter what my feelings are for Kyleigh, she's not here to stay. Once her probation period ends, she'll be on her way back to Seattle and her fancy job. If a pig flying were enough to get Kyleigh and her mother to stay here permanently, I'd help Luke with his ridiculous plan. It'll take more than that for a woman to want to live in this little town. Ms. Green left once. She's not likely to ever make this her home again.

"But Kyleigh could use it to convince her mom to stay. She could say it was fate or something." Luke's expression turns serious. He looks me straight in the eye. "You want her to stay. You won't have to worry about it anymore."

Well, darn. He's overheard me talking with Lucas late at night on our back deck. This is one of the times I hate having my brothers living next door. The entire camp has gone quiet. Less than half the people camping with us this weekend aren't here tonight. The rest will hear about this by morning. Everyone in Hayen Falls will know how much I care about Kyleigh before sundown.

"Um." Kyleigh lightly squeezes my hand and bites her bottom lip.

"Slugger, I'm sorry." How do I talk my way out of this? Do I even want to?

"My mom brought all our stuff with her."

"Wait." I cup her cheek in my other hand. "You're really staying?" This changes everything.

She shrugs. "I don't know what we're doing."

"Now, we really need a pig." Luke grins and rubs his hands together.

I give up trying to talk sense into my brother. Lucas can deal with him for the rest of the night.

"Come on, Slugger. I'll take you and Grace home."

Maybe we can talk if I get her out of here. She and Grace rode with Hadley to the lake.

"That's a great idea." Kyleigh grabs her purse from the back of her chair.

Lucas's phone rings. He holds up a finger, signaling for me to wait. If this is a call to Pete's Saloon, I'm arresting everybody when we get there. After taking the call, Lucas steps into the middle of camp. He's smiling, so it's good news.

"Hayden Falls' newest citizen has arrived. Everybody celebrate! Benjamin Elliott Hamilton is here. Mother and baby are just fine."

The camp erupts into shouts, squeals, and laughter. Miles and Katie have a son. Little Benjamin missed sharing a birthday with Aiden's son by two hours.

Chapter Forty

Kyleigh

I never thought working in a bookstore would be fun. Sure, people say they want to do it. I personally thought it would be boring. Working at Page Turners the past two days has proven me wrong. There's been a steady stream of customers in the shop. Maybe it's because this is a holiday weekend. I don't know, but I'm enjoying it.

Surprisingly, my favorite customers are the children. They're Grace's favorite, too. She's definitely dreaming about babies. Now we just need to reel her guy in. Of course, I need to figure out who her guy is first.

"Kywee, will you read this to me?" Bently, Hannah and Jasper's little girl holds up a book with bunnies on the cover. I love the way she says my name.

"Of course, Sweet Pea." I learned rather quickly during dance class that this is the only pet name she allows anyone to call her.

I take her hand and lead her to the corner Grace set up for children. A row of bookcases approximately three feet tall creates a wall, giving this area a little privacy. Children's books fill the shelves on the store side, and a small loveseat sits against them in the children's area to create stability. A small table and chairs sit in front of the huge window on one side. Davis's Diner is just across the street. In the middle is a rug with a forest scene and baby animals. Several throw pillows lay around the rug. A rocking chair is in one corner, and a beanbag chair is in the other. It's the perfect area for children.

"Where would you like to sit?"

Bently smiles up at me. "Beanbag."

"Great choice." It's my favorite, too. We settle into the huge beanbag chair. "Do you like bunnies?"

Bently nods. "They sweeping."

I lightly laugh. The cover has two sleeping bunnies cuddling. Most of the cover is pink. I heard Grace read this book to a little girl yesterday.

"They're sisters." I open the cover and turn to the first page.

Bently snuggles closer to me. "I hope I get a sister."

Oh my. I look into the shop area and find Hannah talking with Grace at the front counter. She's happy, glowing, in fact. I smile and kiss the top of Bently's head. Somebody just let a family secret slip.

As I read, Bently makes up extra parts for the story. She has me and a few customers laughing as they walk by. This child has a huge imagination. I can't bring myself to tell her that bunnies will never fly. Hannah and Grace watch from the other side of the bookcases. After we close the book, Bently runs with it to Hannah.

"Mama, can I have it, pwease?"

"Of course." Hannah smiles and motions toward the register.

"Yay." Bently bounces up and down.

"Come on, Sweet Pea. Let's go ring this up." Grace takes her hand and leads the way to the front counter.

"Congratulations," I whisper to Hannah.

Her eyes dart around the room to make sure no one is in hearing distance. They're not. I already checked.

"I can't believe she told you," Hannah whispers.

"She let a little hint drop."

"I'm not a hundred percent sure. I have a doctor's appointment this week. If we are, we'll announce it at the Fall Festival." She smiles sweetly at a couple of ladies in the Suspense section. They're too far away to hear us.

"Your secret is safe with me." I point at Bently. "You might want to keep a close eye on her, though."

Hannah laughs. "Thanks, Kyleigh."

She hurries to the front counter to pay for Bently's book. I'm almost positive she and Jasper will have an announcement to make next weekend.

While Grace takes care of the customers in line at the register, I collect the books left on tables and chairs and return them to their places. There are a few areas around the shop to sit and read. Grace offers coffee, hot tea, and hot chocolate to customers. It's not as fancy as Beth's Morning Brew, though. Grace has tables around the shop for people to leave books they've changed their minds about. She says this is better than customers putting books where they don't belong.

Page Turners and nearly every store in town will close at six today. Only the restaurants will open tomorrow. Grace has agreed to go back to the lake with me this afternoon. She's still not sold on camping. I hope she changes her mind. Even if we don't share a tent, the thought of camping with Leo makes me giddy.

I slide the last book into its place and turn to search for more. A new customer walks in. I gasp and freeze. This is not happening.

"So, this is where you ran off to." Scott walks toward me.

"What are you doing here?" I glance around nervously. Most of the customers have left. Grace is still at the front counter.

"You won't take my calls. I had to come find you." He sounds annoyed.

"I don't want to talk to you. I blocked your number, and you shouldn't have come." I spin on my heels and walk to the next row.

"Come on, Kyleigh. You're acting childish. We need to talk." Scott follows.

"We have nothing to talk about."

The bookcases in the middle of the shop are about five feet tall. Grace finally notices me just as Scott grabs my arm and turns me to face him.

"We have a lot to talk about if you'd just listen." He leans close. "I miss you."

I snap my head back. He misses me? Has he lost his mind? He can't be serious. A couple of months ago, I might have fallen for that line. Not now. Not after what he did to us.

"Go home, Scott." I grab another book and put it on the shelf.

"Will you stop?" He grabs my arm and spins me around again. "I came here to get you and take you home."

Home? With him? Whatever sick game he's playing, he can do it without me. He's Brenda's problem, not mine. My home will never be with him again.

"I'm not going anywhere with you." I jerk my arm away and step back. "I don't ever want to see you again."

"Kyleigh." He narrows his eyes and takes a step toward me.

One minute, I'm looking at Scott's angry face. The next, I see the back of a black deputy's uniform.

"Is there a problem here?" Leo's voice is deeper and sharper than I've ever heard.

"No, Officer. I'm just trying to talk to my girlfriend." Scott's a lot friendlier to Leo than he was to me.

Leo turns his head to the side but doesn't look fully over his shoulder at me. "Kyleigh?"

"Ex. He's my ex-boyfriend."

"Do you want to talk to him?" Leo still won't look at me.

"No." My voice cracks a little.

Leo finally turns his head enough for our eyes to meet. I'm not sure what I see in his eyes. He looks hurt and unsure for a moment. I shake my head. I don't want anything to do with Scott.

"Don't worry, Slugger. I got it." He turns to face Scott.

"Wait. Slugger? What kind of name is that?" Scott looks around Leo's broad shoulders. "You leave me for some country cop?"

"I didn't leave you. You brought a woman home and threw me out," I snap. He doesn't get to play the victim here. Grace rushes to my side.

Leo quickly looks at me over his shoulder and back to Scott. "You cheated and threw her out?" He shakes his head. "You're an idiot."

"What's going on?" Lucas demands.

Scott looks between Leo and his brother a few times. "Two of them?" He peers around Leo again. "You sleeping with them both?"

"Why you." Leo draws his right arm back.

I try catching his wrist but can't. Lucas jumps in front of Leo. He grabs his arms and turns Leo to the side.

"No!" Lucas shakes his head. "Trust me. I want to knock him out for that comment, too, but we can't."

"This is unbelievable." Scott jabs his finger at me. "You are not the woman I thought you were."

Leo pushes toward Scott. Lucas spins around and manages to keep his body in front of Leo. Before Lucas can unleash on him, a hand clamps down hard on Scott's neck.

"I thought I told you to never disrespect my wife and daughter again." Dad's grip tightens. "You should have never showed up in my town."

"You're as crazy as your daughter." Scott glares at Dad.

"I'm worse than crazy when someone messes with my family." Dad nudges Scott toward the door.

"You'll regret this, Kyleigh!" Scott shouts. "You've fallen so low. You choose a country cop over me and quit your job to work in a bookstore. Pathetic."

Dad ignores Scott's outburst but doesn't let go of his neck. "Kyleigh, we're going to the Sheriff's Office right now and taking a restraining order on this little punk." He glances at Leo. "I'm trusting you with my daughter. You'll bring her to the Station?"

"Yes, Sir." Leo puts his arm around me. I lean into his side. "I've got her."

Somehow, I get the feeling they mean more than just a ride to the Sheriff's Office. Dad doesn't easily trust. Is he giving Leo his approval to date me?

"Grace, do you want a restraining order to keep him away from you and the bookstore?" Lucas asks.

"Just the shop is fine," Grace replies.

"No. You need one, too. He knows you're connected to Kyleigh. He could come after you to get to her." Leo has a good point.

I don't think Scott would do something like that, but he's changed. He's not the man I fell in love with. He's an idiot to think I'd take him back. Showing up here proves he's irrational. I nod. Grace gives in and nods, too.

"Okay. Deputy Green's not going to wait on this. We'll take Kyleigh to sign her restraining order now, and I'll bring her back. I'll escort you to the Sheriff's Office after closing to sign your papers." Leo points out the window. "Spencer and Aiden will keep an eye on you and the shop."

"Thank you." Grace holds the door for us.

She still has customers so she can't close to go with us. She waves to Aiden and Spencer. Lucas is filling them in on everything.

I grab her hand. "I'm so sorry."

"It's not your fault." She smiles weakly. "Listen to your Dad and Leo."

Leo and I walk behind Lucas past Frozen Scoops toward the Sheriff's Office. They must have been walking around the square when Grace called. The scene inside the bookstore has drawn the eyes of all the nosy people in town. Great. I'll be in the gossip blog again this evening.

"Thank you," I whisper once we're out of sight of the town square.

Leo kisses the top of my head. "You never have to thank me for protecting you."

Chapter Forty-One

Leo

Small towns are supposed to be boring. There's never a dull moment in our little town. If it's not one of our townsfolk doing something off the wall, an outsider comes in and tries to act big and bad.

Scott Jensen was like every other troublemaking outsider. He threatened to sue the Sheriff's Office and have all our jobs. He called his fancy lawyer in Seattle. Their office didn't have anyone in Montana to send to help him. Quinn handled the lawyer over the phone. In the end, a restraining order was placed against him for Kyleigh and her mom. Another was signed for Grace and the bookstore. Mr. Jensen has no reason to be in Hayden Falls. Dad personally escorted Kyleigh's ex-boyfriend to the county line on his way to Missoula and the interstate. Hopefully, that's the last we've seen of him.

Tonight, everyone's happy and having a good time. Everyone but Lucas, that is. He's at the edge of the campsite on the phone. I'll lose my temper if Willows Bend needs backup at Pete's Saloon tonight.

Miles is the only person who won't be camping with us tonight. He brought his wife and son home this afternoon. Aiden and Spencer stopped by after their shift to welcome the family home. They made it to the campsite in time to grill steaks, pork chops, and burgers for dinner. Aiden loves to grill. He doesn't care what time of year it is.

I got here a couple of hours before dark and got a little fishing in. We should have enough for a fish fry tomorrow night. Yes, I brought Kyleigh and Grace with me. We've kept someone close to them all afternoon. The random customers at Page Turners today weren't really random. Most of them didn't even buy anything. I'm not ashamed for sending them. I would have sent more if I could have. I sent every person I ran into that I trusted. This town is crazy, but we do look out for each other.

The party field is going strong. We can hear them from here. The ladies in our camp have gathered to one side. They turned on some music and started dancing. It's cute to watch. Well, I'm only watching one of them. The ladies grab a drink and join us when the song ends.

"That was fun." Kyleigh pours herself and Grace a glass of wine.

Most of the ladies are drinking beer or sodas. Not my girl. She has wine in a plastic cup. It's one of the craziest things I've seen. And my girl? I slowly release a long breath. Kyleigh isn't officially mine. I want her to be. Everyone in town says she is. There's too much uncertainty surrounding us for things to go further. I'm not sure where we stand.

"This is so fun." Grace giggles.

Oh no. Grace has had a little too much wine. It's good to see her laughing and dancing. Grace is sweet and kind-hearted. She wouldn't survive rumors of being drunk. Eli Wentworth will go livid on everyone here if his sister gets hurt or embarrasses herself. We'll need to watch Grace closely tonight.

Lucas ends his call and sits down in the chair on my left. "Hey."

"We get a call?" I hope not. He and I had a couple of beers tonight. We shouldn't be driving.

He sighs and shakes his head. "No. Dad wants us to get a couple of hunting parties together this week. Buck's been spotted on Sam's cameras around the shooting range."

"We can do that."

The hunting parties might not be large on such short notice. Still, there are always people in our community willing to help.

Lucas looks across the campsite. "A few people have seen Phillip and Aaron hunting."

Phillip Crawford is here tonight. Aaron Bailey will join us after his shift ends at Pete's Saloon. Their wives are here. Both ladies are pregnant. I understand why these two are hunting on their own. Buck attacked their kids on Thanksgiving Day last year.

"Who's Buck?" Kyleigh asked.

Hadley, Grace, and Riley tell her about Mags' wild dog. All four ladies almost fall out of their chairs, laughing. Okay. We need to hide the wine. We cannot have a camp full of drunk women. We should assign this task to Luke. He'll stay out of trouble tonight if he's busy. From the looks of these ladies, he'll be busy for a while.

"Would you like to go for a walk?" I offer Kyleigh my hand.

"I…" She grits her teeth and looks at Grace.

"I'm fine." Grace flips her wrist. "Go. Walk. Talk. And other things."

Grace is not fine. She's tipsy. Kyleigh is aware of it, too.

Hadley moves her chair next to Grace. "We'll keep Grace company."

Riley slides her chair over to them. Naturally, Luke follows her over. I grin. He's protecting these ladies without officially being assigned the position.

Grace giggles and points across the campsite. "Sammie, Ally, and Hannah are over there. I can sit with them, so you two can stay with Lucas and Luke."

"I'll walk you over." Hadley loops her arm around Grace's and pulls her to her feet. They walk across the camp and excitedly fall into conversation with their friends. Lucas glares at me.

"Sorry, bro." I just cost him time with his girlfriend.

"Go." Lucas leans back and crosses his arms. "I'll watch things here."

It doesn't matter where we are or if we're officially on duty or not. My brother and I watch over the people around us. The beer in Lucas' hand will be his last one tonight. I've had my last one, too. If Kyleigh and Grace don't stay the night with us, I'll need a clear head to drive them home. I hope they stay at Kyleigh's Dad's house if they go home tonight. I don't trust Scott Jensen to heed Dad's warning to stay out of Hayden Falls.

"Okay." Kyleigh stands and wraps her arm around mine. "I need to go to the restroom anyway."

I turn on the flashlight as we start down the path. The sounds from the party field get louder. Most partygoers will go home or to one of the bars by midnight. The ones who stay will party all night long.

"So, you quit your job." We haven't talked about this since her ex mentioned it today.

"I didn't have a choice," she says softly.

"Why? I thought you were working remotely."

"My manager gave me a month to get back."

We fall into an awkward silence. She lost her job because of my truck. This doesn't sit right with me.

"I'm sorry." I would fix this for her if I could. Lucas and Dad can't figure out why Judge Morgan was so hard on her.

She shrugs. "It's my own fault. I should have stopped us from going out that night."

Kyleigh's mouth falls open when we step out of the forest. The music is loud, and the fire in the pit is high. Devon Reed and Zane Gallagher have one of the fire engines across the party field. Chief Foster allows it during town celebrations if they don't have a call. With the way Four and Pit build fires, the engine is needed at times.

"Wow."

"You've never been to a party at the lake?"

She rolls her eyes and grins. "I was eight when we moved away."

"You were here for the Fourth of July Celebration this year."

"I was at Cowboys," she mumbles.

Right. It was the night we met. The parties during the Fourth of July lasted all week. She could have slipped out here at some point.

"Restrooms are this way, Slugger." I walk her over and wait outside.

"Hey, Leo." Beth Murphy walks into the lady's room. She's had a little too much to drink tonight. She's not to the point where she needs her brother to rescue her.

"Barnes." Theo Carter heads into the men's room. Spencer is going to kill him if he doesn't stay away from Beth.

Kyleigh and Beth come out together, laughing. Beth loops her arm around Theo's. I watch to see which campsite they go to. I'll let Spencer know where she's at.

"Would you like a s'mores?" I point to the firepit.

"No. That would burn our faces off."

"Okay. We can head back to camp." I was hoping to talk with her. You can't have a serious conversation with all this noise going on.

"It's really pretty out here." Kyleigh looks out at the lake and smiles. Does she mean just the lake or Montana?

The lake is one of my favorite places. I glance at the lake, too. Moonlight dances on the water, creating a peaceful scene. The moon isn't full, but it's still bright. The lights from homes across the lake shine through the trees. You can see a glimpse of Miles and Katie's house from our campsite.

"Do you think you're going to stay?" Do I sound desperate for asking?

"Do you want me to stay?"

That stops me in my tracks. I gently turn her to face me. I was afraid this would happen. Women who stay or come here for a man end up leaving within a few years.

"I want what's best for you." I swallow hard. I'll never ask her to stay for me.

"Thank you," she whispers.

I'm not sure why she's thanking me. She wraps her arms around my waist. I lean down and steal a kiss. I pull back before she can respond to the kiss and start walking again. All of a sudden, I'm lost for words tonight.

When we get back to camp, Grace is sitting in her chair outside my tent. She can barely keep her eyes open. Hadley sits next to her. As much as I don't want to, I need to take them home.

"Would you ladies like to stay or go home?" I hope they stay.

"Where would we sleep?" Grace blinks a few times to keep her eyes open.

"You can have my tent. I'll bunk down with Aiden," Spencer offers.

Grace looks over her shoulder at Spencer's tent and up to Kyleigh. "It's up to you."

"We don't have anything to sleep in," Kyleigh says.

"Hold on." Spencer goes into his tent and comes out with a few things. "I have everything I need for the night. You ladies can sleep in these." He hands Grace and Kyleigh t-shirts.

"I don't think so." I snatch the one from Kyleigh and throw it back at Spencer.

Spencer holds his hand up and laughs. "I didn't mean it like that, man."

I glare at my friend. He's lost his ever-loving mind. I storm into my tent to get Kyleigh one of my T-shirts. No man is going to give my girl a shirt to sleep in. Lucas told me he loved seeing Hadley in one of his shirts. I thought he was insane. I get it now. Just the thought of her wearing Spencer's shirt ticks me off.

"Here you go, Slugger." It's a simple plain gray T-shirt, but it's mine.

Hadley offers them both a pair of leggings. "In case you're not comfortable in just a shirt."

"Thank you." Grace wobbles when she stands.

Kyleigh catches her. "I should get her inside."

I give her a quick kiss and hold the tent flap open for them. Hopefully, she'll come back out and sit with us once Grace is asleep. Spencer and Aiden sit across the camp, laughing at me. Jerks.

Chapter Forty-Two

Kyleigh

"Hey!" I jump back and glare at the crazy old man.

My life has become a rollercoaster ride, and I want off. Some horrible new experience happens every week. The Sheriff called yesterday to inform me of the latest horrible news. Leo hasn't worked on his truck this week. He can't. He's out with the hunting party tracking the wild dog. Somehow, Judge Morgan knew. I have to do this week's community service for Sheriff Barnes.

"You're wasting time, girl." The old man cuts his eyes at me as he dips his sponge into the bucket of soapy water again.

"You don't have to sling water all over me." I should dump the entire bucket over his head. He makes me so mad.

"Not my fault you're standing there." He proceeds to wash the front window of Sweet Treats without looking at me.

"Uh!" I can't deal with him anymore. I wet my sponge, grab my squeegee, and move to the windows for Beth's Morning Brew.

If I could snatch the tattered hat off his head and beat him senseless with it, I would. I'd only have hit him once. He's the craziest person I've met in my life.

I'll never understand why Sheriff Barnes thought it was a good idea to make us work together. Meeting Mags in person is worse than I expected. The stories Dad tells about the old man are funny and unbelievable. Everyone says Mags is harmless. I think he's rude and mean. He sure doesn't like me for some reason.

The Fall Festival is this Saturday. Like every celebration in Hayden Falls, the shop owners decorate early and plan their games and prizes. Tourists will begin showing up tomorrow in hopes of finding out what's happening during the event. I'm looking forward to the festival. Dad has talked about it for years. Memories from my childhood are vague. I remember playing with other kids in the park and getting ice cream cones from Frozen Scoops during events, but that's about the extent of it.

Tomorrow, I'll work with Grace at Page Turners again. Hopefully, I can find a job soon. It probably won't be anything my degree will qualify me for. My employment status is two days at the bookstore. Community service isn't employment. I applied for unemployment but was denied. It was a long shot, anyway, since I resigned. I wasn't fired.

The coffee shop has two huge front windows. I'm halfway through cleaning the first one when water splashes on me again. That's it. I've had it with this old man. He doesn't want to work with me any more than I want to with him.

"Stop it!" I throw my sponge into the bucket of soapy water and glare at Mags.

"Just working." The old man basically ignores me and continues washing the window closest to the coffee shop.

People on this side of the square pause and watch us. The old man is grinning. I swear he's aggravating me on purpose. The men putting the stage together in the middle of the square glance our way. At least they keep working, unlike the nosy old biddies on the sidewalk.

"Keep the water in the bucket," I demand.

Mags dips his sponge in the bucket again. He stands and tosses his arms out. Naturally, water splashes on me again.

"Can't. Gotta wash the window with it," he says, like I'm stupid.

"Then get it on the window and not me." I shake the squeegee at him.

"Stop it! Stop it, I say!" One of the nosy old women in the middle of the square runs across the street, jabbing her finger toward me.

What in the world? All I can do is gawk at her. I'm speechless. It makes no sense. She's defending the old man. This town gets weirder by the day.

"You okay, Mags?" She puts her arm around him and looks him over for injury. She's as crazy as he is. Nobody touched him.

"I'm okay, Miss Betty." Mags takes his old, tattered hat off and runs a hand through his long, gray, stringy hair. "Sheriff making me work in hard conditions." He narrows his eyes at me.

"Well." Miss Betty huffs. She glares at me and turns back to Mags. "Let's just go tell the Sheriff you can't work with her."

"I did nothing to him. *He* wet *me*."

Miss Betty scrunches her face up and jabs her finger at me again. "You are nothing but trouble."

Hadley steps out of the coffee shop. "Miss Betty, Mags, you two move along and let Kyleigh work."

Miss Betty gives Hadley the same glare she gave me. For a moment, I thought the old woman would smart something off. Hadley crosses her arms and raises an eyebrow, challenging the woman.

"Come on, Mags. I'll go with you to see the Sheriff." Miss Betty huffs and turns Mags toward Frozen Scoops.

"Their men are hunting my dog," Mags grumbles before they turn the corner. Is that why he hates me?

"You okay?"

I peel my eyes from the odd couple and blink at Hadley. She's back to her happy self.

"What?" I slightly shake my head and motion toward Miss Betty and Mags just before they're out of sight.

Hadley holds her hand up to stop further questions. "Don't try to figure those two out. Nobody understands why Miss Betty Taylor has latched on to Mags."

"Thanks for helping." I turn to face the store window. "Guess I better get back to work." Things will go faster without the old man here.

"Can I get you anything?"

"A job." I lightly laugh.

"If we had an opening, I'd hire you in a heartbeat. How about a Peppermint Mocha?" She knows my weakness.

"Oh, I'd love one." The thought of a Peppermint Mocha has me sighing.

Hadley laughs and goes inside while I focus on my wonderful task. I have to rewash the window now because the soap has dried. Sheriff Barnes only gave us two buckets, sponges, squeegees, and liquid soap. One bucket is for washing water, and the other is for rinsing. The shops around the square give us the water to clean their windows. This system is ridiculous. A spray bottle of window cleaner and paper towels would have been better. Somehow, the old man would have still gotten me wet.

"Well, hello there, beautiful." The man's voice sends a shiver down my spine. I've only met him once, but I'll never forget his voice.

I slowly turn to face Bryson Crane. He looks exactly like I remember him. Worn jeans, an old T-shirt, and boots. All three have grease spots on them. His hair could use a comb. The gleam in his eyes has me taking a step back. Today just added two unpleasant events to my life.

"Why are you here?"

"Passing through. I wasn't expecting to see you." His grin widens. "I still have the door."

Hadley steps out onto the sidewalk with my coffee and grabs my wrist. "I need you to clean the office."

"Yeah." I take the to-go cup she's holding.

"Can I help you?" Hadley asks Bryson.

One side of his mouth lifts in a sly grin, and he looks Hadley over the way he did me at his junkyard. She doesn't flinch. "I'm sure you can."

"Not happening." Lucas steps in front of Hadley. Where did he come from?

"You have no business here." Leo steps in front of me.

"I just stopped for coffee." Bryson holds his hands up. His eyes bounce between Leo and Lucas. It's the reaction most people have when they first meet the twins.

"Sweet Girl, why don't you get Mr. Crane a cup of coffee right quick?" Lucas opens the shop door for her.

"A regular coffee?" Hadley asks.

"With cream and sugar." Bryson nods.

"Slugger, why don't you go with Hadley?" Leo suggests over his shoulder.

"Yeah." There's a lot of male tension out here. I ease my way toward the door Lucas is still holding open.

"I thought you two weren't dating," Bryson says.

"We are now." Leo's voice hardens. "Even if we weren't, I told you to stay away from her."

He did? What exactly happened at that junkyard?

"I'll get my coffee and go." Bryson grins and takes a step back.

I hurry into the safety of the coffee shop and watch the scene outside through the window. The employees and customers are watching, too. This entire town is nosy.

Hadley hands Lucas the to-go cup through the door. "It's on the house. Just get him out of here."

"No charge." Lucas hands Bryson the coffee and points toward Floyd's Market. "Your truck is right there."

"Stay away from her," Leo warns.

"Don't worry, cop." Bryson casually takes a sip of his coffee. He doesn't seem fazed by two deputies glaring at him. "I don't date taken women."

"Date?" Leo literally growls. "Is that what you call it?"

"Bye, cop." Bryson Crane says no more as he walks away.

Hadley and I step outside after the creep leaves. She walks into Lucas' arms. My assessment of Bryson Crane when I first met him can't be wrong if he has this many people on edge.

Lucas takes an incoming call. "On our way." He puts his phone in his pocket and points across the square. "Got an angry customer at the hardware store. Dad's sending us."

Leo drops his head back and groans. He takes my hand and pulls me to him. "Are you okay?"

"Yeah. That man just creeps me out."

"If you see him around again, call the Sheriff's Office if you can't get me." He closes his eyes and softly kisses my forehead.

"Leo." Lucas taps Leo's arm with the back of his hand before running across the middle of the square.

Leo snaps his head toward the hardware store and back to me. Two men are arguing on the sidewalk. Leo looks torn between doing his job and taking care of me. I'm fine now that the greasy mechanic is gone.

"Go." I give him a gentle shove.

"I'll help Kyleigh finish the windows and clean up out here." Hadley shoos him away with her hands.

We watch him run across the square and help Lucas separate the two elderly gentlemen. Grace comes out of the bookstore, locks the door, and runs down the sidewalk toward the hardware store.

"What's going on?"

"Well." Hadley points to the man on the right. "That's Grace's grandfather. Every time Mr. Wentworth goes into the hardware store, Bob Edwards swears he's stealing." She points to the man on the left.

"Should we help Grace?"

"Nope." Hadley motions to a man running down the sidewalk in front of the flower shop and jewelry store. "Her brother, Eli, will handle their grandfather."

Grace and her brother take their grandfather toward the park and out of sight. Mr. Edwards is still yelling at Mr. Wentworth. There must be an old feud between the two men. I highly doubt Grace's grandfather would steal anything.

My mind goes back to the incident with Bryson moments ago. Lucas and Leo got here quickly, and both men were angry.

"Did you call Lucas?"

"I did."

Leo was angry when we left the junkyard in Thorn Valley. He refused to buy the door. Bryson knows Leo won't get it. So, why did he tell me he still has it? Something's off.

"Do you know what's going on with Bryson Crane?"

"No." Hadley motions to the cleaning supplies. We start washing the window. "All I know is Lucas showed me a picture of the man and said to call if I ever saw him in town, especially if he was around you."

"Why would he do that?"

"For Leo." She gives me a small smile. "I don't know the details, but I'll find out. Now, tell me what you remember from that day in Thorn Valley. Maybe you and I can piece it together."

While we wash the windows, I tell her everything. The only thing we can piece together is the fact we both can't stand Bryson Crane. I learned rather quickly that Hadley Lunsford has a temper and one I didn't expect. The greasy mechanic would have worn his free cup of coffee if she had known just how creepy he was. I'm so ready for this day to end.

Chapter Forty-Three

Leo

*L*unchtime took forever to get here today. The Fall Festival is always busy. Something's different today. I feel it in the air. Most of the tourists and townsfolk are happy and having a great time. However, there are a few bad apples in the bunch this year. You'd think Hayden Falls was having a Black Friday Sale, and everything was five dollars.

I head straight to the diner the moment my watch hits noon. The crazy festival goers can be someone else's problem for an hour. Kyleigh is helping Grace at the bookstore again this weekend. They called their lunch orders in. I had Miss Cora add them to my bill. Surprisingly, I walk into the diner and find my little brother waiting for an order, too.

"You picking up lunch for the Station?" I see the names on the bags Miss Cora's setting on the counter. He's not here for the Fire Department.

"No. Katie saw me on the sidewalk and asked if I'd pick up the order she called in. She has the baby at the flower shop." Levi's off duty today. He's not hanging around the flower shop because Katie has her newborn son with her. I've seen who's helping out at Petals today.

"Did Luke take the engine out to the party field?"

Levi and Luke work the same shift. Luke's working today since he was suspended last weekend.

"No." Levi shakes his head. He narrows his eyes until the left one is almost closed. "But the Chief's letting him come up to the square to make an announcement."

Okay. That can't be good. I'm sure my expression looks as pained as Levi's.

"What kind of announcement?"

Levi shrugs. "He said to tell you to be in the square at twelve-thirty."

Levi and I stare at each other for a moment. How does he not know what our brother is up to? Oh, this is beyond bad. Luke has never made an announcement in the square. Sure, he was loud during his partying days, but Luke's rarely serious. Dating Riley changed him. Levi and I gasp and snap our heads toward each other. Oh, man. Maybe our brother's announcement is a good thing.

"Here you go, boys." Miss Cora slides two boxes filled with to-go bags across the counter.

Levi and I pay and leave her a nice tip. Miss Cora is the best server in our little town. I have less orders, so I get the door. Levi's name is on one of the bags. Little brother is having lunch with his girl. Hopefully, someday, he'll take a bold step and turn moments like this into more than friends hanging out with friends.

The center of the square and the sidewalks are buzzing with activity. I nod toward the street behind the bookstore. We'll have to take the long way around. Well, Levi will. My stop is around the corner.

The park is full of families having picnic lunches. The community football game is this afternoon. This will be the first year one of us won't be playing in the game. The Fire Department is grilling hamburgers and hotdogs. Luke roped Riley into helping him sell the plates. Levi and I chuckle and shake our heads.

"Guess I'll see you in about twenty minutes."

Levi looks over his shoulder at his twin. "Yeah. We'll never live it down if we don't show up."

He hurries away when we get to the back door of Page Turners. He can use this street and the one behind the jewelry store to get to Petals faster. I call Kyleigh to let me in. Grace needs to have a doorbell or buzzer installed back here.

"What's going on?" Kyleigh leads the way to the small breakroom.

I slightly lift the box. "Lunch."

"No, silly." She playfully swats my arm.

"Hey, Mrs. Wentworth."

"Hello, young man. I'll take that." Grace's grandmother is running the register today. She reaches into the box and takes her bag.

"You're not joining us?"

"No. I'll watch the store while you and the girls eat."

Three high school girls are helping customers and playing games with the kids. Their orders are in the box, too. Mrs. Wentworth won't be alone out here. I nod and step into the breakroom.

"What's up, Leo?" Grace tosses her hands in the air.

Whoa. A hungry Grace Wentworth is scary. I quickly set the box on the table and slide it toward her.

"Sorry. I didn't mean to keep you waiting."

"It's not that." Kyleigh gets us a soda from the fridge. "We got texts saying Luke needs everyone in the square during lunch."

"Levi just told me Luke's making an announcement."

Grace picks up a fry and points it at me. "Now that's scary."

She's not wrong. Still, we quickly eat our sandwiches and head out to the sidewalk. Luke didn't say we had to be in the center of the square. Besides, he knows the business owners and employees need to stay close to their stores.

Kyleigh's parents join us. I glance around for my family. Levi's on the sidewalk outside Petals with Bailey, Ally, and Sammie. Miles and Katie are there with their families. I stopped in earlier and officially met their newest family member. The little guy already looks like Miles.

Lucas is outside the coffee shop with Hadley and the rest of our family. Even both sets of our grandparents are here. Yeah. This is going to be a big announcement.

Luke's on stage holding Riley's hand. She looks happy. Maybe she's expecting this. Our friends and family look confused. Quinn Martin hands my brother the microphone. Okay. Here we go. Hopefully, Luke won't screw this up.

"Hello, Hayden Falls," Luke shouts. It's not necessary. He has a microphone. "Can I have your attention?"

Most of the people in the square stop. The tourists slow their pace and look toward the stage. Hushed whispers are going around our townsfolk. The gossipers have their phones out recording. That's not necessary either. Megan Sanders in front and center.

"Thank you all for coming. We hope you're enjoying yourselves. I asked my family, friends, and the wonderful citizens of Hayden Falls to be here because I have a couple of announcements."

A couple? Oh, dear. Now, I'm worried. A quick glance at Lucas and Levi confirms they're concerned, too.

"The Fall Festival is my favorite town celebration. At last year's festival, I tried to sell Rocky a hamburger plate." Luke looks at Riley and grins. "Since then, she's become the most important person in my life."

Riley looks around nervously. My heart goes out to her. She wasn't expecting this after all. There's a tarp in front of the stage. Elliott Matthews and Chase Maxwell stand on the sides. Luke holds his hand behind his back. Chloe Hamilton rushes up and slips a bouquet of roses into his hand. She joins Chase and Elliott.

Luke offers the roses to Riley. She looks around again and slightly shakes her head. Oh, no. That's not good. Luke's about to get his heart broken in front of the whole town. Riley loves him. Everyone can see it. Sadly, for Luke, it doesn't look like she's ready for this step. Still, she takes the roses and continues to glance around the crowd. Luke pulls a ring from his pocket and kneels in front of Riley. I look at Levi and motion to the stage. Somebody needs to stop this. Luke would take it better if it were his twin. Levi shakes his head.

Mom and our grandmothers are wiping tears from their eyes. This is going to be a disaster.

Luke gently tugs on her hand. "No. No. Rocky. Stop looking at everybody else. Look me in the eye and let everything else fall away. It's just you and me."

Riley does as he asks. Surprisingly, she smiles, and her nerves settle. As weird as they are, these two calm each other.

"I love everything about you, from our water gun fights and movie nights on the couch to watching you sleep. A year ago, you wouldn't buy my hamburger plate. Today, I'm hoping and praying you'll accept this ring and do me the honor of being my wife. What do you say, Rocky? You wanna throw stones with me for the rest of my life?"

It's the weirdest proposal I've ever heard. Riley closes her eyes and covers her mouth with her other hand. She's crying, along with half the women here. Kyleigh snuggles into my side. I tighten my arm around her and wait to see if my brother's heart gets ripped out. Riley drops her hand. Her smile almost splits her face. This might not be the disaster I thought it would be.

Riley nods. "Of course I will."

Relief washes over me and my other two brothers. The entire square erupts in cheers as Luke slips the rings on Riley's finger. He stands and twirls her around. The tarp is removed, and balloons rise into the sky. My family just officially gained a new member.

"Okay. Okay." Luke gets everyone's attention again. "Thank you for sharing this moment with us." He gives Riley a quick kiss. Luke's mischievous grin concerns me. "Now for the second announcement. Well, it's more like an event."

Riley's grin matches Luke's. That's not a good sign. They glance up for a moment. I follow their gaze to the wire above their heads. What in the world? Why has no one noticed this until now? I follow the wire to the roof of Petals Florist. Pit's standing there. Pit? Oh no. I quickly snap my head to the roof above Sweet Treats. Sure enough, Four is there holding a pig wearing a harness.

"Luke! No! Don't do it!"

My brother ignores my shouts and raises his hand to the roof above Sweet Treats. I miss everything he's saying, but he has the entire crowd looking at Four.

"It's time for a phenomenal moment in history!" Luke shouts.

Half the crowd gasps as Four attaches the pig's harness to the wire. Everyone else is laughing. Kids bounce up and down with excitement. No. They don't need to encourage Luke's madness. Lucas runs to the middle of the street and shouts at Four. Luke nor Four listens to either of us. On Luke's signal, Four gives the pig a hard shove. All we can do is watch as the squealing little pig zooms across the middle of the square to Pit. He unhooks the poor pig and disappears. I'm going to hurt my brother.

"There you go, Mrs. Green!" Luke shouts before handing the microphone back to a stunned Quinn Martin. That'll teach our future Mayor to let Luke make announcements.

Kyleigh and her mother gasp. I don't wait or apologize for my brother. I leave them on the sidewalk and push through the crowd to catch Luke as he leaves the stage. Lucas gets to him at the same time.

I grab Luke's arm and pull him away from Riley. "You're insane!"

"Nah. That was epic." Luke grins. "Now, your girl and her mom will stay."

I slap my hand to my forehead. He's beyond crazy. He can't honestly believe that seeing a pig zoom across the square will keep Kyleigh's mother in Hayden Falls.

"I'm arresting you!"

"For what?" Luke looks as though I slapped him.

I point to the wire above our heads without looking up. "That had to be animal cruelty."

Luke tosses his arm toward Colton Maxwell. "The pig's fine."

Colton and Graham are doubled over laughing. It takes both of them to hang onto the pig. They were in on this little stunt. Lucas goes over and scolds his friend while Aiden gets his brother.

Colton finally composes himself and walks over to us with the pig. "Don't worry, Leo. The pig's fine."

"See? No pigs were harmed in the making of this historical event." Luke scratches the pig's head. "Take *Dumbo* home and give him some treats."

Dumbo? I shake my head. If that's not the pig's name, it is now. Who names a pig anyway?

"Will do." Colton tucks the pig under his arm and walks away like nothing happened. This whole thing is crazy. Colton Maxwell is grumpy. He doesn't laugh or play pranks.

"*Dumbo* is an elephant. *Wilbur* is the pig." I really want to hurt my brother. He's crazy. Yet, I'm the one referencing cartoons.

"Yeah, but that pig didn't fly." Luke slaps his hand against my shoulder. "See ya, bro. Rocky and I are going to go celebrate our engagement."

Lucas stands next to me, glaring holes into Luke's back as he walks away. Neither of us knows what to say. This was one of the craziest moments I've ever seen, and our little brother planned it. Lucas nods toward the bookstore.

How am I supposed to face Kyleigh and her parents after this? I take a deep breath and prepare to meet their angry faces. Instead, I look over to find Kyleigh, her mom, and Grace huddled together in a fit of laughter. Chief Deputy Green is as stunned as I am, but the women are happy. Maybe this wasn't so bad. Finally, Lucas and I give in and burst out laughing with everyone else. One thing's for sure. Our townsfolk will be talking about this day for generations.

Chapter Forty-Four

Leo

The Fall Festival was an event-filled day, and I don't mean just the scheduled events with happy participants or my brother's craziness. The booths and stores around town had games and prizes all day. The stage was busy from the moment Mayor Martin gave his speech at ten this morning until Jake Campbell's Band closed things out at eight. Luke's proposal and the flying pig were the highlight of the day.

Every deputy on the force worked today at some point. Even though our shifts ended in the middle of the afternoon, Lucas and I stayed in town until the stores closed at six. Naturally, Lucas stayed close to the coffee shop while I kept an eye on the bookstore. I don't want Kyleigh too far from me with Bryson Crane and her ex showing up in town.

The Iron Rebels had the department on edge today. They rode through town twice. Thankfully, they didn't stop. Somehow, they managed to bail their little friend, Dawg, out. My nerves settled a little when Aaron reported the gang was all present and accounted for at Pete's Saloon. Let's hope Willows Bend doesn't need backup tonight.

Cowboys and O'Brien's Tavern have kept us busy from the time they opened. I don't know what's going on today. Nearly every call we got was to break up fights or disagreements. It's like the argument at Mountainside Hardware store on Thursday set the mood for the whole weekend.

"Everything okay?" I don't like the worry lines on my brother's face.

Lucas is sitting next to me outside his tent, like always. He's listening to his radio at the calls coming into the Station tonight. If our second-shift guys need backup, we'll have to go.

"Aiden and Spencer are arresting two more, but they're good." Lucas pops the top on a soda. We're on call, so we aren't drinking.

Aiden and Spencer are working a twelve-hour shift today from noon until midnight. This makes six they've arrested. If they arrest any more during their last two hours, they'll be doing paperwork way past midnight.

Kyleigh goes to the coolers and comes back with three drinks. She hands me a soda and sits down on my right. I lean over and give her a quick kiss. I love how comfortable she's becoming with everyone, especially with me. She smiles and resumes her conversation with Hannah. She and Hannah are drinking strawberry-flavored water.

Jasper and Hannah's tent is on my right in Spencer's usual spot. I'm glad they're here tonight because Grace couldn't join us this weekend.

There's a baby boom going on in Hayden Falls. Kennedy and Tara announced their pregnancies about two months ago. Jasper and Hannah made their baby announcement today during the festival. Their daughter, Bently, is super excited. It's surprising she's not here tonight.

The biggest, unexpected announcement today came from E Maxwell. She was going to tell Aiden tomorrow on his day off. Morning sickness hit her hard this afternoon. I don't know why it's called morning sickness. From what I hear, it can happen at any time of the day. Spoiling her surprise a day early was the only way E could stop Aiden from taking her to the Emergency Room.

"Hey, man." Wade pulls a chair up in front of me. He got here about an hour ago. He wasn't planning on camping with us this weekend. When he showed up with his tent bag, Lucas and I helped him assemble it. "My dad and grandma wanted me to ask if you plan on hunting this week."

"Your grandmother doesn't need to be hunting," Lucas mumbles.

"Hey." Hadley gives Lucas a playful shove. At least, I think it's playful.

"She hasn't shot anybody lately." Wade snickers.

"Did you have any luck this week?" Jasper asks.

I shrug and drop my eyes. I've given Dad updates on the wild dog or whatever it is. I've been working closely with the forest rangers since last fall. We don't know a lot about the animal. I've suggested several times that we need to let the public know what little we do know and ask them to remain alert. I've no idea why the press conference hasn't been scheduled yet.

"Are you guys ever going to find it?" I'm not sure if Hannah is asking me or the group as a whole. Every man here and a few of the women have joined the hunting party at some point.

"I thought you'd have it by now. You're the best tracker in the county." Wade takes a sip of his beer.

"That obviously isn't true." Phillip Crawford's eyes lock with mine across the firepit.

"Leo *is* the best," Lucas insists.

"If a crazy old mountain man and a wild dog can stump him, he's not." Phillip has a right to be angry. I don't hold it against him.

"Phillip," his wife, Tara, scolds.

"No, Farm Girl." Phillip's eyes never leave mine. "So, what's the problem, Barnes? Why can't you track this thing?"

"I have tracked it."

Phillip narrows his eyes and slightly tilts his head. "So you know where it is?"

Every eye in the camp turns toward me, causing me to shift in my chair. The forest rangers asked me to let them inform the public. Phillip isn't going to wait for a press conference.

"Not exactly."

"What *exactly* do you know?" Phillip demands.

"Phillip, you need to calm down." Lucas sits up straight, going into cop mode.

"No." Phillip jumps to his feet and points at me. "If he knows where it is, we can finally kill this thing."

"It's not that simple." I hold my hands out as a peace offering. It doesn't help.

"It is. It attacked my son and Peyton. If you've seen it, why didn't you shoot it?"

Tara stands and places her hand on his arm. "Phillip, please."

I'm on my feet now, too. "Because I don't know which one attacked your children."

Everyone freezes for a moment and looks around at each other. Phillip and I never drop eye contact. My temper settles when Kyleigh snuggles into my side. I take a deep breath and wrap an arm around her, pulling her closer. She grounds me in ways I can't explain.

Kennedy Reed Bailey steps forward. "There's more than one?"

I nod. Hopefully, what they learn tonight doesn't send half the town into a panic. People with no business handling a firearm will be out hunting if this gets out.

"Are you sure? You and several others have thought so." Lucas is standing next to me. I nod again.

"How many?" Phillip demands.

I shake my head. "I don't know exactly."

"What *exactly* do you know?" Phillip asks again. He takes several deep breaths.

I'm not trying to make him or anyone else angry. I look around the campsite. The people here are my friends and family. They deserve to know what's going on. They have a right to protect their families. I no longer care what the forest rangers want. They should have already made an announcement.

"I don't know how many are out there because they're not all black. We can't prove anything yet. We need to catch one first, and that's easier said than done."

"I don't want to catch it. I want to kill it," Phillip snaps.

"The one that attacked your children should be put down. The others are skittish and stay closer to the mountains. The forest rangers want to study them. We don't have scientific proof, but I think they're part coyote."

"That would make sense. There's lots of coyotes around here." Wade leans back in his chair.

Tara manages to get Phillip to sit back down. The tension around the campsite eases.

Jasper leans forward, resting his forearms on his knees. "How many do you estimate are out there?"

"I've spotted three black ones and approximately another seven brown and tan ones."

"There's a pack of them?" Kyleigh slides her chair closer and nuzzles into my side. I'm not trying to scare her.

"No. Coyotes aren't social animals. They don't form packs. Their family groups are called bands. I've located five bands around the county and just outside. I believe Buck belongs to one of them. Every time he's been spotted, his trail blends into one of the bands. I haven't found their den yet. They keep moving. If they'd settle down, we'd already have him."

"If these animals are a threat, surely the forest rangers will let us hunt them." Wade doesn't go out with the hunting party often.

Since his grandmother and sister shot Four, Wade's been going with us more, so those two don't. Well, Hadley's done with hunting. Once was enough for her. Their Grandmother, Nancy, refuses to sit on the sidelines.

"When's the press conference?" Lucas asked.

"They'll let Dad know when they're ready. For now, we treat them like coyotes. If they're stalking around our homes or animals, shoot them. The only one that appears to be a threat is Buck." My eyes lock with Phillip's again.

"Why just him?" Phillip is ready to kill them all.

"Because Mags found him dying as a pup and saved him. Buck's the only one that's used to being around people." It's the only useful information Dad and I got from Mags. It explains why Buck is loyal to the old man.

I don't tell them Mags is helping Buck. Everyone thinks he is. They just don't know how much Mags is trying to help him. I've spotted where the lone animal tracks break off from the band. It meets up with a human, and the animal tracks disappear. Mags is carrying Buck. He uses the roads, rivers, and even the lake to try and hide Buck's trail. Levi and I found his little boat hidden in a small bend near his cabin. Mags is getting sloppy and desperate in his attempt to help Buck. It won't last forever.

"Is the one on my brother's cameras Buck?" Sammie Foster asks.

"Yes. He's the only one that roams on his own for long periods of time." I meet Phillip's eyes again. "Keep doing what you're doing. From the tracks I've seen, you and Aaron have gotten close a couple of times."

"Thanks." Phillip nods once. "Good to know."

Those two will more than likely be the ones to cross Buck's path first. Phillip will shoot whether Mags is there or not. Hopefully, Mags won't sacrifice himself to save Buck. We don't need another hunting accident on our hands.

"You want to go for a walk?" Kyleigh asks.

"Yeah." I stand and pull her up with me.

She looks around nervously. "You've got your gun, right?"

Several of us laugh.

"Yeah, Slugger. Give me a second."

After I get my handgun from the tent and slide it into the back of my jeans, under my shirt, I wrap an arm around her and head toward the path. While she goes to the restroom, I can survey the party field. Thank goodness there's been no fighting out here tonight.

"Are we working on Darlin this week?"

"Yes, ma'am. We sure are." I kiss the top of her head and tighten my arm around her.

I'll make sure we work on my truck at least one day every week. Let's just say I wasn't happy when I found out about the little stipulation the judge added to her community service. Dad didn't know all the details until Judge Morgan called him. This has to be what she meant about the judge adding things. Not to worry. I'll make sure she never has to do community service with the old mountain man again.

Chapter Forty-Five

Kyleigh

As hectic and weird as my life has become, I'm starting to settle into a routine. The people here are growing on me. Grace and Hannah have become my best friends. Zoe is the only one of my childhood friends who tries to talk to me. However, her shifts at the hospital haven't allowed time for us to hang out.

Dance class is my favorite weekly activity. Well, outside of working with Leo on his truck. Since he's working day shift again, we get at least an hour in each day. Lucas helped him install the new door yesterday. Their grandfather was extremely happy. He's already planning another trip to the bar with Leo when Darlin is ready.

Leo doesn't let me do any of the hard work. It's okay. I just like being around him. Right now, my job consists of sanding the fenders. I can't wait to see Darlin repainted all blue.

Dance class isn't my happy place tonight. I'm trying to pretend everything is okay. Maybe it is, and I'm stressing for no reason. Leo's here and was my dance partner tonight. That's always great. It was a little hard to relax and enjoy myself with my Alien Parents here. I was shocked when they walked in. Neither mentioned anything today about joining the class tonight.

My parents are a mystery to me. They hugged me when they arrived and acted like being here was a normal thing. When class was over, they hugged me again and hurried to Cowboys to meet up with their friends. I have no idea who they're meeting. My parents haven't mentioned having friends until tonight. It probably has something to do with the invasion that's about to happen.

As always, after class, we have snacks in the breakroom. As always, it's never just snacks. We have a buffet of food on the counter.

"Any luck finding a job?" Grace brings Hannah and me a slice of cake. Well, Hannah has a couple of slices, different flavors of course.

"Not yet." I sigh deeply. Job hunting is so tiring.

As much as I hate doing it, I'll have to apply at Crawford Bank and the banks in Walsburg. The financial companies I applied to in Missoula aren't hiring at the moment.

"A job?" Hannah perks up and abandons her cake. "You're staying?"

"Looks that way." I lightly laugh.

"This is great." Hannah's about to bounce out of her chair. "I was hoping you'd fall in love with our little town."

"If not the town, one of our deputies for sure," Grace teases.

The three of us glance across the room to where Leo and Jasper are talking with Lucas, Hadley, and Wade. It's true. I'm falling for Leo. Is he reason enough to stay here? My mom left for unknown reasons. This town wasn't enough for her at one point. I don't want the same thing to happen to me.

"Your parents seem to be getting back together." Hannah takes the last bite of cake and pushes the empty dessert plate away. She's ready for girl talk.

"I have no idea what's going on with them." At some point, my parents and I will need to have a serious conversation. It's not fun feeling like I'm on another planet. "And I'm not sure where I stand with Leo."

"You two appear to be getting closer." Hannah bites her fingernail.

My eyes meet Leo's across the room. We both smile. I didn't mean to fall for another man so soon after my relationship with Scott ended. Meeting Leo didn't start out great. However, getting close to him was easy. He's not at all what I expected. When he arrested me, I thought he was cruel and hateful. Turns out, he's really sweet and caring.

"He hasn't asked for anything more than friendship and casual dating." I shrug. "He hasn't asked me to stay."

Sounding like a whiny teenager is pathetic. I'm a grown woman. I need to get my life together. The hard conversation with my parents needs to happen whether I'm ready or not. I need to make some plans and set some goals. If Mom stays here, I'll have to return to Seattle alone. Is that something I want to do? I've never been without my mom. I'm not dependent on her. I just don't want to be far from her. After being with Dad for two months, I don't want to be far from him anymore, either.

"I don't think Leo is the type to ask you to stay." Grace looks over her shoulder to the guys and back to me. "You're going to have to make the first big move."

"What? Me?" My mouth drops open for a moment. "I've never done that."

"Look." Hannah puts her hand on mine. "Hayden Falls is a small town. You'll never find all the conveniences you had in Seattle here. If you make this move permanently, it needs to because you want it."

"You did it," Grace points out.

"I did, and I'm beyond happy. I love my husband. Our daughter is amazing. We have a baby on the way, and I love my job." Hannah sighs and looks me in the eye. "But my time here didn't start out great. Everything went wrong at nearly every turn. I had lots of obstacles to overcome. Jasper couldn't stand me at first. We got through all that, and I don't regret giving up my old life in Cheyenne for a minute."

Wow. Her story sounds so much like mine. If Hannah can overcome all her obstacles, maybe I can too. I don't have a home or a job in Seattle anymore. I'm not sure what my mom's situation is. I have four months left of probation. Maybe I should start looking at this little town as a place to live forever rather than one I'm leaving.

"I want you to stay, but Hannah's right. If you stay, it needs to be what you want." Grace's sad expression breaks my heart. I don't want to lose my friendship with her no matter what I decide.

"I'm not against staying." I smile, hoping she will, too. "I'll have to figure a few things out if I do."

"Really?" Grace's eyes light up. There's my happy friend. I nod.

"Well, if a job is one of those things, I might be able to help you out." Hannah props her elbow on the table and rests her chin in her hand. Her little grin gets my hopes up. I don't know what she thinks I can do for her.

"I can't dance," I tease.

"No, silly." Hannah lightly taps my upper arm. "You work in finances, right?" I nod. "Well, Jasper's parents have their own business. With the baby on the way, they want to be more hands-on as grandparents. They've been talking about hiring someone. It'll be part-time at first. If it's okay with you, I'll tell them you're interested."

Hannah spends the next fifteen minutes telling me about Ramsey's Financial Service. Jasper's parents handle the business portfolios for most of the stores in Hayden Falls and a few in Willows Bend and Walsburg. They also do individual taxes during tax season. This will be a smaller scale than Hillsworth Financial, but it's basically the same job. This is right up my alley.

Before we left the gym, Hannah handed me a business card with an appointment time written on the back. She went to Jasper's office and called his parents. They want to meet with me on Monday here at the gym. This is so amazing. For once, I feel like something is going my way.

Leo reaches across the console and takes my hand in his. Riding in his Camaro is nice. I can't wait to ride with him in his truck. He smiles and lifts my hand to his lips. Every kiss he gives me moves him deeper into my heart. I would stay in this little town for him. But I believe Grace is right. Leo won't ask me to stay just for him. Who knows. Maybe after finding a job and having a serious conversation with my parents, I just might take a huge, bold step with this man.

Chapter Forty-Six

Kyleigh

Things are finally looking up for me. Jasper's parents are the sweetest couple I've ever met in the world of finance. Yes, I've met several husband and wife teams. One, if not both, were rude and strictly business. Oh, they do their jobs exceptionally well. However, talking with them will give you a headache.

Mr. and Mrs. Ramsey are completely devoted to Jasper and his family. They're over the moon about being grandparents again. They weren't there when Bently was born. What the little girl's mother did to Jasper and their daughter makes me so angry. If I were still in Washington State, I'd travel to Tacoma and give the woman a piece of my mind.

Jasper's parents aren't missing a minute of Hannah's pregnancy. Trust me. Hannah's grandmother isn't missing a minute either. Mrs. Cunningham was at the gym today to check on Hannah. I love their little family. Their family quickly became a part of mine. They insisted I'm more than just an employee. Yep. I got the job.

Ramsey Financial is well-established in the area. Mr. and Mrs. Ramsey started their company after college. They've been in business for over twenty years. I was impressed with their long list of clients. I thought they were picking up individual taxes at the beginning of the year to fill a slow period and to keep their company afloat. That's not the case. Well, maybe it was in the beginning. They do it now to help out their friends and family.

Their business is based out of their home. Jasper is giving them one of the spare offices at the gym, so I won't have to drive outside of town every day to work. I like this idea. I'll get to see Hannah and little Bently almost every day now. I can't wait to tell Leo. I texted him to let him know I would see him for dinner tonight.

Today is Dad's day off. Surprisingly, his truck is in the driveway. He's usually helping out around the community when he's not working. This is great. I can tell my parents at the same time about my new job.

I rush in the front door and head straight to the kitchen. It's really weird my mom spends so much time in the kitchen. She didn't do this in Seattle. I had no idea she was such a good cook.

"Mom. Dad."

I freeze in the doorway. The aliens impersonating my parents are standing in front of the stove in each other's arms. I'm definitely not on Earth anymore.

"Kyleigh." Dad just grins and walks over to the table.

"Sit down, Sweetie. Lunch is ready." Mom moves three bowls of Teriyaki Chicken and salads to the table.

"You look happy. Did you get the job?" Dad casually takes a sip of sweet tea.

"Yeah." I slowly look between my parents. They're acting like they weren't just caught hugging intimately. "What's going on between you two?"

Mom blushes and drops her eyes. "We've been talking."

"Talking?" Oh, they're doing more than talking. "Are you two getting back together? Are we not going back to Seattle?"

Dad's face goes slack. "You want to leave?"

Now, I'm officially the worst daughter on the planet. My dad looks so heartbroken. I don't know why I brought Seattle up. I'm not sure I want to go back anymore. But Mom concerns me. She's left this little town once already.

"I'm sorry, Dad. I don't understand what's going on. I'm just confused."

"That's understandable. We haven't been upfront with you." Dad rubs his chin and looks at Mom.

"Are you getting married again?"

Well, Sweetie." Mom takes a deep breath and straightens her shoulders. "We never got divorced."

I almost choke on air. Is she serious? "How's that possible?"

"We had an argument. You and I went to my friends in Seattle. No paperwork was ever filed." Mom bites her fingernail.

That doesn't explain much. Oh, I'll need a lot more information before I believe she's serious about staying here.

"What could you fight about that took us away for fifteen years?"

"Um." Mom quickly stands and grabs the tea pitcher to refill our almost full glasses. "I got a job, too."

Oh, no, no, no. She does not get to change the subject. I'm glad she found a job, but this mystery between my parents needs to be solved.

"Mom."

"Kendra." Dad gently grabs her wrist before she can walk away. "She deserves to know."

"Fine." Mom sets the pitcher on the table and drops her head back for a moment. "I thought your dad cheated on me."

"Dad?"

He holds his hands up and shakes his head. "No. I didn't."

Mom presses her lips together and returns to her chair. She looks everywhere but at me while she gets herself together. She's never liked admitting when she's wrong. Guess I need to talk her through this.

"Why did you believe that?"

Mom looks at Dad. He nods.

"He came home a few times smelling like alcohol and perfume. People talk. The night before we left, he came home like that and had lipstick on his cheek."

Okay. I'll have to read between the lines a little. I get the alcohol, perfume, and lipstick. Dad's going to have to explain how those happened. But people talk? Oh, good gracious. She means gossip. Please tell me she didn't fall for gossip. This town didn't have an online blog back then, but word of mouth has always been a thing here. Well, at least she finally admitted it.

"Dad, do you want to explain?"

"There was a lady who lived here for a couple of years. Summer McKay." He pauses and rubs the bridge of his nose. "I've no idea what sent her over the edge. She was drunk more than sober. Nearly every weekend, we had to pick her up at one of the bars. The Sheriff had us take her home or hold her in a cell overnight so she could sleep it off. She usually threw herself at the deputies who showed up.

"A few times, she spilled beer on us while we were trying to take the bottles from her. Her cheap perfume was so strong I swore she wore the whole bottle. She probably tried kissing every deputy on the force, including the Sheriff. And like your mom said, people talk."

I lean back and take a moment to process all of that. As crazy as this little town is, I can picture everything happening. And yep. Gossip played a role in my parent's separation.

I cross my arms and turn to Mom. "Why would you take fifteen years to talk this out?"

Mom huffs and looks away. "Because I'm stubborn and hardheaded."

At least she has the decency to admit that, too. Facing the truth has never been one of her strong suits. I glance at Dad. His eyes focus on Mom. I cover his hand with mine and shake my head when he starts to stand. He wants to comfort her, but Mom needs to get all this out. It'll come back to haunt us if she doesn't.

"Still, fifteen years is a long time." I push for more. Hey. It's for her own good.

"You're right. It was." She lifts her eyes to Dad. "The first couple of years, I was mad. It was easy to believe I was right. Then, I got the job at the lab. I used it and the amount of money I was making as an excuse to stay away. By that point, it was easier to believe the lie than to admit I was wrong. Over time, I figured things were too far gone to try fixing it. I'm sorry."

"And you're fixing things now?" I look between my parents. They nod. I take Mom's hand and squeeze tightly. "Are you sure this is where you want to live?"

A tear slides from her eye. "We should've never left."

Dad waits no longer. He rounds the table and pulls Mom into his arms. Wow. Things are seriously going to change for us now. It's been fifteen years. I've forgotten what it's like to have my parents together.

I stand and wrap my arms around them. They pull me into their hug. I sigh and lean into them. This feels amazing. It's different, though, and I'm loving different right now. I lay my cheek against Dad's chest and look at Mom.

"You can't leave him again."

It would be wrong for her to offer him a chance at being a family again and take it away if she changed her mind later. She needs to be sure this is what she wants.

Mom smiles up at Dad. "I won't. And we kind of have to stay since pigs do fly."

Dad rolls his eyes and growls. Mom and I laugh. Dumbo's trip across the square is the talk of the town. Only the people camping with us during Labor Day weekend know the true meaning behind it.

"I'm getting a shower." I kiss their cheeks and go to my room.

They're falling in love again. They need some time alone. I'm happy for them. I'm just not ready to witness their intimate moments. From the look in their eyes, I'll have to get over that soon. Well, this confirms Mom's not going back to Seattle, and I don't want to go back alone.

Chapter Forty-Seven

Leo

*I*t takes almost two weeks for things to fall back into a normal routine for my family. People called, texted, and stopped us in town to talk about Luke. It got to the point where we avoided going into town unless it was absolutely necessary. Being congratulated on Luke and Riley's engagement was fine. None of us want to talk about the pig anymore. Once again, our discomfort is Luke's fault.

Our Sunday family dinner this week turned into an engagement party. No one knew Luke was going to propose. Mom insisted we celebrate. Thank goodness it's still warm enough to have the party in the backyard. Our parents' house is big, but it won't hold this many people.

Both sets of our grandparents are here, plus several of our cousins. Since Hadley's dating Lucas, her family is here too. Kyleigh and her parents arrived an hour ago. She and I aren't officially dating—yet. I plan to fix that little issue tomorrow.

Riley looks after her aunt and uncle in their family's farmhouse on the other side of the lake. Mr. and Mrs. Anderson aren't sick. They moved back to Hayden Falls earlier this year. Their son feels better having another family member under the same roof. Surprisingly, Ian Anderson is here today. His family in North Carolina didn't come with him, though. Riley's brother and sister from Arizona are visiting for a week. As happy as Riley looks today, I wish her entire family would move back to town.

We're using the outdoor party area Levi built for Mom. We've all helped at some point, but Levi's done most of the work. There are swings, tables, patio furniture, an outdoor grilling area, and a small gazebo. Lights are strung all around. If Levi stops being a firefighter, he can go into woodworking without a problem.

This is Mom's favorite place to relax. During the Summer, we usually find her and Grandma out here when they aren't cooking. The amount of time Mom spends out here has Dad talking about building a small sunroom on the house so she can have a place similar to this during the winter. Levi will probably help with that, too.

Levi, being the baby of the family, does everything he can for Mom. He adds anything to her special oasis he thinks will make her happy. The raised flower beds and planters are new and add a nice touch. He's already building the trellises for the grapevines I mentioned to Mom. She loved the idea of having her own little vineyard. The wooden structures are about twenty yards from the party area. Granddad and I check them out while Kyleigh's listening to Riley's wedding plans.

Deputy Green joins us and offers Granddad a glass of lemonade. "Your wife said to give you this."

"Ah. Yes." Granddad takes a sip as he walks around the five trellises. He's looking forward to having fresh grapes.

Deputy Green turns to face me. "You wanted to see me?"

"Yeah. I wanted to talk with you tomorrow." I called him this morning and set the appointment up.

"We're here now. You don't have to wait." He crosses his arms. "Unless it's police work."

"It's not." I glance at Granddad. He's pretending not to listen.

"Well, then. No need to wait."

"I'm supposed to come to you, not a meeting of convenience." I glance toward the party.

"Leo, if you're embarrassed to ask, then my answer is already no."
He's stern but not rude. He's probably figured out my reason for seeing
him.

I'm not embarrassed. I was, however, hoping to talk with my
grandfather tonight. He's not as hard on Kyleigh as he was in the
beginning. There's still some tension between them, though. I don't
want to hurt my grandfather. But I can't ignore my feelings for Kyleigh
anymore.

I straighten my shoulders and look Deputy Green in the eye. "I want
to ask for your permission to date your daughter."

"Permission?" He raises his eyebrows. "I thought you were already
dating Kyleigh."

"Not officially." It hurts to say those words. I should have already
made my intentions known.

"And you want to ask her to be your girlfriend?"

"I do, and with your blessing."

He glances at Kyleigh. She's laughing with my family. Seeing her
happy and carefree causes both of us to smile.

"You're not asking to marry her?"

I cough and clear my throat. "Not today."

It's true. Love is in the air in our little town. People are getting
engaged, and babies are being born. I've finally stopped fighting my
feelings and admitted to myself and to Lucas on our back deck late one
night just how much I love Kyleigh. I'm a little nervous today. This is
the first time I've asked a father permission to date his daughter.
Kyleigh and I aren't anywhere close to marriage, though.

"Relax, Leo." Deputy Green's hand clamps down on my shoulder.
"I know you care about Kyleigh. She cares about you, too. I appreciate
you asking like this. It's a bit old-fashioned."

"She's special, and it's what a man's supposed to do." I haven't
dated a lot. Hardly ever, in fact. Still, my parents raised us to be
gentlemen.

"She is special." He takes a deep breath and meets my eyes again.
"Thank you for respecting her, but I can't give you my blessing today."

"What?" I can barely get the word out.

"My daughter is one of the most important women in my life, right next to her mother. I know you love Kyleigh. It pains me to see her hurt, but I can't give you my blessing today." He nods toward my grandfather. "When things are settled with him, you'll have it."

I look between Granddad and Deputy Green. "He's not mad at her anymore."

"That's not what I mean." He walks to the closest trellis. "You had a right to be angry. What Kyleigh and her friends did was wrong, no matter what their reason was. I'll never condone what they did. They should be held accountable and pay for it.

"It wasn't Kyleigh's idea, but she took the blame. She's paying for it, and not just financially. She's lost a lot because of this. Some of it, I'm glad she lost. I'm beyond thrilled she's living in my home again and not the city. She was wrong. She's apologized and has worked hard to earn your forgiveness. But what you did was wrong, too. Two wrongs don't make a right, Sheldon. You know that. I know that truck means a lot to you. I promise you, my daughter means a lot more. If she cries one more tear because of this, the damage the bat did will be nothing. I'll burn your truck to the ground. Fix it."

Deputy Green may have kept his voice calm yet stern, but his body shakes with anger. No one has ever talked to my grandfather that way. Well, not in front of me, anyway. Al spins on his heels and storms off before I gain enough senses to speak. What was that about? I slowly turn to face my grandfather. He's fidgeting.

"Granddad, what did he mean?"

"Nothing." Granddad drops his eyes and shakes his head. "I'll fix it."

I walk around the trellises to stand in front of him. "Fix what? What did you do?"

"It doesn't matter. I'll fix it. I'll make the call now."

I gently grab his arm, halting him. "Granddad?"

"I promise. I'll fix it," he says again.

That's not an answer. What could he have done, and who does he need to call? I drop my head back when it finally dawns on me. Kyleigh was frantic when she said the judge kept adding things to her sentence. Granddad is friends with Judge Morgan.

"Tell me you didn't."

"I'm sorry, Leo. I didn't know you'd fall in love with her." He drops his eyes again.

I release a long breath and walk over to the closest trellis. Resting my forearms on the wooden frame, I drop my head. I want to be angry. I probably am. This is my grandfather. I'll never yell at him, no matter what he's done. Deputy Green was right. Two wrongs don't make a right.

"I'm sorry, Leo," he apologizes again.

"She is, too."

Kyleigh has apologized so many times. She's gone out of her way to be nice to my grandfather so he'll forgive her. I won't let her apologize again.

"I did ask him not to go easy on her in court, but I never asked him to add to her punishment. I'll call the judge right now."

"Thanks, Granddad." I don't look up.

"Please don't hate me." Granddad's voice cracks.

I glance over my shoulder. He has tears in his eyes. I believe him. He never meant for things to go this far. I can't watch him hurt, either. I walk over and wrap my arms around him.

"I love you. I could never hate you."

He nods and steps back. "Let me make that call now and help you get your girl."

I give him a sad smile. "Yeah. I'd appreciate it."

He and I have never been in a predicament like this. I don't know how to talk to him right now. Granddad must feel the same way. He nods again and makes a beeline for the back door.

My eyes automatically seek out Kyleigh. She's still laughing with all the women over wedding ideas. Deputy Green raises an eyebrow. Guess he watched everything with my grandfather. I nod and mouth the words *'I'm sorry.'* Al lifts his tea glass slightly before returning to his conversation with Dad and Lucas. Both look confused. I'll have to explain this to them later.

If Granddad gets through to Judge Morgan today, maybe tomorrow, I can ask Kyleigh to be mine. Somehow, I'll find a way to tell her about this, too. I won't keep it from her. Hopefully, she'll still want me.

Chapter Forty-Eight

Leo

Everyone enjoyed my brother's engagement party. Well, mostly everyone, anyway. A few of us were on edge. Thankfully, we hid it well. I wanted to pull Kyleigh aside and let her know what was happening. She was so happy. I couldn't ruin her day.

Deputy Green aimlessly joined in a few conversations. He spent most of his time watching Granddad. Neither spoke to the other for the rest of the party. My twin kept squinting his eyes at me. I shook my head at his unspoken questions. And, of course, Dad watched everybody.

What my grandfather did doesn't sit well with me. In a way, I understand it too. We all want justice when we've been wronged. Sometimes, people go too far. To me, this is one of those times.

I shove the covers back and swing my legs over the side of the bed. The clock on the nightstand says it's two in the morning. Good thing I have today off. Too many things are running through my mind to let me sleep. Tossing and turning aren't getting me anywhere. Might as well make some coffee.

I pull on a pair of sweats and a T-shirt before heading to the kitchen. Since there's no way I'll be able to go back to sleep, I make a whole pot. I'll need several pots to get through this day.

After adding cream and sugar to the biggest mug I can find, I head out to the deck. My brother and I set this area up for grilling and parties. It makes no sense. We hardly ever use it. Luke and Levi's deck and backyard have more stuff than ours. They use theirs often. Usually, Lucas and I join them.

I set my mug on the table before leaning forward and dropping my head into my hands. There's so much to figure out. It gives me a headache trying to sort it all out. Who knows? Maybe I'm overthinking everything.

The back door opens, and Lucas walks out. He sits in the chair beside me with a cup of coffee. I didn't mean to wake him. Hadley doesn't follow him out. At least I didn't disturb her. With Lucas up this early, too, we'll need a lot of coffee today.

"You wanna talk about it?"

"Yeah." I sit up and run a hand through my hair.

Honestly, I'd rather everything work itself out. It might happen in the movies. My life, however, isn't going to let me off the hook so easily. If I want peace of mind and possibly a happily ever after, I'll have to work for it. Besides, talking with my brother usually helps.

"What's going on with Granddad?" Lucas doesn't give me a chance to start.

"Hold up, bros." Luke walks up onto the deck. "We need in this conversation too."

"I'm getting coffee first." Levi rubs his hands over his face as he disappears into the house. Luke probably woke him up and dragged him out here.

Once we all have a cup of coffee and another pot is started, I tell them what happened with Granddad and Chief Deputy Green. We sit and stare at nothing for a long time. Our grandfather isn't perfect. Yet, we've never heard of him going this far.

"But it's fixed now, right?" Luke recovers first.

I nod. "He got through to Judge Morgan late this evening."

"Are you going to tell Kyleigh?" Levi takes a sip of coffee.

I slowly blow out a long breath and lean back in my chair. I've tried to think of a way around doing this. I've come up empty handed every time.

"I don't advise keeping it a secret." Lucas is speaking from experience.

Lucas' plan to keep Hadley safe at the beginning of the year was stupid. I told him so several times. It was his relationship, so I went along with his decision. His plan almost broke him and Hadley beyond repair. Seeing her pain and knowing how bad his was is why I took her to his cabin that day. Lucas' intentions were noble. Still, it caused a huge strain on his relationship with Hadley's father and brother. It's been about eight months. I still don't think Wade has completely forgiven Lucas.

"I have to tell her. Hopefully, she won't hate me," I mumble the last part.

"She won't." Levi stands with his empty cup. "Anyone need a refill?"

"Just bring the pot, little brother." Luke finishes off his coffee and sets the mug on the table.

"Kyleigh's a lot like her dad. She might not be very talkative, but she's got a good heart. She won't hold what Granddad did against you." Wish I was as sure as Lucas is.

"I love her," I say softly.

One side of Lucas' mouth lifts in a cocky grin. Luke is about to vibrate out of his chair. This fool is about to say something ridiculous.

"I thought we cleared that up a few weeks ago." Levi refills our mugs and sits back down.

I nod and drop my head back into my hands. I'm making this harder than it has to be.

"So, what's troubling you?" Lucas asks.

"If it's Kyleigh's feelings, trust me, she loves you too." Luke jumps up. "Be right back." He brings out the cream and sugar Levi forgot.

"I know she has feelings for me. Not sure I'd call it love yet, but it could be one day." I lean back in the chair, hard enough for it to bounce a little. "But will she stay? Will Hayden Falls be enough for her?"

"Will you be enough?" Levi adds. I nod again.

"Look." Luke points at me. Here comes ridiculous. "She has to stay. I ensured she would. I helped a pig fly for you."

I knew it. Sometimes, I swear he doesn't have brains in his head. Since he's a full-time firefighter, he's not as dumb as he acts.

"You had a pig zipline across the square. That's not flying."

"Tomato. Tomahto." Luke tosses his hands up. "It worked. Mrs. Green is staying. There's no way Kyleigh will go back to Seattle without her mom."

"I think Kyleigh's parents are getting back together." Levi quickly covers a yawn. Luke shouldn't have woken him up.

"They're still married." Lucas' statement sends Luke into a round of nosy questions. Kyleigh told me this the night she found out.

"See?" Luke tosses his hand toward me. "Everything is working out perfectly. You have nothing to worry about."

"Look." Lucas wraps his hand around my wrist before I can tell our little brother how much of an idiot he is. "You love Kyleigh. That's huge, Leo. You've liked a couple of girls in college." He shakes his head. "But you haven't loved until now. This is different. It's worth taking a chance. Tell Kyleigh how you feel."

Luke nods. "Lucas and I almost lost our girls by messing around. Don't be like us. Tell her and soon."

Levi and I lock eyes. He gives me a tight smile. He nods and rubs the back of his neck. Of all my brothers, he understands my situation the most. He's scared to speak up for his girl, too.

"I'm going to talk with Kyleigh later today." Hopefully, I won't choke on my words and mess this up. And bigger yet, hopefully, I won't have a broken heart in the end.

"Good." Lucas clamps his hand on my shoulder as he stands up. "You have a big day ahead of you. Let's get some sleep."

Luke and Levi pat my shoulders and say their goodbyes. Levi gives me a sympathetic look. I wish I could fix things for him.

Lucas tosses his hand up, saying goodnight, and goes to his room. There's no way I can sleep. After cleaning my brothers' mugs and starting a new pot of coffee, I settle on the couch to watch Netflix. An episode of *Supernatural* is about halfway through. Hadley obviously picked the last show she and Lucas watched. I click play but don't pay the show any attention.

Lucas was right. Today is a big day for me. Things are moving forward with my truck. With any luck, I'll officially have a girlfriend at the end of the day. Yep. I'm back in high school.

Chapter Forty-Nine

Leo

My big day has finally arrived. It's been less than twelve hours since I talked with my brothers, yet it feels like weeks. Time dragged on while I waited for lunch. I dozed off a few times while sitting on the couch, nothing more than ten minutes at a time, though. Altogether, I maybe got an hour's nap. As antsy as I am, I should probably put off talking with Kyleigh.

We're having a little celebration lunch at my parents' house. Kyleigh, Lucas, Mom, and my grandparents are here. The rest of my family are on duty today. No, my family isn't here to watch me tell Kyleigh I love her and ask her to be mine. I may be taking steps a teenager would to have a girlfriend, but I haven't fallen *that* far back in time.

Today, Ally's picking up my truck. Kyleigh and I have done all we can do. I don't mind working on my truck when I can. I'll never be a mechanic. Painting is definitely out of my skill set.

We hurry out the back door when we hear Ally driving to the barn. The barn doors are open. Darlin is already sitting outside waiting for her. There's nothing wrong with the engine. I won't drive her until she's painted.

While Ally backs the rollback up, I glance over my shoulder at Kyleigh. She's walking across the yard with my mom and grandmother. The smile on her face makes me smile, too. She's gone from the outsider we didn't trust to a member of our family. Yeah, today's the day I ask her to be mine.

"Today's the day, huh?" Ally grins as she hops out of the truck. Did she just read my thoughts? Nah. That's crazy.

"It sure is." I jingle the truck keys at her.

Ally snatches the keys from my hand. "Thanks, jerk." She didn't mean that. The jerk part, anyway.

I lead her to the back fender and point out a few spots. "I wasn't able to buff these all the way out."

"We," Kyleigh corrects. She bounces over and hugs Ally. Thank goodness she found the right group of friends in Hayden Falls. Hers from Walsburg are useless.

"It's not a problem," Ally assures us. "We'll give her a good look over and get anything you guys missed."

A phone rings. Everyone reaches for theirs. Kyleigh narrows her eyes at her screen. She doesn't look as though she wants to answer the call. It best not be her ex. He's not supposed to contact her in any way.

"Uh." She motions over her shoulder with her thumb. "I'll take this inside." She answers the call and rushes into the barn.

"Leo." Ally snaps her fingers in my face. My eyes dart to hers. "I was saying we should be finished in about a week."

Lucas helps Granddad say goodbye to Darlin. Granddad isn't sad today. He's ready to see our truck returned to her former glory.

"Is a week enough time? It's okay if it takes longer. Don't rush the job."

"Relax, Leo." Ally laughs and shakes her head. "Dad and I will take good care of Darlin. Ian Anderson is helping us out while he's in town. A week should be plenty of time."

Ah. Having an extra mechanic would free Ally up to work on my truck. Riley's cousin owns a shop in North Carolina. Riley hasn't said how long he's staying in town. Guess he doesn't like sitting idle while he's here.

Ally motions for me to follow her to the cab of the rollback. She reaches in and pulls out the paperwork I need to sign. The *'paid in full'* stamp on the invoice stops me mid-signature. My stomach twists into knots.

"Ally, I don't want her paying for this."

"She has to, Leo. You know that. You know Judge Morgan will come after her if she doesn't."

Judge Morgan won't add any more conditions to Kyleigh's sentence. Hopefully, after Granddad's phone call last night, the judge won't be monitoring her so closely anymore. The only reason I finish signing my name is because paying the restoration fees was part of Kyleigh's main sentence in court. If she doesn't pay this, she'll be held in contempt of court and will go to jail.

"I still hate it," I mumble.

Ally tosses the clipboard into the truck and smiles mischievously. "If it bothers you that much, you could do little things and some grand gestures for her to make up for it. Oh, let's say, for the rest of your life." She winks at me.

I lightly chuckle. "I plan on it."

"Good man." Ally pats my arm twice. "Didn't doubt you for a minute."

Once Darlin is secured on the rollback, I toss an arm over Granddad's shoulders. Lucas smiles. His eyes flick from Granddad to me. It feels good to see our grandfather happy again.

"When you get her back, we gotta paint the town." Granddad wipes away a happy tear.

"Going to the bar might be great, but I don't think he needs to find a girl anymore," Lucas teases.

"No." Granddad drops his eyes for a moment and lowers his voice. "He found her."

I glance toward the barn just as Kyleigh walks out. My heart drops a little. She looks lost and confused. I run a hand through my hair and lock eyes with Lucas. I have a strange feeling whatever that phone call was about just changed everything.

I hurry to her and put an arm around her. "Hey, Slugger. You okay?" She's not.

Ally senses it, too. She hurries over and takes her hand. "Kyleigh? What happened?"

Kyleigh looks up at me with a blank expression and turns to Ally. "That was my old manager. She's offering me my job back." She pauses for a moment. "With a raise."

"The same manager that doesn't like anybody?" Ally scrunches her face up. Kyleigh nods.

"I thought you took the job with the Ramseys." Mom fidgets with the collar of her blouse. That is not a good sign.

"I did."

"Are you going to take your old job back?" My grandfather wrings his hands together.

Before Kyleigh can reply, Ally gives her hand a little shake. "Hey. Why don't we call Grace and have a Girls' Night at Sammie's apartment?"

"Yeah. That sounds like a good idea." Kyleigh hugs Ally and waves as she gets into the rollback.

She's been offered her job in Seattle back. She'll never find that kind of opportunity here. It takes everything in me to hold myself together. I swallow hard and lock eyes with Lucas. He starts to speak but snaps his mouth shut when I shake my head. The future I was hoping for was just snatched from me. My biggest fear just happened.

"Why don't we wrap things up here so you can get home?" As much as I try to keep the hurt and disappointment from my voice, it's still there.

My family senses the change immediately. They drop their heads and start walking toward the house. Mom and Grandma blink to hold back tears. Even Granddad looks heartbroken. Lucas wants to say something. Thankfully, he quietly walks away. He probably won't go far.

Kyleigh follows me into the barn. "I'm not going home. I'm meeting Mr. and Mrs. Ramsey at the gym in fifteen minutes."

Wow. Things are happening faster than I thought they would. Did she already call them so she can turn in her notice? Fast is probably for the best.

"You go ahead. I can clean things up here." I aimlessly start putting tools and unused parts away.

"Leo?" Her fingertips gently slide across my back. I already miss her. "What's wrong?"

I take a deep breath and turn to face her. Her blue eyes do me in. Somehow, she quietly slipped past all my defenses and into my heart. How do I let her go?

"It's a great opportunity."

"But…"

I cup her face in my hands, cutting her off. "You'll never find a job like that here."

"I know."

"This town is small. There's not a lot to do around here."

"Leo? What…" The pain and confusion in her eyes break my heart.

"You deserve more than this." I can barely whisper the words.

"Wait. You're not…"

"It's okay, Slugger." I gently press my lips to her forehead. If I touch her lips again, I'll crumble to the ground. "I only want what's best for you."

She gasps and steps back. "Really? Why does this keep happening? What's wrong with me?" I don't think she's talking to me.

"Don't be late for your appointment."

Her eyes snap to mine. Confusion has turned to anger. "Fine. Whatever." She spins and storms out of the barn, taking my heart with her.

I turn and grab the worktable with both hands. Watching her go was by far the hardest thing I've ever done. With a loud, agonizing cry, I throw the closest tool at the barn wall. Lucas rushes in and wraps his arms around me from behind before I can throw another one.

"Don't, Leo."

I could break his hold if I wanted to. Right now, I don't have the energy. Instead, I drop to my knees, pulling Lucas down with me.

Chapter Fifty

Kyleigh

Two weeks. It's been two long weeks. Well, technically, tomorrow is officially two weeks. But who's counting? It's been a huge rollercoaster ride with my emotions, none of them good.

Some days, okay, most days, I'm sad and broken. I've had six Girls' Nights with different friends during the past thirteen days. Except for Grace, she's been at every single one. I hate feeling broken, and like I'm not enough. It's hard not to feel this way when two guys dump you within two months. Maybe dump isn't the right word. Leo wasn't actually my boyfriend. I thought we were headed for a committed relationship, though. Guess it was just me.

A few times, I wanted to go to the Sheriff's Office and give Deputy Leo Barnes a piece of my mind and punch him. No, if I punched him, I'd hurt my hand. A bat would help. That would be ironic. I don't own a bat. Neither does my dad. I wouldn't do it anyway, but it's nice to imagine it.

If I'm not broken, crying, or mad, I'm numb. Numb is how I feel most of the time. How I get anything done being on autopilot is a mystery. You can't work in the financial world on autopilot. One wrong number, and you'll mess up someone's portfolio and their life. It only takes one slip-up to lose a client.

"You okay?" Grace pushes the creamer across the table to me. "You zoned out again."

"I'll get there."

There's no point lying to her. She knows I'm not okay. Last night was another broken and sad time for me. Grace and I had a Girls' Night, just the two of us at her apartment. Since the stores were closed on Sunday, we stayed up most of the night talking and watching movies.

I've avoided Leo and his family since I left the barn two weeks ago. It's been hard, really hard. I stopped going to dance class because I couldn't handle seeing Leo showing up and dancing with someone else. Grace said he didn't show up at either class.

I'm also not ready to talk with Hadley and Riley in person. I'm short in my text messages with them. Both ladies never miss dance class. My office is at the gym. I don't stay late on Thursdays. If I'm not finished with a file, I take it home with me.

Yesterday, I wasn't able to avoid the Barnes' or Hadley. It's why I went into sad mode again. Sheriff Barnes called Dad because I wasn't answering my phone. I needed one hour to finish my community service work. You'd think they'd let an hour slide. Nope. Not my luck. Sheriff Barnes assigned my hour at Beth's Morning Brew. It was a setup. I'm sure of it.

Thankfully, I didn't have to make drinks or take orders. I cleaned Beth and Hadley's offices, the small breakroom, and the bathrooms. I threw myself into getting the assigned community service done and only spoke to Hadley when she spoke to me. Yeah, I'm a terrible friend.

Hadley, unlike me, doesn't avoid people or tough situations. Between customers, she let me know how stupid Leo and I were acting. She's absolutely right. I agree with everything she said. I just don't know how to move past whatever this is. Fear? I don't know. Up until now, my life has been simple and easy. I've never had to make bold moves or hard decisions.

Even if I were brave, I can't make Leo want me. I'm sure not going to beg. It hurt a little hearing that Leo is as broken as I am. It makes no sense for him to be sad. He's the one who told me to go.

Hadley was with a customer when my hour was up. I bolted out the door before the ink of Beth's signature was dry on the community service form. For a moment, I thought Hadley was going to run after me. She probably would have if it weren't for Mrs. Hayes' order for the inn.

"Hello, ladies." Hadley slides into our booth next to Grace. Grace hurries to make room for her.

"This is a great idea. We should do it more often." Riley uses her body to push me over. Great. Now, I'm trapped between her and the window.

The only businesses open today are the three restaurants. Grace and I have pigged out on junk food since I arrived at her apartment last night. It's the middle of the afternoon. We decided to come to Davis's Diner for a real meal. Hadley and Riley have no reason to be in town today. I lock eyes with Grace. Oh, yes. She knew they were coming. She probably texted them an invite. Grace Wentworth may be my new best friend, but she's meddling.

"We really should." Grace drops her eyes and takes a sip of coffee.

"What can I get you, ladies?" Miss Cora sets mine and Grace's plates on the table.

"Just coffee," Hadley replies. Riley nods.

Miss Cora hurries back with two fresh cups and refills mine and Grace's.

"You should get that to go." Riley points at my plate.

"Why?"

"Family dinner is in an hour." Riley slides out of the booth. "I'll get you a to-go plate. Grace, you want one, too?"

"That'd be great." Grace smiles sweetly. Oh, good grief. Her acting is so bad. She set this entire thing up.

"You and I need to talk." I jab my finger at her.

"You should talk to Leo." Hadley cuts right to the chase. Of course, this is why they're here.

"I'm not going to the Barnes' family dinner."

"Why not? Your parents are there." Riley hands Grace a to-go plate. She grabs my plate, pops a piece of bacon in her mouth, and starts putting my food into another container. Bacon stealer.

My parents told me yesterday that Mrs. Barnes invited us to dinner. I turned the invitation down but insisted they go. Dad is good friends with the Sheriff. Their relationship doesn't need to be strained because of me. Since Mom has decided she's never leaving Dad again, she needs to reconnect with more of her old friends. She and Mrs. Barnes were friends in high school. They weren't best friends, but they often hung out in the same groups.

My phone dings with a text. I quickly check it. I'm not expecting anyone. I just don't want to have this conversation. I read the message and snap my head up.

Grace slowly sets her mug down. "Your old manager?"

"Yeah."

Riley grabs my wrist. She's not happy. "You're taking that job?"

"No." I look her in the eye and shake my head. "I never intended to take it."

"Wait." Hadley grabs my hand the moment Riley lets go. "You aren't going back to Seattle?"

"No." I shake my head. "My parents and I have been talking since we saw a pig fly across the square." We laugh and cut our eyes at Riley. She was so in on that part. She grins and shrugs. "Anyway. Mom and I are happier here. We're not going back."

My phone rings this time. The caller isn't in my contacts. Taylor just texted from her phone. This number has a Washington area code. Did she borrow someone else's phone?

"You should answer that and bluntly tell her no and to stop contacting you." Grace read my emails from Taylor last night. She agrees the job sounds too good to be true. The offer is very suspicious. Taylor has never done this before. Grace is right. I need to end this nonsense. I hit the accept button and quickly set the call to speaker.

"Hello."

"I hate you!" a woman screams.

I sigh and lean back against the booth. Nope. Not Taylor. "Not my problem."

"If you take that job, you'll regret it," she snaps.

"Uh, Brenda? How did you even know about my wonderful job offer?"

"Because Scott's behind it!" She's still shouting. Everyone in the diner pauses to listen. I don't care this time. "I heard him on the phone with Taylor. He wants you back. He's blackmailing her somehow and paying for your raise!"

"You live with him, right?"

"Yes! And I'm not letting you come back and steal him from me!"

Wow. Scott really is a jerk. He lives with one woman and wants another. This time, our roles are reversed. Brenda has nothing to worry about from me.

"Brenda, not that it's any of your business, but I'm not taking the job. I'm not moving back to Seattle. And I will *never* take Scott back. He's all yours. Now, don't ever call me again."

I end the call and drop my phone on the table. Not too hard, though. Phones are expensive. A round of applause erupts in the diner. Wow. I've never had a whole town on my side before. Well, the whole town isn't in the diner, but close enough.

"Yes!" Riley throws her arms around me. "You *have* to come to dinner now."

"Uh, no." I unwrap myself from her arms. "Leo doesn't want me. He told me to go. I can't face him."

"Oh my gosh." Hadley groans and rubs her hands down her face. It wasn't a happy exclamation. "Smart people can be so dumb sometimes." Her expression hardens. She jabs her finger at me. I don't like angry Hadley. Nope. Not one bit. "Leo wants you. He's madly in love with you. The day Ally took Darlin, he was going to ask you to be his girlfriend."

"What?" I suck in a breath.

"Leo doesn't get into serious relationships because he's watched so many marriages around here fail because this small-town life wasn't enough for one of them. He wants what's best for you. If that's a fancy, high-paying job in another state, then he would never keep you from it. He's done everything he can think of to protect you." Hadley looks to Riley and Grace for confirmation and both nod.

"He broke his own heart to give you the happiness he thought you wanted." Riley can be pretty serious when she's not around Luke.

"Letting me go is protecting me?"

"In his eyes, yes." Riley closes the lid on the to-go box and slides it in front of me.

"He's protected you in several ways."

The three of us snap our heads toward Hadley. What does she mean? Do I really want to know?

"How?" Apparently, I do.

Hadley glances around the diner as she leans forward. Most of the customers have stopped watching us. The ones closest to us take Hadley's glare as their cue to mind their business now.

"For one, he made sure your ex won't return to Hayden Falls. It's probably why the jerk is trying to get you back to Seattle. Anyway, when no one was paying attention, Leo threatened to break both of Scott's arms if he ever touched you again. He got his dad to escort the scumbag out of town.

"Now, speaking of scumbags. This one tops the list. Bryson Crane will probably die if he ever touches you. And not just by Leo. The other three will gladly help. Leo didn't buy the door that day because the jerk offered to trade even for it for a night with you."

I gasp and clamp both hands over my mouth. Grace and Riley do, too. I knew there was more to that situation. Oh my gosh. I might cry. Leo needed that door, but he let it go for me. And the whole dude trading a part for a night with me creeps me out.

"And the biker gang wasn't trustworthy, either. Even Aaron Bailey was scared they'd go after the families of the arresting officers. They're why Leo suggested your dad install cameras at his house." Hadley leans back against the booth. "So, you see, he's been doing everything he can to protect you even before he realized he loved you."

"He loves me?"

Hadley nods. "He fell so hard, he'll never stop loving you."

"And you know all this how?"

"Lucas has gotten up several times to sit on the back deck with him." She shrugs. "I hear things."

"Where is he?" I wipe a tear from the corner of my eye.

"He's at his parents' house for Sunday dinner." Riley slides out of the booth.

"Leo's never had a serious relationship. He knows less about women than Lucas did. You're going to have to make the first move." Hadley stands.

"Take me to him." I'm too emotional to drive.

Chapter Fifty-One

Kyleigh

The drive to the Barnes' house takes forever. Okay. It's about ten minutes. I bounce in the backseat while Hadley drives. Riley's sitting next to her and talks the whole way. It's gibberish to me.

"He's in the kitchen." Riley holds up her phone and shows me the text from Luke. Thank goodness I heard her that time.

The moment Hadley has the car in park, I jump out and run toward the front door. I don't know what I'll do or say, but I have to do something. Luke comes out just as I reach the steps.

"Kitchen." He holds the door open for me.

"Thanks." I wave as I hurry past him.

I run straight for the huge kitchen at the back of the house. My action causes everyone in the living room to jump to their feet.

Mom is helping Leo's mother and grandmother prepare dinner. I catch a glimpse of them from the corner of my eye. It feels like there are more than three women in the room. I don't look to verify. I'm focused on the man with his back to me, looking for something in the fridge. Seeing him makes me tremble, and he's not even looking at me yet. Oh, how I've missed him.

"Mom, where's the salsa dip you made?" The sound of his voice has me blinking back tears. I haven't heard it in two weeks.

The moment he turns around, our eyes lock. I know. I know without a doubt that I want to spend the rest of my life with this man. I was an idiot to go two weeks without trying to talk to him.

"Kyleigh?" Hadley says behind me.

I don't pay her any attention. Who I want is standing in front of me. Nothing is stopping me today. Without a care of who's watching, I rush across the room and throw my arms around Leo's neck. His eyes widen as his mouth falls open. He doesn't get a chance to speak. My lips crash against his.

Shocked gasps go around the room. My name is shouted from several directions. So what if I just shocked the Quiet Barnes and our family members? I even shocked myself. I'm so proud of me. As I said, I. Don't. Care. I love this man. I'm not afraid to show the world just how much.

Leo quickly grabs my upper arms and pushes me away, breaking our kiss. If I weren't as shocked as he is, I'd think he didn't want his family to see us kissing. Note to self. Be mindful of public displays of affection in the future.

"Kyleigh." Leo's eyes flick behind me for a moment.

If he thought the kiss was shocking, he's seen nothing yet.

"I love you," I blurt out.

"What?" His eyes almost pop out of his head as he struggles to speak.

"I love you. I was never going to take the job in Seattle. I decided weeks ago I wasn't leaving. I like it here. I love you. You are a big enough reason to stay. I thank you for everything you've done to protect me. I know why you didn't buy the door." I can't stop the tears. "I love you even more for it."

I throw my arms around him and try to kiss him again. Leo's prepared this time. Instead of pulling me into his arms, he pries me from him.

"Kyleigh, stop."

Stop? Why does he want me to stop? Hadley and Riley said he loved me. Is PDA really this big of a deal for him?

"That's enough!" Hadley rushes over and shoves my shoulder. "Slugger?"

My eyes move from a seriously angry Hadley to Leo. Wait. Slugger? That came from behind me. Only Leo calls me Slugger. My eyes snap to Hadley. She's about to eat me alive. My mouth slowly falls open, and I cover it with my hand. I look back at the man in front of me.

"No," I whisper behind my hand. He nods.

Hadley pushes between us. She pokes me in the chest. Geez. What's with her and poking people?

"I like you, but I never want to see your lips on his again. And don't love him like that." She grabs my shoulders, whirls me around, and points across the room. "That's your twin. Learn how to tell them apart, or you and I will be fighting on a regular basis."

I look over my shoulder at her. "How? They're identical. I could learn their badge numbers."

Hadley laughs. It's pure evil. Angry Hadley returns rather quickly. "That would be great while they're on duty. Lucas' badge number is 1456. Leo's is 2457. Burn them to memory. But what are you going to do in moments like this? They're not in uniform today. Badge numbers won't work."

"I don't know." I toss my hands in the air. "Tattoo their foreheads or something."

Luke bursts out laughing. No one else moves or says anything.

"No." Hadley stomps across the room and pulls an amused Leo over to Lucas. "Let me help you solve the mystery until you figure it out by how they move and act."

"This is ridiculous. They can wear name tags." The brothers cut their eyes at me. Okay. No name tags.

Hadley stands next to me in front of Lucas. She points to him. "This is my twin." She moves behind me and takes my shoulders to position me directly in front of Leo. "This is your twin."

"Okay." My eyes bounce between them. "Nope. Hadley, that doesn't work."

"Geez, girl. You don't pay attention to your surroundings. Life tip here. Never go into a dark alley. You'll die." She spins me to face her and cups my face in her hands. "Look at them very closely. Once you see it, you'll never unsee it." She pats my face a couple of times before spinning me back around.

I study Leo and Lucas' faces. They're the same height. Their hair is the same shade. Their eyes might have a slight difference, but I'd never notice it if they weren't standing side by side like this. Leo's beard looks a little fuller, but I'm not really sure. Ugh! I don't see a noticeable difference.

Hadley runs a finger down the side of my face. She taps my cheekbone just before my temple. I study their eyes again. Nope. It's not the eyes. What about their faces is different? Their faces. I gasp and slap my hand over my mouth again. With wide eyes, I turn to Hadley. Their faces are a little different. Lucas' face is a little rounder. Leo's is a little narrower. She's right. I can't unsee it now. Hadley grins and nods.

Mrs. Barnes laughs. She walks over and puts an arm around Hadley and me. "I'm so glad someone finally noticed."

"What? I don't get it." Luke looks over his Mom's shoulder.

"Shoo." Mrs. Barnes waves him away with both hands. "Help Riley set the table."

"You sure you got it?" Hadley raises an eyebrow. I nod. "Good." She pokes me in the chest again. "If I catch your lips on my twin's again, I'll burn yours off."

Whoa. That sounds painful. I have no doubts she'll do it.

"I'm sorry," I tell her and turn to the twins. "I'm so so sorry."

"I don't know what to say." Lucas does look lost and confused. I highly doubt this has ever happened before. He pulls Hadley into his arms. "I'm sorry, Sweet Girl."

"Not your fault." Hadley presses her lips to his.

Nope. It was my fault. All me here.

"Well, if this is cleared up." Leo offers me his hand. "Would you like to step outside for a moment, Slugger?"

I nod and place my hand in his. After my big blunder, I don't know what to say to him. This will be hard to get past.

"That was epic," Luke says as we walk out the back door. "I got it all on video."

"Of course he did," Leo mumbles as he closes the door behind us.

Leo quietly leads me to the barn. My mouth drops open, and I cover it with both hands this time.

"Oh my gosh. She's beautiful." I hurry over and rub Darlin's hood. I have no idea why I'm petting a truck like it's a dog.

The truck looks even better than I remember before Jenna took the first swing. Well, it was dark when we found Darlin. Still, I could tell then this was a beautiful truck. Ally did an amazing job. The dents we couldn't buff out are gone, and the paint is flawless.

"You both are." Leo spins me around with my back against the fender. His eyes hold mine for a long, silent moment. "You sure you want to live here?"

"Yeah," I reply softly. "After the Fall Festival, my parents and I have had some long, serious conversations. I already wanted to stay. Knowing my mom was staying here relieved a lot of my worries. I didn't want her to go back to alone. Getting the job with the Ramseys showed me I have a place here if I wanted it."

Mom got a job working in the lab at the hospital in Walburg. The pay is lower, but she's more excited about this job than the one at the research lab in Seattle.

"What will you do if Hayden Falls becomes boring?"

After everything Hadley and Riley told me today, his question is understandable. My mom leaving my dad years ago is the perfect example of his fears.

"If that happens, I guess you and I will have to take a week or two vacation and do something different."

"You're not staying because of me?"

"Yes and no." I won't lie to him. "Yes, you're one of my reasons for staying. You're the part that means the most to me. No, because as weird as this little town is, I like it here. And like my mom said, we never should have left."

Leo wraps his arms around my waist and pulls me to him. One corner of his mouth lifts in a sly grin. "Well, Slugger. If you're done declaring your love for me to my brother." I groan and grit my teeth. Oops. "You wanna be *my* girl?"

"Yes, Deputy Barnes. I'd love to be your girl."

This time, I kiss the right twin—my twin. Finally, my world feels like it's falling into place.

Chapter Fifty-Two

Leo

"Come on! We're gonna be late!" Granddad practically runs across the backyard ahead of us.

"Sheldon, you need to slow down." Grandma's warning goes unheard. She turns to me. "Leo?"

"I got him." I chuckle and run to catch up with him.

I reach the barn before Granddad can open the double doors. He's beyond excited. He's worse than a group of preschoolers. Tonight's the night. We're taking Darlin out on the town. Mom said Granddad watched the clock all afternoon. He even called me four times in the past two hours.

Granddad and I swing the doors open and secure them in place. I stand in the doorway and wait for the ladies and Dad to catch up with us. Kyleigh slides under my arm and wraps one of hers around my waist. This is exactly where she belongs. She lightly laughs as she watches Granddad. He places both hands on the hood and drops his head between them for a moment. We give him all the time he needs. With a huge smile, he stands and walks around Darlin, talking to her like the old friend she is. One hand slides over the blue metal, never breaking contact.

"Dad, you behave yourself, and don't give the kids a hard time tonight." My dad opens the passenger door.

"Guess I'll see you guys at Cowboys." Kyleigh lifts up on her toes and presses her lips to mine.

I've gone from the quiet brother to someone who doesn't mind public displays of affection. Mom says it's progress. I guess it is.

"Yeah." With one hand on her hip and the other on the side of her neck, I kiss her again. "I love you, Slugger." I've never said those words to a woman I'm not related to.

"I love you, too." Kyleigh waves to everyone and starts toward the door.

"Where you going, Slugger?" Granddad calls out.

Everyone glances around at each other. Kyleigh freezes in the doorway. Granddad has never called her that before.

"Um." She motions over her shoulder with her thumb. "I'm meeting you guys at the bar."

"No, ma'am." Granddad walks over and takes her hand. "You're riding with us." He leads her to the passenger door. I hurry around to help her inside. Granddad swats my hand away. "I can help a pretty girl into our truck. You drive."

Kyleigh slides to the middle of the bench seat. Granddad climbs in next to her. He grins and rubs his hands together when the engine fires up. He leans out the window and kisses Grandma. They've done this for years. It's sweet to watch.

"See ya in a few hours, love." He gives her another quick kiss.

Kyleigh thinks it's weird when she sees her parents in romantic moments. It's not for my brothers and me. Dad and Granddad have never hidden their love for their wives. Now, Mom's parents are a little more modest. They'll hold hands and hug in front of people, but that's about it.

My family waves and shouts 'bye' and 'have fun' to us as we drive out of the barn. Granddad is happy as a lark. If his grin gets any wider, his face will break. Kyleigh shoulders shake as she silently laughs at Granddad. The moment is perfect.

"I can't believe you've had Darlin back for two weeks and haven't taken her out yet."

Granddad's expression goes blank for a moment. He and Kyleigh stare at each other. "We were waiting for you."

Kyleigh snaps her head toward me, her mouth slightly open. I nod.

"You didn't have to do that." She squeezes Granddad's hand.

"It wouldn't be right without you, and Leo refused," he mumbles the last part.

She looks at me again. I shrug. It's true. I wanted her with us for the first ride and many more after this.

"Thank you." She kisses my cheek.

"Hey." Granddad taps his left cheek. "I could use one, too."

"Of course, Mr. Barnes." She leans over and kisses his cheek.

"It's Granddad to you, Slugger."

She looks at me again. I nod. Granddad has been kinder since he found out beating up Darlin wasn't Kyleigh's idea. Jenna Owens best hope she never crosses Granddad's path. He'll be giving her a piece of his mind. Granddad sat down last weekend with us and told Kyleigh why Judge Morgan was so hard on her. He didn't want her blaming me for his mistake. It was an emotional conversation. I thought I'd cry, too, when they forgave each other and hugged.

"What's going on?" Kyleigh leans forward as we drive through the square.

Groups of people line the sidewalk. They, along with everyone walking around the square, wave and shout. Granddad rolls his window down and happily waves back. He probably set this up. It's okay. He can have this moment.

Kyleigh laughs and snuggles into my side. She lays her head on my shoulder. I glance over her head at Granddad. We share a knowing look. Yeah, this is the benefit of having a bench seat he said I'd learn someday. It feels good having your girl next to you while driving.

If I thought the scene in the square was crazy, the one at Cowboys is worse. Our friends and family members are waiting in the parking lot. Blue balloons lift into the air. Luke. Of course, it's Luke. I'm going to have to hurt him one day. The balloons weren't enough for my little brother. Luke and Riley stand on each side of the entrance of the parking lot. They set off confetti bombs as we pull into the lot. Yeah, I sound grumpy. Secretly, I like this.

I drive to the far side of the lot. My usual spot in the corner is empty. I pause and stare at it.

"Is that?" Kyleigh points to the old blue beat-up truck in the next space.

"Skip Rodgers?" I nod.

Granddad flips his wrist a couple of times to motion me on. "Park somewhere else."

Kyleigh presses her lips together. She wants to laugh. So do I. It is kind of ironic the sleazebag is here tonight.

"Good idea." I find an empty spot next to the building, three spaces from the doors.

Granddad gets out and offers Kyleigh his hand. "Come on, Slugger. Time to celebrate." Once Kyleigh is on her feet, he playfully points at her. "No bats."

She laughs and shakes her head. "No bats, Granddad. I promise."

"Good." He looks at me with a face-splitting grin. Yeah, he likes her calling him Granddad. He winks at Kyleigh. "And be sure to kiss the right grandson."

"Uh." Kyleigh drops her head back. "I'm never going to live that down."

"Nope." Granddad leads the way to the doors. "I'll be telling your children about it."

Kyleigh and I pause. We look at each other and back to Granddad as he continues walking like nothing just happened. Kids? Oh yeah, but they're a long way off. Neither of us says anything and hurry inside.

I take Kyleigh's hand and follow Granddad to the bar. His friends have his favorite stool waiting for him. They've been to the house twice this week to see Darlin.

I tap the bar with my hand to get Noah's attention. "Their first two rounds are on me."

Noah nods and fills three mugs from the tap. Kyleigh, still holding my hand, wiggles to the beat of the music. I don't usually dance in public, but tonight, I'll be dancing with my girl every chance I get. I can't tease Lucas about leaving us to dance with Hadley anymore.

"You stay out of trouble." I pat Granddad's shoulder.

He grabs my arm and looks past me to Kyleigh. She's watching the dance floor or the band. Jealousy flares like a monster. She can't be swooning over Jake Campbell and his band.

My grandfather smiles up at me. "I told you Darlin would help you find your girl."

"Yeah." I glance at Kyleigh and back to him. "And on the very night you said it would happen." Granted, it didn't happen the way we thought it would, but it happened.

Granddad nods once and turns back to his friends. I place my hands on Kyleigh's hips and move her through the crowd in front of me. Cowboys is packed tonight.

"Come on, Slugger. Let's get you to your friends."

"I can walk to the table by myself," she says over her shoulder.

"No, ma'am. It's my job to get you there safely."

We weave through the crowd until we reach the three tables pulled together for her friends. Wow. It looks like all the ladies are here tonight. She hugs Grace and Hannah. The other ladies shout their hellos.

Beth Murphy is already drunk. Yeah. Brady Maxwell was in the news today. I look to the upper level. Spencer sits up straighter than usual. His eyes zone in on his little sister. It'll be a long night for him.

I help Kyleigh hop up on her stool and cup her cheek in my hand. Her smile and the excitement in her eyes stir up emotions within me I shouldn't have in public.

"Delivered, safe and sound."

"Thank you, Deputy, for protecting me across this dangerous tundra." She tosses her hand toward the front doors.

Oh, she has no idea how many wolves are between this table and the front door. None of the local guys will get out of line. They know every man on the upper level will take pleasure in hurting them if they mess with the women at this table.

I lean close. My lips hover above hers. "I'll spend the rest of my life protecting you."

Whatever she was about to say gets cut off when my lips press hard against hers. I don't end the kiss until she's clinging to me and out of breath. Oh, I meant what I said and the kiss. It was also to show the wolves in here that she's mine.

"Well, you can have the first dance." Her breathing isn't normal yet. It takes her a moment to get the words out.

"I get all your dances."

"I don't need a partner to line dance."

"Okay."

"And after Grace has a couple of glasses of wine, she likes to dance."

The women at this table often dance together as a group. Every man in the bar watches them when they do.

"You can dance with Grace, but no men."

She looks past me to the bar. "Granddad might want to dance."

I can't help but laugh. "If you can convince him to dance, you're more than welcome to dance with Granddad."

"Shoo, Barnes! It's Girls Night!" Beth Murphy shouts.

Yeah, I need to let her have some fun with her friends. Mine are waiting on the upper level. I press my lips to hers again. I keep this kiss short and sweet.

"I love you, Slugger."

"I love you, too, Deputy."

"The first slow song, I'll be back for you."

"If you don't hurry, I'll meet you halfway." She gives me a quick kiss and turns to face her friends.

Every man I know watches me walk across the dance floor to the steps for the upper level. Lucas, sitting at the table next to me, snickers. The moment I sit down, Tyler shoves a beer into my hand. Wade takes a napkin, rips it in half, and dramatically drops it on the table.

"Man card officially gone. Boom!" Wade throws his hands in the air. He's as crazy as Luke. Every man on the upper level bursts out laughing.

My eyes go straight to Kyleigh. She smiles and waves. I wink and take a sip of my beer. Yep. Man card gone. She owns every part of me. It's okay. Because of her, I finally know what love and happiness are.

If she'll have me, I'll spend the rest of my life protecting her. I'll just make sure to hide all the bats if we have a son who plays baseball. A son? Now, my grin almost splits my face. Yeah, I want a son and a daughter.

Hello, My Lovely Reader,

I hope you enjoyed Leo and Kyleigh's story. Thank you so much for reading this book. I love Leo and hope you do, too. His story took a little longer than I expected to write. Apparently, when I made him the Quiet Barnes, he took that literally. He talked to me in little moments, but finally, his story came together. I can't wait to hear what you think about him.

Hayden Falls is one of my favorite series to write. I love small-town stories. They're full of so many different characters. Some are funny, some smart, some crazy, and a few you want to drop off a cliff. There are happy moments, sad moments, and moments you wonder if that really happened. It's perfect.

Today, the Quiet Barnes has fallen. There's one Barnes left. His story isn't next, though. Next, be looking for another Hayden Falls Christmas story with little updates on a few of our couples and families. After the Christmas story, we'll return to Tennessee and The Dawson Boys. Well, unless someone in Hayden Falls decides to jump in with their story ahead of time. Let's hope not.

Thank you again for reading *Protecting You ~ Hayden Falls ~ Book Two*. Stay tuned. There's so much more coming this year. Please check out the Follow Me page. I'd love to connect with you. I have reader groups where you'll get information faster. I have giveaways in the groups, too. If you don't mind, will you consider leaving a review for this book on Amazon, Goodreads, and/or BookBub? I'd love to see them. Until next time, I hope you find lots of great books to read.

Happy Reading,
Debbie Hyde

Follow Me

Here are places to follow me:

Sign up for my Newsletter:
www.debbiehyde-author.com

Facebook Page:
Debbie Hyde Author

Facebook Groups:
Debbie Hyde Books – This is my reader's group. I hold giveaways in the group often.
For the Love of a Shaw – This group is dedicated to the series. I hold giveaways here, too.
Debbie Hyde's Book Launch Team – I would love to have you on my book launch team! The team gets all my book news first. They sometimes help with cover designs. The Team can get FREE ebooks for an honest review. Join me today!
The Fireside Book Café – This is a book community group with various Authors and books from every genre. We hold Giveaways here, too.

Instagram:
www.instagram.com/debbie_hyde_author

Twitter:
Debbie Hyde5

TikTok:
debbie_hyde

Background Cover Photographer

Thank you to the wonder Carrie Licano Pichler! Carrie is the photographer of all the cover backgrounds for this series. Every picture is from the beautiful state of Montana. Carrie does Landscapes, Portraits, and Weddings. If you're in Montana, please connect with her. You won't regret it! Be sure to thank you for these cover photos.

You can find her at:

Website: carriepichlerphotography.weebly.com

Facebook Group: Carrie Pichler Photography

Hayden Falls

Forever Mine ~ Book One
Aiden and E

Today, I'm going home to a town that wrote me off years ago. Home to watch the woman I love marry someone else. I'm not going to survive this.

Only With You ~ Book Two
Miles and Katie

My career was strong and sure. My personal life was a mess. My only regret was keeping her a secret. Winning her back won't be easy, but I have to try.

Giving Her My Heart ~ Book Three
Jasper and Hannah

The dance teacher annoys me at every turn until she twirls her way into my heart and my daughter's. Now, I need to find a way to get her to stay.

Finding Home ~ Book Four
Luke and Riley

I was the fun brother until my twin almost died in a fire. Now, I'm a mess. Then she came along. I'm charming, but am I enough for her to stay?

Listening to My Heart ~ Book Five
Phillip and Tara

My family took the biggest part of my heart from me. A piece I didn't know existed. After nine years, the woman who holds every piece of my heart returns, bringing a huge secret with her. This time, no one will keep me from her.

A Hayden Falls Christmas
    Spend Christmas in Hayden Falls. Enjoy a short story about the five couples we've met, plus two of the town's beloved families.

Falling for You ~ Book Six
Lucas and Hadley
    I'm a career-minded deputy. I wasn't looking for love. Until my little brother butted into my love life, I never even noticed the woman right in front of me.

Finally Home ~ Book Seven
Aaron and Kennedy
    If I had known joining the Army would have cost me her, I never would have enlisted.

Protecting You ~ Book Eight
Leo and Kyleigh
I'm the quiet brother. Nothing gets under my skin. Well, not until a little brunette swings her way into my life and changes everything.

A Hayden Falls Christmas ~ Two is Coming Soon!
Book Nine is expected by Fall 2024!

The Dawson Boys

Holding Her ~ Book One
Harrison & Tru
Losing her destroyed me. One letter gave me hope. Like a man on a mission, I went after her.

I Do It For You ~ Book Two
Bryan & Dana
Sometimes, slow, steady, and sweet are not the best way to go. Did I wait too long? Did my plan fail? I don't know, but I'd do anything for her.

Everything I Ever Wanted ~ Book Three
Calen & Daisy
"Get out!" I've shouted those words every day. Does she listen? Not a chance. She challenges me. She tests me. How did she become everything I ever wanted?

Book Four is expected Spring of 2024!

For the Love of a Shaw

When A Knight Falls ~ Book One
Gavin & Abby

The future Earl will battle his long-time enemy more than once when he falls for his nursemaid. Will Abby marry the wrong man to save an innocent girl?

Falling for the Enemy ~ Book Two
Nate & Olivia

Nathaniel Shaw takes a job to prove his worth to his father. He loses his heart to the mysterious woman in his crew only to discover she isn't who she claims to be.

A Knight's Destiny ~ Book Three
Nick & Elizabeth

Nicholas Shaw is a Knight without a title, but he's loved the Duke's sister for years. When Elizabeth needs protection and runs away, Nick goes with her rather than sending her to her brother.

Capturing A Knight's Heart ~ Book Four
Jax & Nancie

The rules of society don't bind Jackson Shaw. He's free to roam as he pleases until he stumbles across a well-kept secret of Miss Nancie's. Will Nancie guard her heart and push him away? Or has she truly captured this Knight's heart?

A Duke's Treasure ~ Book Five
Sam & Dani

The Duke of Greyham, Samuel Dawson, has loved Lady Danielle Shaw for years. Dani stumbles into his darkest secret, leaving Sam no choice but to steal her away.

A Knight's Passion ~ Book Six
Caleb & Briley

Caleb Shaw feels lost, alone, and misunderstood. His mind is haunted by his past. While running for his life, he devises a plan to save Briley. The bluff is called, trapping them together forever.

A Mysterious Knight ~ Book Seven
Alex & Emily

Alexander Shaw had no light, peace, or love if he didn't have her. The day she sent him away almost destroyed him. Emily's trapped in her father's secrets and can't break free no matter how much she wants to. Alex will risk his life to free hers.

Other Books by the Author

Forest Rovania series: Middle-Grade Fantasy
Written with: Nevaeh Roberson

Jasper's Journey ~ Book One
Forest Rovania's only hope begins with an epic journey.

Women's Christian:
Stamped *subtitle:* Breaking Out of the Box
Her *subtitle:* Beautiful, Loved, Wanted, Matters, Priceless!
Her: Beautiful, Loved, Wanted, Matters, Priceless! Guided Study
Journal.

Blank Recipe Cookbooks:
My Thanksgiving Recipes
Store all your holiday recipes in one place. Choose from 4 cover
designs.
Burgundy, Orange, Peach, and Cream & Burgundy.

My Halloween Recipes
A great place to store fun children's recipes.

Acknowledgments:

Thank you to my awesome *Toon Blast* gaming friends, Four!, Pit, and Mags! You guys gave me some great character names for this series. Stay tuned! I'm sure those guys will be doing a lot more throughout the series!

Thank you, Carrie Pichler, for being our Montana Photographer for this series. All the background photos are really from Montana. Carrie is an amazing photographer!

Thank you, Nancie Alewine Blume, for being my beta reader.

Thank you, Wendy (Winnie) Sizemore, for bouncing story ideas with me.

A Montana School Transportation Law from the 1960s stated that if a student rode a horse to school, the principal had to take care of it. This law has been used for Senior Day pranks in Montana several times.

A very special thank you to the members of the *Facebook* group *For All Who Love Montana.* Your stories are so great! If you liked or commented on the post for stories, I have included your names here. It meant a lot to me that you took the time to share with me. Christine Migneault, Tammie Duran, Jim and Coleen Larson Done, Andrea Phillips, Joy Rasmussen, Kelli Vilchis, Sandra Stuckey, Sarah Jobe, Gracene Long, Dennis Fabel, Deb McGann Langshaw, Janice Berget, Ruth Collins Johnson, Roxanna Malone McGinnis, Shawn Wakefield, Alan Johnson, Judy Shockley, Danielle Mccrory, Larry Campbell, Maureen Mannion Kemp, Nancy Ray, Jerry Urfer, Kris Biffle Rudin, Holly Good, Vic Direito, Mozelle Brewer, Joseph Hartel, Cheri Wicks, Stephanie Schuck-Quinn, Travis Frank, Kamae

Luscombe, Dianne Eshuk Ketcharm, Patty Ward, Tina Griffin Williams, Steve Kline, Jim Lidquist, Christina Mansfield, Glen Hodges, Teri St Pierre, Lalena Chacon-Carter, Eric Wolf, Jennifer Ahern Lammers, Marilyn Handyside, Lynnette Graf, Arianna Dawn Fake, Cody Birdwell, Doug Jeanne Hall, Mary Thomas.

Debbie Hyde

About the Author

Debbie Hyde is the author of the Historical Romance *series For the Love of a Shaw*. The seven-book family sage begins with Gavin in When A Knight Falls. She is currently working on *The Dawson Boys* series and the *Hayden Falls* series. Both series are Contemporary Romances. A couple more series are in the works.

Debbie has a love for writing! She enjoys reading books from many different genres, such as Christian, Romance, Young Adults, and many more. You will always find wonderful, clean stories in her fictional writings.

She enjoys using her talents in cooking, baking, and cake decorating when not reading or writing. She loves using her skill as a seamstress to make gowns, costumes, teddy bears, baby blankets, and much more.

Debbie started Letters To You on Facebook after God put it on her heart to "Love the lost and lead them to Jesus." This wonderful community of amazing people allows her to continue her mission to Just #LoveThemAll.

Debbie would love to hear from you and see your reviews!

Made in United States
Troutdale, OR
11/19/2024

25036013R00181